LUCKY LADY

PRAISE FOR BOOKS BY PAULLA HUNTER

Brittle Bones: "Another fun, humorous, Darcy Moreland mystery! Hunter, again, weaves a compelling story about skeletons found buried underneath an old house. A serious and talented reporter, Darcy can't wait for her police detective boyfriend to solve the crimes and goes digging, putting herself and others in peril. Her sleuthing takes us back to World War II, family squabbles, and lost lovers. Throughout this delightful novel, Hunter's marvelous sense of humor kept me chuckling. I recommend this book."

Mariko Tatsumoto, Author of **Blossoms on a Poisoned Sea**

"*Rough Ride* busts right out of the chute, and it twists and bucks until the last page. It's a fun inside-view primer that serves as a "behind-the-chutes" tour of the largest outdoor rodeo in America."

C.J. Box, #1 New York Times best-selling author of **Shadows Reel**

"Get ready to enjoy a modern wild west mystery with a spunky new heroine. Reporter Darcy Moreland will gallop into readers' hearts with her action-packed debut in Paulla Hunter's Rough Ride. Cops, cowboys, rodeos and murder take center stage."

Laura DiSilverio, national best-selling and award-winning author of the Readaholics Book Club Mysteries, Swift Investigations series, and Incubation Trilogy

LUCKY LADY

Darcy Moreland Mysteries, Book 3

PAULLA HUNTER

CAVEL PRESS

Kenmore, WA

A Camel Press book published by Epicenter Press

Epicenter Press
6524 NE 181st St.
Suite 2
Kenmore, WA 98028

For more information go to:
www.Camelpress.com
www.Coffeetownpress.com
www.Epicenterpress.com
www.paullahunternovels.com

This is a work of fiction. Names, characters, places, brands, media, and incidents are either the product of the author's imagination or are used fictitiously.

Cover design by Scott Book
Design by Melissa Vail Coffman

Lucky Lady
Copyright © 2024 by Paulla Hunter

Library of Congress Control Number: 2023950884

ISBN: 978-1-68492-167-6 (Trade Paper)
ISBN: 978-1-68492-168-3 (eBook)

I dedicate all my works to God, St. Philomena, my husband, Roger, my daughter Stacie, my son of my heart Zach, and my three beautiful granddaughters, who have always encouraged me and loved me through this journey of mine. I could not have done this without you.

ACKNOWLEDGMENTS

I WANT TO THANK MY CHEYENNE Critique group: Elizabeth Roadifer, Jeana Byrne, Michael Shay, Dean Petersen, Tina Olson, and David Hopkinson. They were kind but thorough in their critiques of this book. If there are any mistakes in this book it is solely my fault.

I would also like to thank Michael Kassel, Associate Director/ Curator at the Cheyenne Frontier Days Old West Museum who spent time researching the underground tunnels under Cheyenne and explaining them to me.

CHAPTER 1

THE ARCTIC NORTH WIND BLEW PELLETS of snow down the back of Darcy Moreland's wool coat as she jumped from the Channel 23 News van onto the slick downtown pavement in Cheyenne, Wyoming. Her new snow boots slipped on the mosaic inlay depicting Chief Little Shield in front of the Prairie Hotel.

She waved at Jeannie Carson, who was peering out of the plate-glass window of the hotel's coffee shop.

"This must be the place," she hollered back over her shoulder at Bill Netters as she yanked her angora scarf tighter around her neck. "Jeannie was the one who called and said a small crowd was milling around. For people to stand around in this cold . . ."

"Yeah, yeah. I know the drill, Calamity," Netters muttered as he battled to control the large video camera against the blustery winter wind. "But if this turns out to be nothing, you're buying me several beers tonight." He hitched the camera onto his shoulder and followed Darcy across the street towards where a group of about 10 or 15 people were huddled on the sidewalk in front of Thompson's Furniture.

Shouldering her way toward the front, Darcy recognized Annie, her hairdresser from the Hair Affair around the corner. Annie was standing with another woman from the salon behind a phalanx of tall, broad-shouldered men who had obviously piled out of the pool hall up the street.

"What's up?" Darcy shouted over the wind, puffing clouds of white frosty breath in Annie's ear.

"Dunno, I can't see." Annie stomped her feet to warm them and hugged herself against the cold.

Darcy pushed through the crowd. "Sorry guys. TV news." She turned and pointed to Netters behind her. Netters glared at her and pulled his blue Cubbies' cap low over his eyes. She thought she heard him growl but ignored it as she forged ahead.

Darcy focused on a man with sparse, salt and pepper hair wafting in the wind. He was leaning half out of one of the double glass doors of the massive three-storied building. Dressed in shirtsleeves, a vest, and a loosened tie, his face was red with either cold or temper.

"Please. Please," he shouted to the crowd. "This is just a vandal's prank. I've called the police and I'm sure they will ask you to leave."

Darcy waved Netters into position and grabbed the mic.

"Hi. Darcy Moreland KYCH Channel 23 News. Can you tell me who you are and what's going on here?" she said into the mic, then thrust it under the man's chin and waited for his response.

In Darcy's experience, when caught in a crisis like this, people either went nuclear or told you the unvarnished truth. She braced herself for either reaction. The man's icy gray eyes narrowed into slits. He stepped fully out of the doorway and glanced down.

Darcy followed his gaze. At first, she saw what looked like a large boulder covered in matted brown fur. When she spied the puddle of darkening blood pooling beneath it, her heart tripped, and she fought the urge to gag.

Shifting to the left, she glanced down and stared into sightless liquid brown eyes the size of silver dollars. The objective, analytical side of Darcy's brain registered two black horns jutting from the sides of the skull and the black triangle of a nose as big as her hand. The rest of her brain, however, went code red and she yelped and staggered back a step.

"Oh, my god! It's a . . ."

The man smirked at her shock. "Just so. A bison's head."

Up the street at the State Capitol building, there used to be a complete stuffed bison in the rotunda before the restoration, but that differed vastly from the bloody, smelly lump at her feet.

Darcy's sherry-colored eyes scanned the small group of people standing stoically watching. Pulling herself together, she asked, "Do you know who might have done this?"

"Not a notion." The man turned back toward the unblocked half of the door, yanking it open.

Darcy squeezed in behind him, passing the mic back to Netters without looking.

"Sir, may I talk to you for a moment?" She raised her hands in the air to show they were empty. Netters followed her in and dropped the camera to his side. "No cameras, just talk." He didn't tell them to get out, which she supposed was progress.

It was only minimally warmer in the poorly lit building. Darcy barely had time to spin once and note remnants of old carpeting heaped in the corner stripped from the dark wood floors. Milky winter sunlight pooled on the grimy floor from the enormous picture windows that wrapped around the entire front and corner of the building. The air smelled stale and dusty.

Someone pounded on the door.

Darcy watched as the slim man with the ramrod back let in two police officers. She recognized Tom Quinn and Ken Meeker.

The man spread his stance and raised his chin. "It is about time you arrived," he said. "My name is Latham Kellogg and I represent a consortium that has recently purchased this building. I would be grateful if you would call the sanitation department and have that disgusting thing removed from the front of the building before it attracts even more attention." He turned and glared at Darcy and Netters as they stood in a small patch of sun filtering in from the window facing 16th street.

"My God," Kellogg said, turning to the officers again. "We already have the local media sniffing around." He gestured behind him carelessly.

One of the officers squinted into the showroom.

"Oh hiya, Darcy."

"Hi, Tom," Darcy raised her hand in greeting. She knew Tom Quinn more from dating Detective Hank Nelson than from doing news reports. Most of what Tom dealt with was civil complaints, few of which were newsworthy. Until now.

"As gratifying as this charming confab is," Kellogg glanced from Tom to Darcy as if to punctuate his displeasure, "I want that repulsive piece of offal removed without delay."

"Sorry, sir. We'll clear it away as soon as possible," Tom said. He nodded to Ken Meeker. Darcy watched through the window as Officer Meeker went to his cruiser and called in.

"When did you discover the . . . uhm . . . head, sir?" Tom asked. Taking out his notebook, he poised his stubby pencil over the page.

Kellogg flicked his eyes in Darcy's direction, and she pulled Netters closer to the window as if studying the outside commotion.

Satisfied that they had some small bit of privacy, Kellogg answered, "About 10 o'clock this morning. I had come in through the alleyway door and was working at my desk in the back." He gestured toward the back east corner where the glow of a small desk lamp and tiny space heater was all that softened the black shadows.

"I started noticing people walking by and then stopping. I went out to see what the stir was about . . . and then I called you."

Darcy was taking her own notes. "Does your consortium have any enemies?" she asked. "I mean is there anyone who resented that you bought this property . . . or maybe resented what you plan to do with it? What *do* you plan to do with it, Mr. Kellogg?"

"None of your business, young lady. If you will excuse us." He steered Tom toward the back, but Darcy and Netters followed.

Darcy crossed her arms and said, "I just thought you might want to diffuse the tension, if there is any, that is. If someone feels strongly enough to dump a bison head on your doorstep, I'm thinking their behavior might escalate if they have doubts, they're making an impression. Don't you think so, Officer Quinn?"

Kellogg spun back to face her. "There is no tension, young lady. It is a case of simple vandalism."

"Darcy," Tom stepped toward her, then lowered his voice, "I know you're just trying to get the story, but you're not helping. Go stand by the door and I'll give you a statement later if I can."

"Okay, Tom," Darcy responded with sunny enthusiasm. "Sorry, didn't mean to get in your way." She wandered up toward the front doors. Netters followed her.

"What the hell do you think is going on?" Netters whispered to Darcy.

"I haven't got a clue," she whispered back as she glanced at the shadowy figures of Tom and Kellogg.

"I don't give a damn who is responsible. I just want that nasty . . . thing taken away!" Kellogg's voice rose to a full bellow.

Tom snapped his notebook closed and tucked it back in his pocket. "We'll do our best, sir," he promised.

The front door opened. A gust of wind pushed Officer Meeker into the room. As he passed, Darcy saw he was holding something wrapped in an old, dirty newspaper.

"What do you make of this, Quinn?" Meeker handed the paper to Tom who grimaced but gently unfolded the newsprint.

"What on earth?" Tom moved over to the window and Darcy drifted closer.

Peering over his shoulder, she saw an arrow nestled in the folds of the stained newspaper. The arrow looked like an artifact from a museum rather than a modern hunting arrow. Quinn began refolding the paper, but Darcy stopped him.

"Tom, what paper is that? It looks old too."

Quinn rustled the pages open again. Darcy spotted the masthead of the *Cheyenne Chronicle*. It was dated 1972. A fifty-one-year-old newspaper.

"Looks like an article about some Native American occupation at the Bureau of Indian Affairs property," Quinn answered absently as he scanned the brief article.

Darcy reached across and pointed. "Look at the list of demands, Tom. They underlined one in pencil."

Tom brought the paper closer and read, "Native American land must be rightfully returned to Native communities practicing traditional, spiritual, and ecologically respectful lifestyles."

"I don't get it." Darcy looked up in time to see Latham Kellogg blanch.

Clearing his throat, he recovered. "Nothing but radical claptrap. Officer Quinn, how long will it take you to resolve this issue?"

"We've already called for a crew. I'll double check. Excuse me." Tom turned his back and took out his phone.

"Um . . . Mr. Kellogg," Darcy continued to follow him to the back of the store, "what do you propose to do with this store? More furniture?"

"Hardly," Kellogg replied as he slid behind a massive oak desk and pointedly closed his laptop before Darcy could get a thorough look, but she caught the headline, "Native American Property Rights."

"Are you a representative of a tribe or something?"

Kellogg pulled his shoulders back and raised his chin. "Ms. Moreland, is it? What I am, what I do, and where I do it, is none of your business." He stood now, trying to intimidate her. "Please leave. Officer Quinn!"

Darcy held up her hands in mock surrender. "Okay. Okay, but you're just delaying the inevitable. I'm guessing you'll want positive press in the future." Darcy pulled a business card from a case in her back pocket. "Just call me. I'm always interested in helping good causes."

Darcy turned to go, waved goodbye to Tom on the way out, and signaled Netters to follow. Once they got into the van, Netters packed the camera away, then turned to her.

"So, what's going on?"

"I don't know. I only glimpsed his screen, but it had something about Native American Property Rights. What do you suppose that guy is up to? He doesn't strike me as a typical activist. I bet he doesn't even own a pair of Birkenstocks."

Netters snorted. "Well, I got some shots of the bison head and the sanitation guys as they tried to load it onto a truck."

"Good," Darcy dropped the van into gear. "Let's go back to the studio and I'll do a lead in for your video for the 5 o'clock."

DARCY FILLED THE REST OF HER AFTERNOON taping the lead and convincing her boss, Zach Horton, that the bizarre story should be hers.

She had originally come to work at KCHY because Zach was an old college friend and living and working in a large city had lost its luster. When Zach asked her to come work with him and cover Cheyenne Days rodeo last July, she had jumped at the chance.

She stayed on at KCHY as a reporter. After her work on the rodeo murders and solving the mysteries of the two bodies in the basement, she was promoted to an being an investigative reporter. She slipped into the role like a favorite pair of jeans.

Of course, she typically covered the prerequisite small-town station's store openings and/or closings, and pothole patrol, but occasionally, a juicy story landed in her lap, like last Fall's bones in the basement story. She knew from experience that at a larger station it often takes years to establish an impressive enough body of work to have a shot at such a good story.

"I don't know what the guy's up to, Zach, but I'll bet it's nothing good." She leaned over and pointed to the video Netters shot. "See how his eyes shift?"

"It's not every day you get a bison head dropped on your doorstep. He was probably already rattled. And although it saddens me to say it, you have all the sensitivity of a starving pit bull when you go after a story. Hell Darcy, you scare *me* and we're friends."

"But Zach, he was researching Native American property rights. Isn't that weird?" She gulped down a sip of cold coffee, grimaced, and threw the cup away.

"Maybe it's his hobby. Maybe he's a lawyer for some tribe. Did you ever stop to think of that?" Zach shuffled some papers on his desk.

"Nope, I asked him. The bloody bison head coupled with the arrow and newsprint seems to preclude a happy coincidence, don't you think?" Darcy leaned across Zach's desk.

"I think you're taking colossal leaps to form conclusions that aren't substantiated. Get me some solid information about Latham Kellogg, what he's doing in town, and then we'll talk."

"Whatever you say . . . *Boss*." Darcy bounced upright, pleased she had won round one.

"I deeply appreciated your sarcasm. Now get out of here."

Darcy laughed and left. At least Zach hadn't said no outright. If she could find out more about Latham Kellogg, this had the makings of a fascinating story.

She squeezed into her tiny office and grabbed a legal pad to jot down a few notes. She listed: arrow, bison head, property rights, call Carol Simms. She chewed on her pencil.

Carol was an old friend who lived in Minnesota and specialized in tribal litigation. Darcy flipped open her phone and scrolled through her contact list. She punched Carol's number in and got voice mail.

"Carol? Darcy Moreland here. I need some information about Native American property rights. Can you help? Call me back."

She nudged her chair back from the desk and propped her feet up, prodding the small, desiccated ivy plant her mother had given her to brighten up her space.

What could be going on? The bison head was a dramatic message, like the horse's head in the guy's bed in the *Godfather* movie. She shivered.

And the arrow. She remembered something from her Western Lit class about how arrows could be used symbolically as declarations of war.

Darcy swung her feet from the desk onto the gray-green linoleum floor, walked three steps to the door, then paced back, flopping back into her chair.

She knew the two tribes original to the area were the Arapaho and the Cheyenne. The Arapaho had long since settled on the Wind River Reservation clear across the state, and the Cheyenne were in Oklahoma.

Why would either tribe want Thompson's old store? she wondered.

Grabbing her pink eco-bottle from the corner of her littered desk, she titled it back and emptied it.

"Damn it! What am I missing here?" she asked aloud as she looked at her list. She began writing in the margins, working occasional keywords like 'property rights,' 'Native American treaties,' 'follow the money,' and 'who is the consortium?'

When her phone rang, she jumped and grabbed up the receiver.

"Moreland," she said. Darcy always answered her business phone formally; you could never be sure who was calling. Management currently was not paying for caller ID.

"Simms," came the crisp reply, followed by infectious laughter. "I understand you need to probe the depths of my legal expertise."

"Do you have any?" Darcy bantered as she tilted back her chair.

"God, my father hopes so. He paid a small fortune for it. What do you need?"

Darcy filled Carol in on the events of the afternoon, then waited while she heard Carol scratching notes on her end.

"I think you have a genuine mystery there, Darcy. Your instincts are right. The head and the arrow are probably at best a warning, at worst a promise. There are a few militant Native American organizations around who are vigilant about protecting their rights. Do you know any FBI agents out there? They keep a close watch on the more radical groups in the area."

Darcy added FBI to her list. "That's a good idea," she said. "Do you know anyone around here who specializes in Native American law?"

"In Cheyenne? Not off the top of my head. You're more likely to find someone with that specialty up by Riverton or Lander by the rez."

"Yeah, that's what I thought." Darcy wrote 'rez' on her list.

"I wish I could be more help. I can do a little general digging for recent cases and let you know what I find out."

"Thanks, Carol. That would be a big help."

Darcy looked at her list again. She wondered if she could cold-call the FBI. Doubtful she'd get much. Maybe Hank would know someone. Sometimes having a boyfriend who was a local police detective was a plus.

She speed-dialed his number and leaned back in her chair.

"Hi Hank. Do you know anyone in the FBI?"

"Aw hell, Darcy! Are you in trouble again?"

CHAPTER 2

"R EAL CUTE, NELSON. No, THIS IS about the bison head dropped in front of Thompson's Furniture this morning. I want to talk to someone about radical Native American groups, and I thought an FBI agent might steer me in the right direction." As she spoke, Darcy doodled stars in the margin of her notes.

"The only one who comes to mind is Stuart Johnson. I think he's still in Cheyenne."

Darcy added the name and boxed the FBI designation.

"Thanks. Should I use your name or pretend I've never heard of you?" Darcy knew Nelson would be mildly irritated by the implication his professional reputation might be even a little grubby.

"You do what you think best, but I'd tamp down the sassy attitude. FBI is notorious for not responding well to what others think is funny."

Darcy grinned wider. Direct hit, she thought.

"Good to know." she rose to her feet. "Will I see you tonight?"

His voice dropped to a deeper register, guaranteed to make her stomach rumble, "What do you have in mind?"

"Nothing fancy. Pizza and beer at Abby's. She just got back from visiting her sister in Omaha."

"I won't be able to be there until around six. Do you want me to check with Tom Quinn about the investigation, or do you want to do that yourself?"

"I hope you're not implying I'd tempt you with the promise of good pizza and cheap sex for police information."

Hank laughed. "Just so I don't have to turn down either, I think I'll let you do your own leg work. See you at six."

Darcy was still smiling as she dialed the number for the FBI. Having Hank in her life made her feel alive. He was the justification for every shred of sexy new lace underwear she owned. Besides being sexy, he was fun. Just an all-around picture-perfect guy, she thought, smiling to herself. Well, except when he wasn't.

Having Hank in her life was another reason for her to stay. Since they had met during a murder investigation in July, their paths had crossed several times and eventually they had started dating. She didn't know where the relationship was going, she only knew that she felt warm and fuzzy when she talked to him, and he made her laugh. Darcy recognized they needed to have a conversation about what their relationship was and what it wasn't. She just didn't know how to start that conversation.

It took mere moments to get through to Stuart Johnson.

"Agent Johnson? This is Darcy Moreland from KCHY Channel 23 News calling. I'm working on a story about a severed bison head left in front of Thompson's Furniture store."

"Yes, Ms. Moreland. How can I help you?"

"They left the head along with an arrow and an old newspaper that dealt with the occupation of the Bureau of Indian Affairs office in 1972."

"I'm aware of that, Ms. Moreland. What did you want to know?"

"I was curious about radical Native American groups around Cheyenne and whether they might be responsible."

"I would hesitate to guess Ms. Moreland. We have no definitive evidence indicating who was responsible."

"Agent Johnson, Detective Hank Nelson, gave me your name." She disliked using Hank's name, but she was getting nowhere.

"And I'd be happy to give you general background information, but nothing specific to this incident. Will that work for you?"

Darcy took a deep, calming breath and exhaled slowly, "Okay. Can you give me an overview of some of the Native American groups active in the area right now?"

"Well, there's the American Indian Movement, and the newer Native Youth Movement. We consider those the most aggressive organizations, but there are many splinter groups also active. Some are fairly covert."

"But surely not so covert that the FBI doesn't know who they are and what their agenda is," Darcy prodded. She tapped her pencil on the paper, leaving little dots.

Johnson laughed. "I'd like to help you, Ms. Moreland, but you can understand that when we are investigating covert organizations; the key word is covert."

"So, you are telling me the FBI can't identify any group who might use intimidation to further their agenda? May I quote you?"

Johnson paused before answering, "You might say the FBI recognizes that any group, if pushed hard enough and long enough, can and does resort to intimidation occasionally. That is not a federal offense. The bureau is, as always, cognizant of the welfare and safety of American citizens and is monitoring this situation carefully."

Deciding to cut her losses, Darcy finished jotting down notes. "Well, thanks for the no-details-details."

Johnson laughed. "Why don't you call Dr. Richard Barton? He's an expert on all things native and historical in this state. We sometimes informally consult him for background or summary information. He works for the Wyoming State Museum. You can tell him I referred you."

"Thank you, Agent Johnson. I appreciate your help."

With that, Darcy hung up and skimmed the contact information on her laptop. She dialed the museum number, asked for Dr. Barton, but was forced to leave a callback number.

Darcy glanced over her notes. She wasn't sure where to start first.

There was Latham Kellogg. Who was Kellogg and what or who comprised the consortium that had bought Thompson's Furniture?

And why would anybody care? Why especially some disaffected Native American group . . . or someone wanting to appear to be?

Darcy remembered how Kellogg had paled when he heard the reference about returning Native American land.

What could Thompson's Furniture possibly have to do with Native American land? And why would Kellogg be looking up information on Native American Property rights?

Then, there was the not-so-veiled warning of the bison head. Darcy drew circles around "bison head" in her notes.

Could they be from the same group that took over the Bureau of Indian Affairs 50 years ago? Or were they just referring to old demands made to the Federal Government?

Darcy couldn't focus on a clear path forward. Luckily, her phone rang.

"Darcy Moreland," she answered.

"Hello. This is Dr. Richard Barton from the museum. I'm sorry I wasn't available earlier. We're knee deep in building the newspaper digital reference access, and I'm afraid we've gotten distracted."

"Well, I appreciate your calling me back, Dr. Barton." Darcy flipped to a clean page. "I'm trying to do some background research on any militant Native American groups in the area. Stuart Johnson suggested I call you."

"What is this regarding?" Dr. Barton sounded faintly confused, as if shifting from the academic to the practical was an effort.

"There has been what appears to be a protest in front of Thompson's Furniture Store earlier today, complete with a bloody bison head and an article about AIM taking over the Washington BIA headquarters. I was wondering if you might have some insight into this protest." Darcy chewed on the end of her pencil as she waited for Dr. Barton to answer.

"An intriguing question, Ms. Moreland. Over the last few decades, there have been numerous protest organizations, so it would be difficult to pinpoint precisely who is responsible."

Darcy drew a box around Barton's name in her notes, then slashed a line through it.

"Well, thanks for your time," she mumbled, discouraged. Darcy was halfway to hanging up when she heard him still talking. She raised the phone to her ear.

". . . annoying because it is similar to the way things progressed in what they call the Old Time."

"I'm sorry Dr. Barton?" She picked up a pencil just in case.

"I was just saying some things never change."

Darcy was scribbling notes to herself in a combination of texting shorthand and phrases. "In what way?"

"In the Old Time, the whites wanted to deal only with 'the chief' which proved difficult. Although various tribes had leaders, they did not empower those leaders to speak for the entire tribe. It frustrated the whites who couldn't understand the pure democracy that thrived in those communities. Every man had a voice—consensus, which takes an enormous amount of time to achieve, was always the paramount goal."

"You're saying Native Americans groups today still try to reach consensus?" Darcy clarified as she scribbled 'consensus' in her notes.

"Yes . . . but every man has a right to mount his own protest without tribal knowledge or backing. Case in point . . . just as if you wanted to protest taxes in Wyoming, you wouldn't have to have the agreement of all the taxpayers in the state."

"This could be the work of an entire group . . . or one person. Is that what you're telling me?"

"I'm sorry, but yes."

Darcy checked her notes, looking for any specific detail. "There was an old arrow found at the site and—"

"A ubiquitous symbol for war," he cut in, suddenly sounding slightly excited. "They may initiate some kind of confrontation. Anything else?"

"Just the newspaper article found with the arrow I referred to earlier," Darcy answered. "There was a passage underlined declaring one of their demands was the return of lands to Native Americans."

There was a long pause.

"Dr. Barton. Are you still there?"

"Yes. I'm sorry, I was thinking. Although not an original demand, I'm curious about what possible connection Thompson's Furniture would have to Native American land."

"I talked to a man named Latham Kellogg who claims to belong to a consortium that bought the building, but he was reluctant to share any information about their plans for its use."

"If you don't mind, Ms. Moreland, I'll delve into it and see if I can come up with anything. I'll call you if I find anything."

"Fantastic! You have my number here, but my cell number is (307) 555-1379."

"I'll see what I can discover. I'll admit, I quite love these sorts of mysteries."

Darcy laughed. "You and my friend Abby. She likes 'the game's afoot' excitement of the Sherlock Holmes sensibility. I prefer answers myself."

"Well, I'll try to find you some Ms. Moreland."

"Thanks again," Darcy said as she hung up.

Darcy wanted to find station manager Zach Horton and tell him what she had so far; although it was still next to nothing, she wanted to let him know she was digging.

Zach was in his office, feet on his desk, ankles crossed, chewing on an unlit cigar.

Darcy grinned. It tapped into some fond memories of working for him at the University TV studio.

He'd tested her, making her report on the Ag department porcine division, and interviewing the second assistant wrestling coach who made a pass at her. He was another reason she had decided to stay in Cheyenne. He never let her slack. He made her a better reporter.

"What are you smiling at?"

Darcy laughed and came farther into his office. "Old memories."

Zach dropped his feet to the floor. "What do you want?"

"I thought I'd let you know what little I've found out about the bison head."

"Which is?"

"Nothing solid yet, Boss," she answered as she slid into a side chair. "I've talked to the FBI and a guy at the State Museum, but so far, no leads."

"Really? Who did they think did it?"

"The FBI doesn't seem to have any theories they're willing to share with me, but Johnson steered me to Dr. Barton at the State Museum who is going to dig up whatever references he can find."

"Yeah, well, stick with it. It's bizarre enough to be interesting."

"You got it." Darcy stood to leave.

"That doesn't mean work on it exclusively. I need you to pinch-hit on the noon slot. Cary has to get a root canal."

Darcy winced. "Yuck. I had that once. It is no fun. I'll be happy to sit in. Who's co-anchor?"

Zach shuffled papers on his desk, refusing to look her in the eye.

Realization hit her a moment later. "Oh, no, you don't! You will not make me sit with Adkins and make nice-nice at noon."

"Darcy, I don't have anyone else. Meredith threatened to beat him up on air if she ever had to work with him again."

"I'm with Meredith." Darcy glanced at Zach. He looked frazzled and discouraged. Finally, she sighed, taking pity on him. "Okay, just this once. But, damn, Zach, what does it say when none of the female reporters want to be around him?"

"Cary seems to manage him okay," Zach looked up at her.

"Because she showed him the gun she carries and asked if he'd like to sing soprano in church next Sunday. Hell Zach, Cary scares *me*. If I were running this station . . ."

"Well, you're not," Zach said.

"I know, but don't you think it's time to have a come to Jesus meeting with his uncle and suggest this might be a poor career path for his nephew?"

Zach stood and leaned across his paper-strewn desk. "Yeah, well, why don't you explain to Arnold Christenson that no one wants to work with his sister's only child? Should go over well. What part of small-town-small-station don't you get?"

"Okay. Could you at least tell Adkins to dial down the attitude?"

Zach held up his hands in surrender. "I'll do my best." He sat down heavily.

Darcy looked at her watch. "Alright then. I guess I'll throw myself under the bus in the interest of station solidarity right after I get some lunch."

"That's all I can ask." Zach was already picking up his phone as she left.

DARCY SQUEEZED INTO THE TINY CORNER booth in a small sandwich place with her Pepsi and Garden Salad and took out her notebook.

Reading over the sketchy details only caused more questions to crop up. There was something grisly about this whole incident.

Whoever had left the bison had probably butchered the poor animal and left the rest of its body in the field. Trophy-picking was sick; killing an animal for reasons other than food was abhorrent. Even she knew that.

A full-grown bison was too large for a couple of men to hoist onto the back of a pickup. If they did, wouldn't someone see them do it, or at least the carcass they left behind?

Darcy circled her note *'bison body???'* and dug into the cavernous bag. She rooted around for the newest model smart phone her folks had bought her. It was a lifesaver when she had to look something up and was away from her desk. She Googled Bison/Cheyenne and got a hit.

She punched in the number for Bison Bob Carson's Ranch, or 2-Bar-B Ranch, as the locals called it. Apparently, it was a working bison ranch and tourist stop just south of Cheyenne. It was also the closest source she knew for bison on the hoof.

"Bison Bob's Ranch. How may I help you?" asked the treacle-laced voice.

"Hi. This is Darcy Moreland from KCHY Channel 23 News. I was wondering if I could talk to Bison Bob?" Darcy winced. Just saying Bison Bob aloud made her back teeth ache.

"May I inquire what about?" asked the sweet-spoken receptionist.

"A bison head deposited in front of Thompson's Furniture Store earlier today . . ."

"Holy shit!" Miss Chirpy had left the building.

"Exactly."

"I'll go get him right away."

Darcy heard the clatter of the dropped phone and retreating shouts for Bob.

Moments later, a gravely deep voice exploded in Darcy's ear, "Bob Carson here. What the hell is this about a bison head in front of a furniture store? Exactly what are you accusing me of?"

"I am not accusing you of anything, Mr. Carson. I am a reporter with Channel 23 News, and I'm trying to track down the potential source of the bison. Have you had any reports of a discarded carcass on your ranch this morning?"

"No. But I'll damned well put the word out."

"Do you know any other ranchers around here who raise bison?"

"No one else has our size operation."

Darcy looked at her watch and ground her teeth. It was 11:20, and she had to get back to the studio.

"Mr. Carson, I'm sorry but I have to go. If you find anything out, will you please call me at the news station? (307) 555-0628."

"Sure will. I'll check around. Those are expensive animals."

"I sympathize, Mr. Carson," Darcy replied before she hung up. She'd call him back tomorrow if he didn't call her first.

CHAPTER 3

Darcy barely had time to fluff and buff before she zoomed onto the news set.

"Nice of you to drop by Moreland." Adkins looked up briefly from the primping mirror he was holding.

"Didja miss me?" Darcy threaded the mic cord up under her blouse and clipped it. She skimmed the copy before her and checked the placement of the prompter. She focused on the floor director as he counted down and straightened as the lead-in theme song played before fading.

Adkins sat up straighter and faced the camera. The "Welcome to the KCHY noon newscast," went smoothly, but when Adkins began the first story, he had trouble reading the prompter. Darcy thought he sounded like a seven-year-old in a reading circle.

"And here is Darcy Moreland with your Channel 23 weather . . ." Adkins cued her.

Darcy dutifully read about temperatures in the 40's and wind chill in the polar zone. She glimpsed Zach watching from behind the cameras.

She paused slightly after the weather report, waiting for Adkins to take the next lead to tape. When he didn't, she took over.

"There was some discussion at the City Council meeting last night regarding the rejuvenation efforts in downtown Cheyenne. Here is Meredith Markham, to bring us up to date."

The video played with Meredith giving a brief report about the wrangling among a few progressive council members and the handful of hide-bound small business owners clashing as usual.

"That was my lead in!" Adkins hissed at Darcy.

"Then you should've taken it," Darcy whispered back. She was dying to expound about dead air on television, but the floor director cued live feed.

Adkins, ignoring the script, turned to Darcy. *"I understand, Darcy, that you're looking into a gruesome story about a cow's head found downtown . . ."*

Trying to ignore the gleam in Adkins' eyes, Darcy faced into the camera. *"Well Adkins, that's almost right. Somebody left a bison head in front of Thompson's Furniture store early this morning. I will have more details on the five o'clock news."*

She turned back and grinned as if thanking Adkins for the plug on her story. Adkins saw Zach's scowling face, and thankfully said nothing. The rest of the show finished without incident.

Once the director signaled a wrap, Darcy yanked the mic down and out through her blouse and slapped it on the desk.

"Do not ever go off script again," she said to Adkins.

She pushed past Zach, muttering for his ears only, "Never again."

She slammed the door behind her as she stormed into her cramped office and plopped down in front of her computer.

Scrolling through her emails, she erased all the junk messages. Then, she saw that she had an email from Dr. Richard Barton. She clicked it open.

"I found a reference to a discovery a year ago of a body buried under the subfloor of Thompson's. Native American woman and child. Tribe unidentified. The remains were moved and interred in the cemetery here. Am still scrounging for circumstances. Will let you know. R.B."

Which would mean what? Darcy thought. Why wouldn't they be interred on the Wind River Reservation? She let out a growl of frustration. She didn't understand the intricacies of the Native American culture she had lived around all her life. How could she be so ignorant? Well, there is always the internet, she thought.

She pulled her laptop closer and dashed off a short thank you to Dr. Barton. Then she typed Native American Burials in the search bar. A long list flashed on the screen. She picked a site for the NAGPRA because she knew the governmental love for all things acronymic.

She had to skim a bit before she learned it stood for Native American Graves Protection and Repatriation act.

Whew! No wonder they used an acronym. She highlighted and copied bits of basic information to a research file.

A federal law was passed in 1990, which outlined a process to return human remains or cultural items to either lineal descendants or affiliated tribes.

"If the remains are inadvertently discovered, then consultation is necessary prior to excavation under an Archaeological Resources Protection Act permit. If remains covered by the law are discovered, they will stop the project for 30 days while the review and consultation process proceeds."

She read the information carefully. Inadvertently discovered meant unearthed accidentally, she guessed. But what would that mean for the bodies that Dr. Barton referred to? Did it mean that there were no living relatives or associations with a tribe? Why would that make a difference one way or the other?

Her cell buzzed and twitched on her desk. She saw it was Abby McNeil calling.

"Hi Abbs. I was going to leave to get the pizza and beer right after the 5 o'clock report."

"Good. I am dying to ask you about that bison head, but I'll just force myself to be patient," Abby sighed dramatically. "Hey, I have an idea. I'll pick up the stuff so you can get home faster."

Darcy laughed. "For an old lady, you have no more patience than a two-year-old," she said.

"Sixty-one is not old. I'll have you know that the sixties are the new forties and the whole despotism of ageist tyranny . . ."

She was working her way into a lather, Darcy thought. "Yeah, yeah. Got it. You'd better get a large pizza or two mediums, because I invited Hank."

"Okay. The usual?"

"Hmm?" Darcy was scribbling some notes on her promised report.

"Toppings," Abby said with her slow patronizing retired teacher voice.

"Oh . . . yeah. Uhm the usual, I guess. Hank likes black olives and hamburger on his. Would you mind doing half-and-half?"

"Not at all. I'd better go now and get the beer before your report. I'll just have the pizza delivered; I don't want to miss anything. Bye."

"Bye," Darcy mumbled into the phone. She looked at her notes. She didn't have much, but she could stretch the material to maybe two minutes in addition to the video Netters had shot this morning.

She consulted with Netters about what parts of the video to use and tweaked her report, double-checking with Cary, who was anchoring the 5 o'clock news.

"I hear you had fun with Adkins at noon. I'm guessing my root canal was less painful, but I appreciate you covering for me," she said.

"I could've done better if I'd had your gun. As it was . . ." Darcy shrugged and let the sentences hang.

Cary laughed. "That only works if he thinks you'll really shoot him."

"I'm almost there." Darcy shifted around Cary and tossed her notes down on the desktop.

"How long do you think it will run?" Cary asked as she made some notes on the top margin.

"We have a little video from this morning, and I haven't found out a lot more about it since then, so I'm guessing about a two-minute report, but longer if you want to ask questions."

"Yeah. I always think questions add a nice flourish."

"Okay. See you in fifteen." Darcy headed for the makeup area to see if she needed any repairs.

She brushed her honey blond hair until it crackled and then slipped on some pink lipstick and gloss. She was camera ready.

Perched on a stool out of camera range, she reviewed her notes. So far, it wasn't much of a story, but she felt a small shiver on the back of her neck . . . a sure sign that it was worth digging into.

She half listened to a recap of the stories she and Adkins had done at noon. She perked up when Cary cued her:

"Darcy Moreland investigated a report of a severed bison head left by the front doors of Thompson's Furniture store this morning."

Darcy sat up straight as a camera swerved to her.

"Yes, Cary, it was a gruesome sight. The enormous head almost blocked the front doors of the empty furniture store. Latham Kellogg spoke with us briefly as a representative of the building's new owners but was unwilling to comment about any projected use the consortium had determined for the historic building.

Later, Officer Ken Meeker found an antique arrow and an old newspaper report about a protest in 1972 at the Bureau of Indian Affairs office in Washington D.C.

Darcy watched the video play on the screen. Netters had captured the two police officers and Kellogg looking at the newspaper and arrow.

"Officer Quinn told Channel 23 News that the investigation is ongoing, and as usual, we are asking our audience to call the police if they have any information about this incident."

"Darcy, where did the head come from? Do the police have any information?" Cary continued to question.

"Not that I know of Cary. I called a local rancher. He is very concerned and will check if any of his animals are missing. They are expensive animals and the old rustling laws are still on the books. I will keep digging."

"Well, keep us posted, Darcy. Interesting story." Cary shifted slightly, indicating that the live report was finished.

The camera shifted away, and Darcy removed her mic and handed it to a floor tech nearby. Half listening to Cary in the background as she finished the news, Darcy tiptoed across the gray cement floor. She really liked everyone at the station . . . except Adkins. Her jaw tightened as she thought of him.

She knew at a small station like this, turnover was endless, but Adkins was unemployable anywhere that nepotism wasn't a factor.

As she pushed out the studio door, she thought that maybe she should hang around with Cary more . . . a gun toting lady with an attitude that terrified Adkins—Darcy liked that about her.

She made quick work of packing up her notes and laptop before heading out the front door with an over the shoulder wave to Wendy, the station's hard-working receptionist.

It took Darcy exactly 5 minutes to drive to the refurbished Algonquin building, even in the blowing snow and heavy traffic typical of February in Cheyenne.

The white columned porch designed to look imposing instead looked like a young girl dressing up in her mother's clothes . . . you understood the effort even if it made you grin.

As she climbed the concrete steps, avoiding the patches of dark ice in favor of salty grit tossed onto the middle of each step, she felt bone weary. She was glad Abby, her friend and former high school English teacher, lived on the first floor and would already have Mac, Darcy's Cairn terrier, at her place.

The moist warmth from the radiator hissing in the far corner of the hallway smelled rusty and did nothing to dispel the bitter chill from the opened door.

Amber lights in the shape of candle flames flickered energetically but did not scatter the deep shadows on the faded hall carpet.

Darcy saw a spill of golden light from Abby's door, which was ajar.

Pushing through she shouted, "Abby, how many times have I told you not to leave your door open like this?" She slipped out of her coat and hung it on the hall tree.

Abby darted into the brightly lit living room from the kitchen, looking flushed and unrepentant. "About a million . . . give or take. Don't get your knickers in a knot. I knew you and Hank were on the way. It was just a matter of who got here first." She held up two frosty mugs.

Darcy toed off her new boots by the door, bumped the door

closed, and grabbed the beer as she stepped over Mac who acknowledged her only with a tail wag.

"Or . . . it could be the serial killer who attacks careless old ladies who think they still live in the last century." Darcy plopped on the sofa.

"Or a police detective who can just walk in since the door is *still* unlocked," Hank added with a pointed glare at the two women.

"Don't fuss, Hank," Abby said as she handed him the other beer and headed for the kitchen for one for herself. "It isn't like it's downtown Chicago, you know."

Hank sat on the sofa, gripped Darcy's neck with his free hand, and pulled her to him for a deep kiss. Darcy wasn't sure if it was passion or temper. Either way, she liked it.

CHAPTER 4

DARCY SANK INTO HANK'S SIDE. Her heart zinged into a Texas-two-step, and she heard herself murmur something like, "Uhmm." Being incapable of articulate speech at the end of a long day was a bonus.

He smelled of pine, cold air, coffee, and Hank. She snuggled closer as the kiss deepened. She relished the feel of his arm pulling her tighter, and she wrapped her hand around the back of his neck.

"Don't make me throw water on you two," Abby's voice blared behind them. Darcy opened her eyes and slowly pushed Hank away.

Abby cackled on her way to her chair. "Teacher voice always works." She dropped into her favorite overstuffed Chesterfield chair, being careful not to slosh any of her beer. Once settled, Abby signaled to Mac to come up. The little terrier sprung into Abby's lap but looked guiltily at Darcy across the low-slung marble-topped coffee table.

"Damn it, Abby!" Darcy said. "How many times have I told you? Mac is not supposed to be up on the furniture."

"Mac is not *on* the furniture, he's on me," Abby said, stroking the scruffy black and tan hair behind Mac's ears.

"Give it up, Darcy," Hank said. "Abby's with him more than you are. You'll never win."

The doorbell rang. Darcy pushed herself free of the sofa and headed toward the door, muttering about being surrounded by traitors.

By the time she paid for the pizza, slapped it on the coffee table, took a piece, and sat back down, her good humor was almost restored.

"Interesting start to your day, Darcy?" Abby wiped a splotch of red sauce from her chin. Her blue eyes sparkled.

"Don't try to be coy, Abbs. You have no talent for it."

Darcy made her wait while she washed her bite of pizza down with a gulp of beer. She leaned forward, cupping her mug with both hands.

"Okay, here's the story. Someone left a bison head in front of Thompson's store. That's pretty much all we know."

"Your report had more information than that," Abby sputtered her outrage. "I waited all day to get the inside story, and I want it now!"

Darcy lifted her mug in a mock toast, ignoring Abby as she said to Hank, "See? Patience equivalent to a two-year-old."

Hank grinned since the taunt was not aimed at him. "I'm in a worse position, Abby. I didn't even get a chance to see the report before I came."

Somewhat mollified, Abby glanced at Darcy, who nodded slightly.

"Well, as I understand it," Abby began, "a bison head, an arrow, and a newspaper were left in front of Thompson's Furniture Store. The guy . . ." Abby looked inquiringly at Darcy.

"Latham Kellogg," Darcy supplied.

"Yes. Latham Kellogg was in the building and called the police. He wouldn't say why the group he represented bought the building."

Hank reached for another piece of pizza. "Not wanting to share information with the media in general, and Darcy in particular, is not a crime. Though we both know she wishes it were."

Darcy jabbed Hank in the side with her elbow. "Go on Abbs. I'll be interested to see what else you got out of my report."

"Let's see . . ." Abby picked a slice of black olive off her pizza and ate it while she tried to remember the information in the report. "Oh, I know. A local rancher is going to see if he's missing any animals. And then you implied whoever was responsible might be charged with rustling."

"Good job, Abbs. Anyone else need more beer?" Darcy asked, heading for the kitchen. Hank and Abby raised their almost empty mugs in the air.

As soon as Darcy took her seat and passed Hank and Abby a bottle each, Abby leaned forward, her blue eyes snapping, "There had better be more to the story, young lady." She grunted as she twisted off the cap and poured the foamy beer into her mug.

"Not much more. I called my friend Carol Sims, who works with Native American issues back in the mid-west and asked her to send me information on treaty property rights. She was the one who suggested I call the FBI." Darcy glanced at Hank. "By the way Hank, FBI Agent Johnson is so by the book, I think he has an index."

Darcy drank, burped softly, and said to Abby, "Hank suggested I contact him about activist groups in the area."

"Was he helpful?" Hank leaned back against the cushy pillow.

"Not particularly. He didn't give me much more than I got off the website. But he implied there could be some AIM activists in the area."

Hank sat forward and turned Darcy's shoulders so she faced him. "Get that thought right out of your head. Some of those radicals can be aggressive and violent. I'd think you'd learn some caution from your last big investigation of the bodies in the basement."

"But that was just a . . ."

"A radical group with an agenda," Hank finished for her. "The American Indian Movement fits that criterion, or at least has in the past."

"I know what I'm doing, Hank. It's sweet of you to worry about me, but I am being careful." Darcy pushed free and stood above him. "Investigating a story is part of my job. I don't get to pick and choose what is dangerous or not just as you don't."

Hank closed his eyes briefly. He took her hand and pulled her back down into his lap. "I'm just asking you to be cautious when investigating this story."

Darcy felt something relax inside her. Her insides went all melted caramel when Hank used that tone. "Alright, I promise to be careful."

"Isn't this nice?" Abby shifted in her chair and looked from one to the other. "I always feel better when you two get along. Now continue, Darcy. What else did you find out?"

"Agent Johnson told me about a guy at the State Museum who's supposed to be an expert in native history. His name is Dr. Richard Barton. Do you know him, Abby?" Darcy gnawed on the remnant of a cheese-filled crust.

"I think he did a presentation at my ladies' club last month. It was called 'Soiled Doves: Prostitutes in the Old West.' He was funny, interesting . . . and rather handsome as I recall. Does that sound about right?"

"I have no idea. I just talked to him on the phone." Darcy looked over at Abby and raised an eyebrow.

Abby turned crimson and shot out of her chair. "Not everyone in the world has a basket full of raging hormones like you, Darcy," she snarked as she stormed into the kitchen.

Hank shifted closer to nibble on Darcy's neck. "Do you have a basket full of raging hormones? Let's take them out and play."

Darcy nudged him away just as Abby returned with a plate full of cookies.

Abby still seemed flustered as she passed around the plate, and Darcy felt a frisson of guilt.

"Sorry, Abby. I shouldn't tease you."

Abby dismissed the comment with a wave of her hand and sunk back down into her chair. "Perfectly alright, dear, but what did he have to say?"

"He just confirmed what I already suspected about the possible symbolism, but he didn't give me much more until he called later this afternoon. He told me last year a construction crew unearthed the bones of an older woman and a baby when they replaced part of the foundation under Thompson's store."

"Really?" Abby leaned in.

"They buried them in Lakeview Cemetery, and Dr. Barton said he'd have to check to find out why."

"Of course, they'd be buried in the cemetery. Where else?" Abby sat back again.

"More properly on the Wind River Reservation, because they were Native American remains." Darcy watched with some satisfaction as Abby's eyes widened by just a fraction. She loved surprising her old teacher.

"Were they recent?"

Abby's question was soft and breathy, and Darcy knew she was remembering bones found under an old house last fall. Darcy almost hadn't survived that investigation.

She laughed with false bravado. "No, no. Dr. Barton said they thought the bodies were from around the 1800's. A grandmother and child."

"Oh, dear." Abby nibbled her cookie.

"How is it relevant to the bison head?" Hank asked.

"I don't know yet, but I'm sure going to try to find out. I'm up for my six-month review and I'd like to come up with a good story."

"Try not to *become* the story, will you please, Calamity?" Hank said.

Darcy opened and closed her mouth twice, trying to reply with either something scathing or funny, but nothing occurred to her. The truth was, she had earned the nickname Netters had given her; wherever she went, calamity followed.

"Okay, point well taken," she said finally. "But I'm pretty sure this is nothing more than an intriguing political protest."

"What's your next move?" Abby asked.

"I'm going to do some research about the political and social agendas of some Native American groups—" she held up a cautionary hand when Hank looked poised to interrupt, "on the internet mostly and from second person sources like Dr. Barton for now."

Abby got up and began cleaning up the debris of the meal. "Well, if you need any help . . ." she said as she carried the pizza box and plates into the kitchen.

"Thanks," Darcy answered. Then she had a scathingly brilliant idea. "Hey Abbs, maybe you could help . . ."

"Whatever I can do. You know that, Darcy." Abby came in and sat down on the edge her chair.

"I'm slated to do a story on the argument about the city Christmas tree and where it should be located now that they have the mini park downtown."

"What's the problem?" Abby asked.

"The folks at the depot want the tree in the plaza so it will bring folks into the brewery and out of the cold. Worked well last year."

"No, I mean what's the problem you want me to help with?"

"Because I'm going to be tied up tomorrow, I was wondering if you could go over to the State Museum and see if Dr. Barton has found anything."

Darcy watched a light pink flush wash over Abby's face and bit the inside of her cheek to keep from smiling.

"I don't think I could be much help," Abby said.

"Of course, you could. You know what I'm looking for. How might the bison head, the arrow, and now the bodies, be connected? You have a better-than-average grasp of local history—"

"Damned with faint praise, thank you very much," Abby said. "I hasten to point out any historical expertise I might have has been from reading rather than living. I'm not as old as all that, you know."

"Abbs, I could use a second pair of eyes on this. You love history and you like Dr. Barton. What's the downside?"

"The downside is I have no credentials to be asking Dr. Barton or anyone else questions and wasting their time."

Darcy propped her elbows on her knees and leaned in. "Abby don't be silly. How many years have you paid taxes in this state?"

Abby opened her mouth to answer, but Darcy cut her off.

"Lots!" Darcy thumped her half-empty mug on the table for punctuation. "And the State Museum is there for all citizens any time they have a question. Isn't that true, Hank?"

"Leave me out of this." Hank crossed his arms.

"Coward," Darcy snarled at him. "Seriously, Abby. It would be a big help. I just need some background information. Please?"

"Okay. But don't blame me if I don't ask the right questions," Abby said.

It took Darcy a scant five minutes to sketch out notes for possible questions.

Darcy passed the list to Abby. "Feel free to skip any of these or add your own."

"Not on your life," Abby glanced down at the list. "I'm following this like it's a grocery list for a diabetic."

Darcy laughed and swooped in for a kiss on Abby's soft cheek. "You're a sweetheart. Thanks, Abbs."

"Get out of here, the two of you." Abby took her list and stuffed it in her handbag by the door.

Darcy dug in her purse for her keys when they reached her apartment.

Hank stood back as she pushed through and turned on the overhead light.

In contrast to the worn gentility of Abby's apartment, Darcy's home left no doubt that it belonged to a young and complex woman who spent little time at home.

The brightly hued pieces of art on the walls were matted and framed. A variety of Denver Art Museum posters, favoring a blend of bold prints by an artist from Colorado University, hung on neutral walls. Softer watercolors tucked in corners or rested on spaces in the two large bookcases flanking the non-functioning fireplace.

Stacks of magazines littered most of the flat surfaces. Books lying face down teetered on mounds of unanswered mail and unpaid bills. On plain oak side tables, small oriental cloisonné vases and a carved jade ball rested. Family heirlooms.

Clean, but cluttered.

"Ever thought about recycling some of this stuff?" Hank asked as he riffled through a stack of ubiquitous gossip glossies.

"Don't start, Hank. I know where everything is and I'm not through reading them yet. When I am . . ." Darcy pointed to a conspicuous blue bin resting in the far corner of her bay window dining area furnished with a bistro table and Bentwood chairs.

Darcy dropped her oversized bag and coat on the brown super suede sofa and tossed her heels in the corner by the door. She walked to the door to her bedroom and turned, striking a Mae West pose, "Now we can either discuss home renovation, or you can join me in the bedroom."

Hank slipped out of his jacket and began unbuttoning his jeans. He scooped her up in his arms, walked the few feet into the bedroom, and tossed her onto the rumpled bed. He followed her down and rested on top.

Hank nuzzled her neck while unfastening the tiny buttons marching resolutely to the bottom of her white blouse, which barely skimmed the top of her dress slacks.

By the time he released the last button he had pushed the light covering to the side, Darcy skimmed out of her slacks and flung them off her ankles onto the floor leaving her barely covered in a pink froth of lace.

"I do love an eager student," Hank mumbled in her ear as he tried to slide his jeans off.He stopped a moment later. "Damn it!" Hank sat up looking so frustrated it made Darcy laugh.

"Malfunction?"

"Boots," Hank said as if it were an expletive. He wrestled his jeans back up, crossed his foot on his knee one at a time, and tugged the offensive boots off.

He turned, and looked down at Darcy sprawled on the bed, dropped his jeans and boxers. Darcy was not laughing anymore.

CHAPTER 5

H ANK LEANED OVER AND UNFASTENED HER BRA, dragging it languidly up and off. Darcy arched in response to the rough flick across her distended nipples. He easily inserted his hands under the lace of her panties, slipping them slowly down the insides of her thighs, caressing them with his fingertips. He dropped the panties in a pink puddle.

Darcy rolled out from under him to sit on the edge of the bed. "Hank, what are we doing?"

Hank twisted to sit next to her on the bed. "If you have to ask, I must be doing it wrong."

"No, I mean, you always feel good, but what is our relationship? Are we friends with benefits? Committed lovers? Uncommitted lovers?"

"I wasn't prepared for this pop quiz, but I would say we are committed lovers. We date exclusively, spend time together, and make love occasionally as our jobs permit."

"But where is this going?"

"If you're asking if I love you, the answer is yes. Do you love me?"

"Yes. Absolutely! But I have seen relationships fizzle just because the couple was marking time."

"I don't think either of us is capable of marking time. I think we need to be better at not getting our careers tangled up with our love lives and our sex lives. We need to learn how to merge like a motorcyclist in rush hour traffic."

"You think we are merging?"

"Yes, I do," he said before he kissed her and pushed her flat on the bed.

IN THE EARLY HOURS OF THE NEXT MORNING, they raided Darcy's refrigerator. Hank, elbows on the bistro table, ate the remains of a KFC leg while Darcy tore pepperoni slices off a slice of cold pizza.

"What the hell are you smiling about?" Darcy asked. She sat on one of the bentwood chairs facing Hank across the tiny table.

"Abby had it right. You *are* a basket full of raging hormones."

"My hormones weren't raging until you stirred them up."

"Complaining?" Hank arched a dark bow.

"Commenting."

Darcy stared at the man across from her. Dark hair and eyes so blue they jogged her memory about needing windshield washer solution in her car. The early morning sunlight from her small kitchen window made him squint a little and the shadow of his beard created the illusion of danger.

It wasn't all an illusion, she thought. Hank could be confrontational and inflexible, which probably made him a good cop, but not necessarily a wonderful boyfriend.

"What's the matter?" Hank asked.

"Nothing. Just wondering how much of you is cop and how much is . . . just Hank."

"What brought this up?" Hank got up to throw his chicken bone into the trash under the sink.

"I don't know. Morning-after musings. Just thinking about merging a cop with an investigative reporter."

Hank brought the coffee to the tiny table and poured refills.

"Okay, probably a discussion best saved for a long evening over wine." Darcy kissed Hank's cheek on the run.

"Gotta get ready," she said, and disappeared behind her bedroom door.

Hank watched her retreat, then finished the cleanup. He chuckled as he wiped down the counter.

Darcy amused him when she flew off on conversational tangents. He knew from experience she would claim simple curiosity if he called her on it, but Hank recognized it was more.

She loved solving puzzles, and, as Hank had realized early on in their relationship, he was a puzzle to her. Hell, he was a puzzle to himself. He ran a still-damp hand through his hair and caught sight of his rumpled reflection in the window. He hoped Darcy stayed curious about him. He loved that about her.

Darcy heard the door close and said into her mirror, "Man's as bristly as his beard in the morning." She smoothed moisturizer on a rosy abrasion on her cheek.

An hour later, she breezed through the frosted doors of KCHY Studio, pulling with her the blood-numbing cold of the early morning.

She blew on her hands and stomped her feet, trying to warm them as she stopped by the front desk.

Wendy, the office manager, laughed. "You'd do better to get some warmer gloves and boots," she said.

"Yeah, but where's the challenge?" Darcy responded. "Anything interesting going on?"

"Yeah, Zach wants to see you in his office as soon as you come in."

Darcy stopped stomping her feet and stepped gingerly out of the small puddle she had created. "Did he look happy or mad?" Darcy asked.

"He poured himself a big cup of coffee, told me to tell you he wants to see you, and went back to his office," Wendy said.

"Hmmm. A big cup of coffee doesn't bode well," Darcy mused as she unwound the multicolored scarf from around her neck.

"Hey! I make that coffee," Wendy protested.

"I know, and you do miracles with the pig swill they provide you but . . ."

"Not exactly Starbuck's?" Wendy finished.

"Not exactly coffee," Darcy corrected.

Darcy stopped by her office and tossed her coat and scarf over her chair. She rifled through the small stack of 'While You Were Out' slips by her keyboard. One from Dr. Barton, one from Carol, and one from Agent Johnson at the FBI. She chucked them back onto her desk.

Once she inserted herself into a chair in front of Zach's desk, she could feel her neck muscles tighten.

"What's up, Boss?" she tried for a light tone.

"Before I tell you . . ." Zach hesitated and took a deep gulp of coffee.

Darcy sat straight up. "Do not tell me I'm fired. I know I can be abrasive sometimes, but I can try to tone down—"

"Darcy, it's nothing like that. Uncle Arnie wants Adkins to work with you on the investigation about the bison head."

"What?" Darcy practically catapulted out of her chair.

"Sit down, Darcy. Arnold Christenson is convinced if Adkins could uhm . . . sort of intern with a first-rate reporter like yourself . . ."

"No roses are coming from this request." She leaned across the desk and glared.

"I need you to be a team player, Darcy," Zach said.

"That's code for, 'Please don't scream when we throw you under the bus. You'll frighten the bystanders.'"

Zach laughed. "True enough but screaming isn't going to change anything either. Mr. Christenson is convinced Adkins could take over the station one day if he received some good training."

"Then send him to college. Hell Zach, that's where we learned."

"I suggested that, but he said Adkins wasn't academically gifted—"

"Code for he can't get into a college program. . . ." Darcy kibitzed.

"—and would learn more with a hands-on approach," Zach finished, ignoring Darcy.

"I'd like to give him a 'hands on approach'. I'd like to hand him right out of here." Darcy flopped back onto her chair.

Zach tried unsuccessfully to look stern, then gave it up, allowing a huge smile to spread across his face. "Me too!" he agreed.

"But Uncle Arnie owns the station and if he wants to turn it into a home-schooling opportunity for his nephew, I think we have to accommodate him."

"What exactly does accommodate mean?"

Zach shrugged. "Just treat him like an intern."

"Really?" Darcy sat up as she imagined sending Adkins on Starbuck runs and having him pick up her dry cleaning.

"But treat him fairly," Zach cautioned. "Try to teach him about investigative journalism. Let him follow you around. Take some time. Explain why you do things and what you do. Or better yet, explain what you don't do."

"You know what they say about trying to teach a pig to sing . . ."

"Yeah, I know, 'It wastes your time, and annoys the pig.' But give it a shot."

Accepting this was one battle she could not win, Darcy stood up to leave. "So, when does the Moreland College of Journalism open its doors?"

"Right now," Zach said. "I already briefed Adkins. If it's any consolation, he wasn't pleased with this arrangement either."

Darcy stopped at the door and said, "Yeah, it helps a little."

The good mood was long gone by the time she got to her office and found Adkins ruffling through the notes on her desk.

"What are you doing?" Darcy asked very quietly.

Startled, Adkins straightened, once he realized it was Darcy.

"Oh hi, Darcy," he said and stacked her phone messages in a bright yellow pile. "Isn't it going to be fun working together?"

Darcy slapped her hand over the messages. "Adkins," she said through gritted teeth, "do not touch anything on my desk. Do not touch anything on anybody's desk. That's rule number one. Follow it. It may save your life."

Adkins slid out of her way as far as he could in the minuscule office. "They really should give you a larger office, Darcy. Ya want me to talk to Uncle Arnie?"

She sat behind her desk. "Rule number two: do not mention Arnold Christenson's relationship to you. Got it?"

Adkins nodded.

Darcy went on, "Mr. Christenson owns this station. He is our employer. He wants you to intern and learn from me. These are the facts. In journalism, we deal with facts."

"Ah gee, Darcy. Can't we just get along?" he perched on a corner of her desk.

"No, we can't just get along. You do what I tell you to do, listen when I explain something, and stay the hell out of my way."

"Now listen here, Darcy," Adkins puffed up his chest like a fish. "Uncle . . ." Catching the warning spark in Darcy's eye, he paused and then began again. "I want to learn how to be an investigative journalist," he amended.

"That's a start. Sit down."

Adkins sat in the straight-backed wooden chair. When Darcy said nothing, he cleared his throat. Darcy read her messages.

Dr. Barton said he had some more information about the hasty burial. Darcy scrawled 'Abby' on the bottom and placed it by her phone.

Next, she looked at the message from Carol. She wanted Darcy to call her about a 'wrinkle in the law'—whatever the hell that meant. Darcy put it under Dr. Barton's message.

Adkins cleared his throat again. Darcy slanted him a look, her mouth pulled tight. "If you're sick, go home."

"I'm not sick. I just don't know what I'm supposed to do."

Darcy relented. Maybe this won't be so awful after all.

"Okay Adkins, here's the deal," Darcy waved the phone memos in her hand, "These are all calls from people I've contacted about the bison head story."

Adkins looked as if he was trying to remember what that story was about, but he didn't interrupt, so Darcy continued, "This is from a guy at the State Museum." She slapped it down as if dealing cards. "This is from a lawyer friend of mine about Native Americans and the law." Darcy glanced up at Adkins to see if he was still paying attention. He was. "And this is from Agent Johnson of the FBI about Native American activists in the area."

Adkins peered at the messages in front of him.

"So?"

"Choose one to follow up on."

Adkins looked at the messages once more. "I think I'll tackle the FBI guy," he decided as he held up the note.

"And testosterone wins over history and law once more!" Darcy said.

"Huh?"

"Please tell Agent Johnson you're calling back for me. Write down any information he gives you and bring it back here. Okay?"

"Got it." Adkins headed toward the door.

"And Adkins?"

"Yeah?"

"He's doing us a favor. Be nice."

Adkins made a break for it. Darcy leaned back in her chair and dialed Carol's number. She answered on the third ring.

"Darcy. Took you long enough," Carol said by way of greeting.

"Had a minor crisis this morning. I got saddled with an intern."

"Woo Hoo! A Gofer. I want one of them."

"You wouldn't want this one. Owner's nephew."

"Ouch! Who did you misuse and abuse? Was it fun?"

Darcy dropped her feet to the floor. "Your glee about my misfortunes is at best unsettling and at worst scary. Why do you assume I got saddled with the him because I screwed up?"

"Ah. Good point."

"It just so happens Mr. Christenson wants his nephew to learn from the best."

"Couldn't afford NYU?"

"Couldn't pass the ACT." Darcy sipped her now frigid coffee.

"Tough break . . . but I got a little tidbit for you that might lead to something."

Darcy snatched a pencil from a red, chipped mug that held a hodgepodge of writing utensils. "Great. Let me have it."

"When I was looking for precedents—that's lawyer talk—"

"Carol!"

"Wow, you're getting cranky. Are you getting enough sleep?"

Darcy thought about last night and Hank. She didn't answer.

"Your silence is as loud as a squeal. You're getting something, but it's not sleep. Now's not the time, but you'd better bring me up to speed soon or the well of friendly legal advice is going to dry up."

"I'll call you this weekend, I promise. Now give."

"I found a suit filed by the Lummi Nation in Washington State. It basically states that when Native American remains are discovered, the contractor is obligated to inform the tribe, the city, and the state government."

"Is the regulation the same in Wyoming?" Darcy was scribbling notes as quickly as she could.

"Doesn't matter because the Native American Graves Protection and Repatriation Act states that if bodies or even body parts are found, the project has to be stopped for 30 days."

"What's this got to do with Native American Land Rights?"

"Well, if a notification wasn't made and no archeological study was ordered, the land could revert to the original owners."

"Really?"

"I said *could* revert . . . Whoever brought that kind of claim would need a lot of money and some high-powered lawyers."

"Neither of which are in significant supply for Native American tribes," Darcy said.

"There are many precedents of tribes winning some kind of reparation because bodies had been disturbed, but rarely, if ever, do they get their claim on the land back."

"Thanks Carol, it's definitely something I can dig into. And I promise I'll call you this weekend."

Darcy hung up and looked at her notes. This may lead nowhere, she thought. She picked up the message from Dr. Barton and dialed Abby's number. No answer. She dialed the number for Dr. Barton and got a receptionist.

"I'm sorry," the insincere receptionists trilled. "Dr. Barton is in consulting and cannot be disturbed. May I take a message?"

"Please tell him Darcy Moreland from Channel 23 returned his call. Thank you."

She hung up and tried to decide whether she needed coffee or the bigger blast of an energy drink. She felt like she was fading fast.

She pushed away from her desk just as Adkins slammed in.

"Honest to God, Darcy, I don't know where our taxpayer dollars are going if that's the kind of service a citizen can expect from the FBI." Adkins collapsed in the chair in front of her.

"What happened?" Darcy felt her stomach clench.

"Nothing. I swear to you I just called the guy—"

"The agent. You call them agents," Darcy corrected, hoping to penetrate his dense gray matter.

"Yeah. I called the *agent*," he mocked her tone, "and the jerk wouldn't tell me anything."

The clenching pain rose from her stomach to her head. She rubbed her temples, trying to ease it. "What exactly what did you say?"

"I said I was returning your call and he should give me all the information and I'd get it to you if it was important enough," Adkins paused as if he were expecting a reward for protecting her time.

"Adkins, Agent Johnson doesn't owe you or me anything. He was helping me investigate background on activists in the area."

"Geez, Darc . . ."

"Don't call me Darc. You don't know me that well."

"I could always call you Calamity like Netters does."

"Do not call me anything but Darcy or Moreland if you prefer," Darcy said.

The clang of the telephone saved him from a lecture about professionalism.

"Moreland," she answered then listened silently.

Her face flushed red. She kept answering, "Yes sir, yes sir, sorry sir," as she glared at Adkins.

Adkins wisely fled her office.

CHAPTER 6

ABBY MCNEIL FELT POSITIVELY EFFERVESCENT. SHE was eager to start researching Native American issues for Darcy, especially if it meant she could meet with Dr. Richard Barton at the State Museum.

She had called the museum early this morning and arranged an appointment to talk to him at 11:00 o'clock. She had dressed with care. She could not abide ladies of a certain age who dressed like they were in high school. She had taught high school for enough years to know that even youthful bodies looked ridiculous in some choices, never mind . . . less youthful bodies.

She had heard "jeans and a cute top"—Darcy's idea of fashion advice—but this occasion called for understated elegance . . . casual chic. She donned a nice set of gray dress slacks paired with a simple silk blouse and a bright scarf. She fluffed her short salt-and-pepper colored hair and put on a layer of understated peachy colored lipstick.

During the short drive to the museum, Abby reviewed her memory of Dr. Richard Barton. She recalled he was attractive and well groomed. She liked that in a man, she thought as she locked her bright yellow VW. It beeped companionably back at her.

It was formidably frigid out and the wind pushed against her stiffly as she battled her way to the door. Once she reached the front desk, she unbuttoned her gray wool coat and fluffed her hair once more before addressing the young lady at the front desk.

"Good morning, my name is Abigail McNeil. I have an appointment to speak to Dr. Barton," she told the receptionist.

"Oh yes, here you are," the receptionist replied as she pointed a long, pink fingernail to a log line in her appointment book. "If you will wait for just a moment, I'll let him know you're here."

Abby wandered over to a display case off the entrance hall. She had just leaned forward to read the labels on a map of the Lewis and Clark Expedition when she heard, "Ms. McNeil?"

She popped up and turned. Yes, she thought, she had remembered what he looked like correctly.

Dr. Barton was almost a foot taller than Abby, and she enjoyed looking up at him. He looked positively dapper in cordovan loafers, mercilessly creased khaki slacks, and an impeccably tailored navy blazer over a white shirt open at the neck. His white hair fringed a mostly bald head. Abby was pleased he had not surrendered to the fad of shaving off all his hair. His eyes were a soft green, enhanced by tortoise-shell glasses perched low on his nose.

Abby flushed. At first, she thought it was a hot flash, but then recognized the effects of male magnetism. Even now, she would sometimes meet a man who made her heart feel like it had slammed over a speed bump. It always surprised her.

"Call me Abby," she said.

"Well then, Abby, I go by Barton. Never could abide the nickname Dick for obvious reasons—and Richard sounds like I am a butler. What can I do for you?"

"Ah . . ." she trailed off.

Barton gallantly took her elbow and began moving her down a softly lit hall.

"There is something intimidating about being in a museum. All this harvested historical debris so out of context and displayed like a shoe sale at Sears." He laughed softly as he led an entranced Abby through a rat's warren of twists and turns. Finally, he stopped at an office with his name and title stenciled on the frosted glass insert of the door.

Barton ushered Abby inside, and she took a glance at what she had already expected to find. The office was as precise as the man who inhabited it.

Along the back wall marched four lawyer's bookcases displaying a colorful array of leather-bound tomes from another era. Abby's English-teacher-heart soared.

In front of the bookcases was a polished desk, either an antique or an excellent reproduction, Abby thought. Abby ran a tentative finger over the satin finish as she took the seat Barton gestured her into, a burgundy leather club chair in front of the desk. She assumed Barton would retire to sit behind his desk, but he slid into the chair next to her. Abby was sure she could feel the heat from his knees as he faced her. She felt "the flush" again, and silently ordered herself to get a grip.

"The reason I'm here, uhm . . . Barton," she stammered.

"If I may, Abby," Barton reached for a folder on his desk. He handed it to her as he explained, "I did some digging about the grave for the Native American woman that was found during the construction . . . no pun intended."

Abby began looking through the information Barton had assembled. Her shyness disappeared when she glanced at the pages. "It says here the Native American Graves Protection and Repatriation Act of 1990 requires if you find historical artifacts at a construction site, the contractor must notify the people responsible and shut down for a thirty-day investigation. Did this happen?"

"No," Barton leaned closer. "Instead of calling the state archeologist to identify the bones as Native American, which should be standard operating procedure, the county coroner took possession of the bones and cleared the site."

"You mean the contractor could continue to dig there?" A chill slithered down her spine. "Are we talking illegal or just immoral here?"

Barton smiled grimly, "I admire a lady who cuts to the heart of the thing. If I had to guess, I'd say a little of both. The coroner is supposed to ensure the compassionate and dignified disposition of human remains. If the memos I've found can be believed, James

Frye, the county coroner at the time, ignored any obligation to the deceased. His successor found the bones piled in a cardboard box and in a corner of the office."

Barton spread half a dozen irregular slips of paper across the shiny surface of his desk.

Abby placed a newly manicured nail on top of one slip and pulled it toward her. She glanced down at the cramped writing and squinted, trying to focus on the letters that seemed to fade and dance on the page.

Recognizing the problem, Barton snatched his glasses off, and offered them to Abby.

"Allow me . . ."

At first, Abby thought to decline, but curiosity quickly triumphed over vanity. She slipped the still warm glasses onto her face, mentally chiding herself.

The words stopped swimming, and she deciphered the note.

RE: Bones @ Thompson's ID'd as antelope or small elk. Check @ arrangement.

"What does that mean?"

Barton glanced at the memo. "It appears to be a reminder for James Frye regarding how he identified the bones."

Abby shot him her annoyed teacher look. "I can read that much. I meant about James Frye and arrangements."

Unflappable, Barton said, "I think if you try for more precision in your questions, our communication will advance more felicitously."

Abby blinked, opened her mouth to retort, then closed it again. She was clear that Barton had just impugned her communication skills. On the other hand, he had insulted her with such a pleasant voice and affable attitude—not to mention an excellent vocabulary—she could not scrape up enough irritation to be truly affronted.

"So sorry, Dr. Barton," Abby answered and was assured that her return to formality had not been missed. "I live alone and have formed the unhealthy habit of talking to myself when I have a conundrum to solve."

"I beg your pardon, Abby." Barton reached across the small space and placed his hand softly over hers. "I am afraid I have become particularly pedantic in my old age. It comes from being the most experienced on staff and dealing with, well, youth."

"As I am a retired teacher, I certainly understand."

Abby dragged her hand away slowly. She was having trouble concentrating with him touching her, but she did not want him to be offended either. She handed him back his glasses.

"Very gracious of you." Barton left his hand, covering part of the notes.

She looked at Barton and then down at the notes. "Is there any chance that I could get a copy of these notes to take to Darcy?"

"No chance at all, unless you agree to have dinner with me this evening."

Abby felt her heart constrict and her breath catch. An objective part of her brain was trying to remember the last time she had been asked out on a date. Her memory flew back to just after her husband's funeral when Vincent Marcos called her to see if she wanted to go out, but he'd just been interested in selling her more insurance.

"What do you want me to buy?" Abby prayed she had just thought it but could see from Barton's face that she had said it aloud.

"Not a thing. I just think we would have an interesting time getting to know each other. Are you actively involved with someone?"

Abby liked the thought that Barton looked distressed at the idea, "No. No. Nothing like that. I just don't date much." *Much? Any!* Her merciless internal voice corrected.

Barton laughed—a deep, rolling laugh that crinkled his eyes and flashed his fillings.

"I am oddly pleased to hear it. Will you go to dinner with me?"

Barton leaned in closer. Abby smelled a hint of British Lyme Cologne. Its crisp, clean scent seemed to clear her head.

"Well," Abby said, "if it's the only way I can get copies for Darcy. I really would do almost anything for that girl."

"I was just teasing about the copies, Abby, but not about dinner. I'd like you to come without coercion, if possible."

"Then, yes." Abby felt her face go crimson but was powerless to stop it.

"Wonderful!" Barton stood up from his chair. "If you'll wait just a moment, I'll go copy these for you. I'll only be a minute."

Abby barely had time to wander over to the bookcases behind the desk to look at some of the titles before Barton returned. He handed her a folder with several pages.

"Feel free to make notes on any of these with any questions you might have, or have your Darcy do it, and I will endeavor to clarify anything I can."

"Thank you so much, Barton. I can't tell you how grateful . . ."

"Not at all," Barton cut her off. "I'll pick you up at 7 o'clock if that would be alright. Where do you live?"

Abby, who had started to walk toward the door, turned and said, "I live in the Algonquin Apartments on 18th street, Apartment 101. Do you want me to write it down for you?"

"No, I have it. I must admit, I am thrilled that you don't live in one of those new subdivisions like Pony Ridge with those horrible names for the streets like Strawberry Roan or Pinto. Just too Hollywood for me."

Abby laughed. "Me too."

"You see, we already have something in common."

They had reached the front of the building. Barton stopped and took Abby's proffered hand in both of his. "Until this evening then."

Abby thought she murmured a halting, "Uh huh," but she wasn't sure. She was out of the building, but for a moment confused about how she had gotten there. A brisk bitter wind blew her coat open and riffled her hair and she came back to her senses.

"No fool like an old fool," she muttered, not sure if she was talking about Barton or herself.

Latham Kellogg was just finishing a detailed email to his clients. He couldn't wait to return to his plush offices in a New York high rise, he resented the need to keep his clients informed at all. He was handling all the pesky little details in this backwater cesspool of a town. That's what his clients were paying him to do, wasn't it? He didn't feel the need to tell them he had placated the local police and dismissed the symbolism of the bison head and arrow as meaningless corporate vandalism.

He most assuredly would not tell them of the annoying transactions and new demands from the former county coroner, the City Councilperson, and the legislator. They were all so irritatingly skittish about the publicity.

The watery, late afternoon sun had been dodging behind clouds all day and added to the darkening gloom in the cavernously empty store. He jacked up the space heater another notch and began gathering the papers to fax to his clients.

He cursed his hotel's lack of a fax machine. He would be obligated to drive his rental car to the office center the front desk girl had told him about.

The shadows crept across the floor, making him feel almost claustrophobic. Kellogg thought he heard a soft squeak and a muffled rattle behind him from the back room. He even imagined the temperature drop, sending an icy draft up his spine and making him shiver.

He shifted around in his chair and squinted into the vicinity of the back room.

"Anyone there?" he called out. He listened for an answer, straining to hear even a whisper of movement.

Nothing.

Kellogg chuckled. This town was making him crazy. The sooner he got out of this mudhole, the better he would like it.

He slipped several manila folders into his custom leather briefcase. He loved the feel, the satisfying click of the latch. He loved anything that was expensive and exclusive. It was how he eased his conscience about the things he had to do. What good was an Ivy League education if you couldn't parlay it into wealth and comfort? Both of which were in short supply in this place.

He leaned down to switch off the heater. It wouldn't do to burn the place to the ground after all the trouble they'd gone to acquire the building and begin the renovations.

As he stood back up, he thought he heard another scuffle and spun around.

"Who is it?" He franticly opened the small drawer in the desk and pulled out the Smith and Wesson 638 Airweight revolver he had hidden there.

"I'm armed!" he shouted frantically, his voice echoing through the empty space.

He felt a slick film of sweat coating his palms. He clutched the black grip tighter but noticed with disgust that his hand shook.

He swung around in a full circle but couldn't see anything in the dark corners. He concentrated on the surrounding air, trying to sense any movement. More sweat pooled and slithered down his neck. He blinked hard, as if it would improve his sight, but it didn't.

The loud screech of a floorboard had him firing toward the sound, emptying two rounds into the blackened floor, spattering the air with shards of wood and dust, but nothing else.

His stomach roiled. He tried to call out again, but all he could manage in his fear was a breathy, "Please!"

He cleared his throat and tried again, wheezing out, "Please, please don't hurt me. I'm just a lawyer. Just a hired lawyer."

No answer, but Kellogg could feel someone or something pressing closer. He edged back and felt the desk rap the back of his knees. He lost his balance and slapped the top of the desk to right himself but froze.

He felt the rough rasp of a rope from behind tighten around his neck and clawed at it, dropping the revolver to the floor with a clatter.

A violent jerk slammed him across the top of the desk. Kellogg kicked out and struggled but could not loosen the pressure of the rope.

As the rope tightened, Kellogg's vision blurred. He felt compelled to see his attacker, and he opened his bulging eyes with effort and turned his head. He saw instead the metallic glint from a .22 pistol as it passed into his periphery vision.

At least they weren't going to kill him with his own gun, Kellogg thought just before he felt the cold barrel pressed into his temple. His world exploded.

CHAPTER 7

D ARCY WAS BEGINNING TO HAVE a serious meltdown. She didn't know how she was going to be able to trust Adkins, let alone teach him anything. His arrogance and sense of entitlement made her angry.

She had just spent fifteen minutes on the phone with FBI Agent Stuart Johnson, saying almost nothing but "Yes, sir" and "No, sir" while he lectured her on how things are done and not done at the Federal Bureau of Investigation.

"I understand, Agent Johnson. What I was wondering was if this bison head incident might be consistent with some kind of Native American protest or not."

"As a matter of fact," Agent Johnson said, "I tried to tell your boy there has been an escalation of petty vandalism lately. Mostly graffiti on walls, etc. But yes, I would say this incident is consistent with the heightened rhetoric we've been seeing around town."

"Is there someone I could ask for more information about these issues? Do you know who is responsible for the vandalism?"

"We have people we watch closely, yes."

Agent Johnson isn't going to give me something for nothing, Darcy thought.

"I would like to have accurate information. Do these activist groups have a local spokesperson here? Someone who wants their concerns or demands made known?" Darcy flipped to a page not covered with doodles.

"Your desire for accuracy, Ms. Moreland, is commendable. As you might expect, though, the FBI is not in the habit of providing a forum for fringe radical groups."

Darcy hated dealing with government types. They relied on canned answers and rarely demonstrated a sense of humor.

"Ms. Moreland?" Agent Johnson's voice sounded impatient.

"Sorry, sir. What did you say?"

"I said you might want to talk to Mary Blue Feather. She works for the state as a staffer for the Tourism Board."

"She works for the state. Is she considered a member of the radical group?"

"Not Mary, but her son John has had a few run-ins with the law. As a matter of fact, Ms. Moreland, it would probably be best if you didn't mention that you got her name from me. Mary's not exactly a fan of the Bureau."

Did she hear a tiny trace of humanity in that stone-cold bureaucratic voice? "You sound like you know Mrs. Blue Feather."

"Mary is passionate about her people. I admire that and the way she tries to work inside the system. As for her son . . ."

"John?" Darcy asked to double check her notes.

"Yes, John. Mary raised him right, but when he was a young teen, she sent him to the reservation more frequently to live with her brother Michael and his wife. To learn the 'Old Ways' as she called it."

"And you think that was where John was radicalized?" Darcy probed. Call it faith in her intuition, but Darcy was sure there was something personal going on here.

Agent Johnson was silent.

"Agent Johnson? Are you still there?"

"Yes Ms. Moreland, I am. I think that is all the information I can give you. Hope I have been of some help. Goodbye."

It was tantalizing to think about a possible connection, Darcy thought. Mary Blue Feather and Agent Johnson. Was the connection built on respect for a worthy adversary like Sherlock Holmes and Moriarty—or was it perhaps something more personal and complex? She doodled a faint heart enclosing the names in her notes.

She was scanning her list of governmental agencies when her office phone rang, and Darcy jumped.

"What?" she answered.

"Darcy? Wendy. The Police Scanner says there's a 10-31, a suspected crime in progress, at Thompson's. Dispatch says shots fired."

"How long ago?"

"Just now. I knew you were working on that, so . . ."

Darcy threw on her coat as she simultaneously grabbed her bag. "Wendy, you are the best damned office manager EVER!" She slammed the phone down and sprinted out the door.

The drive was short, but she had to park a block away because of the police blockade. It was not an easy hike with residual ice on the sidewalks, but she was determined to get the story. She had tagged Netters on the drive, and he was supposed to meet her there ASAP.

She squirmed through a crowd gathered on the periphery, then spotted a patrolman she recognized from a murder she covered last summer.

"Officer Cummings," she greeted him with enthusiasm.

The young patrolman began to smile, then recognized her and stiffened. "Ms. Moreland. Will you please step back?" He turned his tall, wiry body to block her.

"Ah come on Randy! Last summer wasn't my fault. I didn't mean to get you in trouble."

"Two weeks of desk duty on the graveyard shift," Randy Cummings stated obdurately, as if he was remembering the humiliation.

"I'm sorry. I was just trying to do my job."

"Me too. Now please step back."

Darcy scanned the area. She saw Tom Quinn and tried to catch his eye. Tom finally turned toward her, and she saw Hank Nelson just beyond Quinn.

Hank finished his conversation with Quinn and walked over. Because he was tall, his stride ate up a lot of ground.

"Couldn't stand being away from me?" Hank smirked.

"I'm here about the 10-31. What happened?" Darcy asked.

"Officially, there has been some evidence of violence. The CPD is investigating."

"And 'unofficially'?" Darcy pushed.

"Unofficially and off the record," Hank said and then waited for her nod, "Latham Kellogg has been shot in the head."

"Oh my God!" Darcy drawled the words out in a long, dazed breath.

"Exactly. Someone executed him with a couple of bullets to the head."

"Who would do that? I didn't like the man, but I wouldn't wish that on him." Darcy's eyes followed the stretcher carrying Kellogg's body to the ambulance.

"That's what we're trying to find out. Basically, all you can report is that there was a shooting, and the victim can't be identified. You know the drill."

Distracted, Darcy was not listening carefully. "Executed? Did you say executed?"

Hank felt the familiar tightening at the base of his skull that always occurred when he dealt with Darcy the reporter. "Perhaps a poor choice of words," he hedged.

"Or perhaps an apt description of the murder scene," Darcy said. "Was it the head shots that makes you think they executed him?"

Hank took her arm and steered her away from the crowd to stand in the alleyway north of the building.

"Keep your damned voice down!" he hissed at her.

"You must have some reason to think it was an execution rather than a crime of passion, as they say."

Hank glanced past her into the alley, and Darcy turned to follow his gaze.

Two officers were stretching the yellow crime scene ribbon across the graffiti covered back door.

"We think the killer entered from the alleyway. No forced entry. Either Kellogg was expecting company, or the lock was picked."

Darcy angled toward the door. Hank stopped her, turning her back around to face him. He fixed her with an uncompromising glare.

"Oh, no you don't. The crime scene is off limits to you until the investigation is complete. I'll let you know what I can when I can."

Over Darcy's shoulder, Hank saw an officer coming toward him with evidence bags in his hand. He left Darcy standing in the alleyway.

"Detective Nelson," the officer handed Hank two plastic bags.

Following routine, Hank checked them for identification information, case number, description of contents, and initials of the officer clearly visible on the opaque top of the evidence bag before he looked at the contents themselves.

The top bag held a crow feather, almost blue-black in color. The second contained a scribbled note Hank could read through the plastic: it read "Fly or Die."

"Where did you find these, officer?" Hank asked.

"Uhm . . . ah," the young officer stuttered a little, then cleared his throat with a small cough. "They were laying on the victim's desk, sir. See, I made a note on the bag."

Hank held it up into the gray light and tried to steady its flapping in the wind. "I see you did. Good work, Carson."

Carson left with his shoulders slightly squared and his head high.

"What is that?" Darcy came up behind him.

She reached to take a closer look, but Hank was faster and managed to move the bags out of her reach.

"Evidence, Ms. Moreland, and none of your business." Hank was facing her now, using his six-foot two frame to intimidate.

Darcy refused to back away. Instead, she raised her chin a notch. "Ever hear of the public's right to know?"

"Heard of it. Not a fan. Please leave or get behind the barrier."

Darcy was about to launch into an argument when she saw Netters in the crowd. She turned back to Hank.

"Could we at least do a stand-up with the back door behind us?"

Hank looked down the alley at the door covered in yellow tape. "I guess it won't hurt anything, but then get out of our way. Okay?"

"Okay," Darcy agreed reluctantly as she waved Netters over.

"No juicy tidbits from your Detective?" Netters asked, watching Hank disappear around the corner.

"Nope. Though he agreed to letting us film by the back door. Come on." Darcy strode out.

They set up the shot, and Darcy pulled her scarf tightly around her neck.

"Levels?" Netters said.

"'The cure for boredom is curiosity. There is no cure for curiosity.' How was that?"

"Another Dorothy Parkerism?" Netters asked as he adjusted his focus.

"See how quick you are?" Darcy said. "Look at him, a rhinestone in the rough."

"Hilarious, Darcy. Can we get this done? My fingers are turning into popsicles here."

"You got it."

Darcy pushed her hair behind her ears to keep the wind from blowing it in her face. She watched Netters' fingers do a silent countdown, then point.

This is Darcy Moreland reporting for Channel 23 News at the site of an apparent homicide. Cheyenne Police Detective Hank Nelson has declined to comment on the details of the case. We do know the sound of gunshots was heard coming from inside Thompson's Furniture Store about twenty minutes ago. Police, alerted through an anonymous 911 call, arrived at the scene shortly thereafter. The victim, a white, middle-aged man, was apparently shot to death. Identification is pending notification of next of kin. We will continue to follow this story. This is Darcy Moreland, Channel 23 News.

Darcy signaled Netters to cut.

"How was that?"

Netters was packing up his camera. "Fine. Let's get back to the station. I think I'm freezing from the inside out."

Darcy wrapped her scarf tightly over her head and ears just as a gust of bitter wind pelted her with gravel. She yelped and ran up the block to her car.

Back in her cramped but blessedly warm office, Darcy peeled off her gloves, coat, and scarf, throwing them on the only other chair.

She wanted to write some notes while they were fresh in her mind. Darcy had glimpsed the black feather and gotten a quick peek at the note.

She hadn't had time to read the note and anyway it was partially obscured by the bag with the feather, but she had noticed it looked like it had been scrawled with a wide-tipped magic marker type pen. No namby-pamby fine line rollerball for this killer.

She also wrote "grease" in her notes. While she had been doing the stand-up, it annoyed her to discover she had been standing in a small puddle of motor oil or cooking oil. It didn't matter which. The killer, if he entered from the back, would have left tracks.

She thought briefly of calling Hank to tell him, but then decided against it. She'd mention it to him next time he came over if they hadn't already found it.

Darcy toed off her soiled shoes, making a mental note to clean them in the restroom later.

Execution, Hank had said. That meant the precise placement of shots almost certainly at close range. When people shot in the heat of passion, shots flew all over the place. She had heard of a case where someone had emptied an entire clip and only managed to wound their target.

The feather seemed to her to be an echo of the bison head and the arrow. But she wasn't sure why. She knew a crow's feather could symbolize death or dying because the birds themselves were carrion feeders. Biology 101. Was it a threat that was carried out?

She wished she could have read the note. She thought of calling Hank but dismissed it immediately. She needed to do her own digging.

She thought of Abby and wondered how her meeting with Dr. Barton had gone. With this murder, it was essential she have access to someone with historical expertise on Native Americans.

If Latham Kellogg had been executed by someone in the Native American community, Darcy wanted to know who, and more importantly, why. That was how Hank's job and her's differed. Hank had to know who and how to make a case. That was important for the news too, but what made it an actual story was the human dimension. That was her job as a journalist.

Why would someone kill Latham Kellogg? And why was the empty furniture store in the center of it all?

Darcy glanced at the yellow, pink, and blue sticky notes surrounding her monitor and plastered on her desk. Stuart Johnson's tip about Mary Blue Feather caught her attention.

She googled the site for the Wyoming Tourism Board and dialed. After going through two gatekeepers, someone finally patched her through to Mary Blue Feather.

"Ms. Blue Feather?"

"Yes?"

Her voice sounded tentative, so Darcy rushed into her spiel.

"This is Darcy Moreland from Channel 23 News. I was told you might be an excellent source for some background information on a story I'm covering." Darcy waited, but there was only silence.

Finally, "Who did you say referred you?" Ms. Blue Feather asked.

"Well, I didn't say exactly. I guess I could look that up in my notes, but I don't want to waste any more of your time than I have to."

"What do you want to know?"

"I'm doing a story on the bison head left in front of Thompson's Furniture store. Do you know of any Native American involvement in this? Would there be some issue I'm not aware of that they are protesting?"

"Why do you assume it is a Native American protest?"

"There was an arrow, and a clipping left as well. The article was about the occupation of the Bureau of Indian Affairs building in Washington in 1972."

"Well, that sounds compelling alright. Was there anything else? There wasn't any property damage, was there?"

Ms. Blue Feather sounded guarded. If her son was active in some radical fringe group, Darcy could sure understand why she was hesitant.

"No," Darcy hedged. Not initially, at least, she added silently. Mary would learn about the murder in the same building soon enough. "Just the bison head, an arrow, and the news clipping."

"Well generally speaking, an arrow can sometimes imply war, and a broken arrow can imply peace. I recall hearing some details of the protest in Washington, though I was just a kid at the time."

"Anything you can tell me would help," Darcy encouraged.

"I think the issue was the return of Native American land. Oh, and also, that it needed to be returned to traditional and ecologically respectful native communities. I only remember those terms because I had to look them up. Nothing much came of it though."

"Is the land Thompson's sitting on Native American land?" Darcy held her breath. That would go a long way to explaining some things, at least.

Mary Blue Feather laughed. "Well, technically, all the land around here was ours, but I don't think we're getting it back, do you?"

"Probably not," Darcy admitted. "I was told your son John associated with a . . ." Darcy tried to think of a tactful way to ask the question.

Mary Blue Feather filled the silence. "You've been talking to Stuart Johnson." It was a statement Lent, not a question. She didn't wait for confirmation, just continued, "Yes, John is associated with a traditional Native American group, but that doesn't make him a radical."

"I didn't mean to imply he was. I just thought he might know if there are some issues about the Thompson store affecting land rights or Native American issues."

There was silence.

"Ms. Blue Feather?"

"I'm here Ms. Moreland. I am trying to decide what you are interested in. Do you want to know about the so-called radical pro-testors who you think might be responsible for the bison head and the implied threat? Or do you want background information about Native American causes and grievances?"

Darcy thought for a moment. If she wanted Mary Blue Feather's help and insight, she had to be dead ahead honest.

Darcy said, "Both."

Ms. Blue Feather was quiet once again. Darcy's nerves stretched. She didn't want to lose what could be an excellent source.

Finally, Mary Blue Feather chuckled, then laughed out loud. "Well, you're honest at least."

"I try to be. So, can you help me?"

"I will ask my son if he knows anything, but I must be honest as well, Ms. Moreland. If what he tells me implicates him, I will not likely tell you. Is that understood?"

"Yes, ma'am. I wouldn't ever use confidential information given to me to implicate you or your son, Ms. Blue Feather, but you don't know that about me yet. It's unfair, but I must ask you for blind trust."

"Call me Mary and I will call you Darcy. I'm not worried about myself, but I'm not always sure what John is up to these days. I'll try to get the information for you though, if there is any to be had."

"Thank you, Mary. That would be a big help. Just call me at the station if you find anything out. And thanks."

"I will call you if I can."

Darcy glanced down at her notes. "Oh Mary. One more thing. What might a crow's feather symbolize for a Native American?"

Mary hesitated and then said, "Some Native Americans see the crow as the left-handed guardian and keeper of the sacred law. It might symbolize some religious atrocity or breach of sacred law. Why?"

"I don't know yet, but I was afraid it was something serious like that. Thanks again." Darcy hung up. She had a bad feeling about this.

CHAPTER 8

THE REST OF DARCY'S DAY WAS A HODGE-PODGE of meetings and editing sessions. She updated the story with more details from Hank, and on the five o'clock report, she gave the victim's name. Turned out Latham Kellogg had no next of kin. Darcy felt unaccountably sad about that. She stacked up her notes and headed home.

Darcy knew Abby was waiting as usual in her cozy antique-filled apartment along with Mac, her Cairn terrier. Abby asserted her innocence to charges of alienation of affection when it came to Mac, but Darcy knew it was a fact.

Truth was, Darcy felt guilty about all the time she had to be away from Mac, and it was a blessing to have Abby as company for him. Today she felt blessed, knowing if they had killed her like Kellogg, there would be family, friends, and her sweet fur-ball who would miss her. Here she was grounded with friends, family, and a very significant other.

Gently pushing on the unbolted door to Abby's apartment, it did not surprise Darcy when it swung wide. Darcy shut her mouth and the door without saying a word. She recognized a hopeless cause when she ran headlong into one.

She had barely shrugged out of her heavy coat when Mac rushed up to her and barked enthusiastically. Darcy stooped down and lifted him up. She snuggled into his neck for a moment, savoring his unconditional love.

"I thought I heard the door open."

Abby bustled in holding a green-colored vase with mauve and white flowers. She placed it in the center of an attractively set table.

"Oh Abby, are you having company? I'm so sorry. You should have said something. I could have gotten Mac out of your hair earlier."

For a moment, Abby fussed with the vase to place them in the exact dead center of her round dark oak table. Then, she looked up.

Darcy saw how pretty Abby looked. Her blue eyes sparkled and the slight flush on her cheeks lit up her face in a most appealing way.

Abby wiped her hands on a frilly organza concoction that Darcy supposed would be called an apron, but barely qualified.

"To tell the truth and shame the devil," Abby began as she walked over to Darcy and led her to Darcy's favorite spot on the settee and made her sit. Abby dropped down beside her, turning her body to face Darcy as if preparing to tell a state secret.

"I invited Doctor Barton to join me for dinner tonight. I'd hoped you and Hank would come too so it wouldn't make me look too forward," Abby said then continued, . "He asked me to dinner after our meeting, but I called him later and invited him here. I haven't dated in centuries. I need some support."

Darcy looked around the room as if trying to figure out where she was. "Have we slipped that far from the woman's movement? What is this 'so I won't look too forward' nonsense? He asked you first. You just rearranged the details. Nothing forward in that."

Abby squared her shoulders. "Darcy Marie. I have asked a favor from you as a friend. I am terrified and I don't appreciate your mockery."

Uh oh, Darcy thought. This is a serious, no teasing zone.

Darcy stood and took Abby's hands. "I'm sorry for how I said that to you."

"Of course." Abby squeezed Darcy's fingers. "But would you mind calling Hank and inviting him as well? Tell him we're having pot roast."

"Abby, wouldn't you rather just have Dr. Barton all to yourself?" Darcy asked.

A look of panic crossed Abby's face. Where had her stalwart, unflappable friend gone?

"I can see that is not an option." Darcy pulled out her phone and paused. "Abby, I may not be Hank's favorite friend right now."

Abby was heading toward the kitchen, and she turned back around. "Oh Darcy! What have you done now?"

"Why do you always assume it's my fault?" Darcy said.

Abby shot her a jaundiced eye with a twitchy arched brow.

"Okay. So, I showed up at a murder scene and got a little inquisitive. . ."

"Aggressive?" Abby supplied.

"Inquisitive," Darcy reiterated, "about some evidence. You know how Hank gets about evidence."

"I seem to recall. Just call him and apologize. I am sure he'll forgive you. By the way, who was murdered?"

"Didn't you watch my five o'clock story?"

"I fear not. I was busy getting this feast together. Who died?" Abby asked again.

"Latham Kellogg. I didn't see the body," Darcy shivered at the thought, "but Hank said he'd been executed. He later tried to wiggle out of that description . . . but I wouldn't let him."

"No doubt contributing to being scratched from his favorite friend list," Abby finished. "Call him right now. Maybe my pot roast will soothe the savage breast."

"That's music, Abbs, but thanks for the help."

Darcy speed dialed Hank's cell. He picked up on the second ring.

"Waiting for me to call?" she asked.

"I figured it was just about time for your curiosity to ram into third gear, so yes. I was expecting you."

"You don't sound friendly."

"Murder has that effect on me. What do you want, Darcy?"

"Not me. Abby. She invited Dr. Barton to dinner, and she would like us to be the buffer couple."

"I don't think I'm in a buffer frame of mind."

"This is for Abby. She told me to tell you she's made pot roast." There was a silence on the other end for a long moment. "Hank?"

"I'm weighing Abby's pot roast against your company."

"What's the matter with my company?" Darcy jumped up and paced.

"Nothing usually, but when you're on a story, you're like a pig in quicksand."

Darcy stopped. "I beg your pardon."

"I just mean you flail around until you either get out or go under."

"I never go under."

"But you admit to the flailing?"

"If by that you mean I am persistent and focused, then yes."

"What are the chances you can go all evening without interrogating me about the murder?"

"Pretty good, right now."

"Good enough for me. I'll be there at 6." Hank clicked off before she could say anything more.

Darcy tossed her phone onto the coffee table.

"Is he coming?" Abby called from the kitchen.

"At 6," Darcy said. She set out wine glasses, opened a nice Shiraz, and put it on the table.

The doorbell rang. "Oh dear. I'm not. . . uhm. . ." Abby sputtered nervously.

"I'll get the door," Darcy told her friend. "You find your composure."

Darcy swung open the door and greeted Dr. Barton, taking his coat and jaunty English style cap.

"Don't see too many of these around here." She draped them on the hall tree.

"Yes, I found it in a little shop at Victoria Station in London and I wanted something to keep my head warm." He patted his bald head.

Darcy laughed and led him into the living room, poured him some wine. She was just about ready to go in search of Abby, when the doorbell rang again.

"It's Hank," she shouted to Abby and opened the door.

Hank walked in and hung up his coat. Darcy closed it behind him, introduced the two men, and left them to find Abby.

"Everyone is here, Abbs. What are you doing?"

Abby was guzzling a glass of what looked like water. The silly grin on Abby's face when she had finished the last gulp was proof positive that it was not water.

"What are you drinking?" Darcy picked up the glass and sniffed. "Wine?" she asked, grateful it was not vodka.

"Yes," Abby confirmed and stirred the gravy. "I am way over twenty-one. Problem?"

"Not if you're still able to get this dinner out there."

"Perfectly able. Why don't you put the peas and salad on the table, and I'll finish this off?"

Darcy lifted both bowls and paused. "Just don't finish the wine while you're at it."

Abby gave a little salute just as Dr. Barton came to the door of the kitchen. Abby dropped her hand and stirred the gravy faster.

"Anything I can do to help?"

"Well, yes. You could slice the roast and take it out to the table. Thank you, Barton." He took the roast and left. Abby took another small swig of wine.

As soon as everyone was seated, pouring the wine, and passing the food around became the priority. Except for inane pleasantries, no one said much. The dinner was delicious.

Finally, Hank couldn't stand the silence anymore. "So, Dr. Barton, I understand Darcy is using you as a background source on the story she's working on."

"Please, just call me Barton. I dislike titles. And yes. Darcy sent Abby to talk to me today about the story. By the way," he lifted his glass in Darcy's direction, "thank you."

Darcy nodded. "I just hope it isn't an imposition."

"Absolutely no trouble at all. I'm enjoying the experience." His eyes slid to Abby.

Hank, fascinated with the interaction, asked, "Did you and Abby know each other before today?"

"Yes," Abby said.

"No," Barton said at the same moment.

"That is, I knew of him from a talk he'd given at my ladies' club. We never really met until today," Abby explained as she pushed her peas around her plate.

"Would you mind if I picked your brain a little too?" Hank asked Barton.

"Not at all. I hope I can help."

"Today a man was murdered, and while investigating the crime scene, we found a black crow's feather and a note that read . . ." Hank paused for effect. Darcy was leaning slightly forward, her mouth faintly opened in surprise. This was fun.

"For heaven's sake, Hank, what did the note say?"

Irritating Darcy was a bonus. "All it said was 'Fly or Die'. Would that have any significance?"

"The note, no hidden meaning that I'm aware of other than as a warning, but the feather, perhaps. It might have significant Native American meaning, but then it could also just be where the killer wants to place the blame."

"Actually Barton, I talked to a woman named Mary Blue Feather today, and she said the black crow's feather might be symbolic for the guardian of sacred law," Darcy said.

"Well, Mary would know," Barton mused. "She is a veritable compendium of information about Native American cultural lore."

"And evidently, Darcy is a veritable compendium of surprises," Hank said.

JOHN BLUE FEATHER HAD JUST WOLFED DOWN a couple of greasy burritos. They were delicious but sat in his gut like a layer of concrete. Oh well. They were cheap and filling, and he had more important things on his mind.

He grimaced as his ancient printer groaned and scratched as each cheap recycled sheet ran through. The flyers, though, were impressive, he thought. Stark boldfaced-black on white with a red slash running in a jagged diagonal from the top right-hand corner to the bottom left as if it was a lethal wound.

ANOTHER MASSACRE screamed across the top of the flyer. The text was clear and unequivocal. John read it through again. He had tried for a reasoned tone rather than the hyperbolic rhetoric that dominated so many protests.

The headline and gash were simply to grab attention. The message was important. He scanned the piece, looking for any over-the-top verbiage. The word "annihilates" jumped out at him, but in context he thought it was fair.

He pushed his long, straight black hair behind his ears impatiently. He wished he had something to tie it back.

He skimmed the flyer some more. Obliterate, eradicate, and exterminate, all good words, he thought as he sat cross-legged on the worn carpet of his small pay-by-the-day hotel room three stories above Lincolnway.

John did not mind living on the cheap if it meant he could make a difference for his people. He knew his mom was worried, but he also knew she respected him for choosing his own path. He wished she could admire him like the warriors in the Old Time.

Mothers being mothers probably always worried about their sons. That would not likely change anytime soon.

There was a sharp knock at the door. John looked at his watch. It was close to five pm. Thomas Kingman and Jack Bowles were not due here until seven.

"John Blue Feather. This is the police. Please open the door."

John felt his heart jump into his throat. He grabbed his shearling coat by the collar. It was his only coat, and it had belonged to his dad. He would escape with the coat or die trying, he thought.

The banging grew steadily louder until it felt like an echo in John's heart. He scrambled to gather all the flyers in a wad and stuck them into one of his voluminous coat pockets. Then, he ran to the grimy double-hung window. He threw it up with so much force it slammed back down again.

"Blue Feather. We're coming in." The door shuddered on its rotted hinges.

As John tried to climb out of the small window onto a foot-wide ledge, he saw the door shake violently, then crash open. Three cops swarmed into the room, the barrels of their guns pointing in three different directions.

"There," one of them shouted and rushed to the window.

John did not have enough lead-time to inch his way to the fire escape ladder a few feet away before one man leaned out, grabbed the cuff of his worn jeans, and pulled.

"Come back inside, son. We just want to talk to you."

John tried to kick him free and almost lost his balance on the slim ledge. "I'm not your son. And I know how 'we just want to talk to you' works."

John kicked out again. There was only room for one cop to lean out, and that gave John his only advantage. The bitter winter wind made his bare hands ache. When the next blast of wind, filled with hard pellets of snow, hit his face, he grimaced and lowered his head.

The cop had a death grip on his jeans. John could not throw him off. He wished he had his knife, then dismissed that notion as idiotic. He usually carried his knife in his boot and there was no room on the tiny ledge to stoop to retrieve it.

His leg was jerked back once again, and John struggled to keep his precarious balance. His hands gripped the rough surface of the brick building. He stretched his free arm out trying to grab the rusted fire escape ladder just out of his reach.

He inched his booted foot as far as he could. John stretched again, gripped the ice-cold iron bar of the ladder, and pulled with all his strength.

"Be careful," the cop yelled at him. "You want to fall? Come inside. We'll talk."

John knew he could probably use the leverage of his hold on the ladder to yank the cop all the way out of the window, but he just wanted to get away.

He kicked once again, but the cop held tight. Too late, John heard the window in the next room slam open. Before he could do anything, a burly cop reached through the open window, grabbed him around the waist in a not so friendly bear hug, and dragged him into the adjoining room. He landed hard on his side and the pain exploded from his hip down his leg.

Both John and the cop floundered on the floor for a moment, trying to regain their feet. The shooting pain in his leg hampered him, but John leapt up with a rush of adrenaline.

The cop who had pulled him in grabbed John's leg and tripped him as he tried to run. John fell with another bone-jarring thump onto the floor. Before he could recover, they flipped him onto his stomach and jerked his arms halfway up his back. John felt the cold steel of handcuffs and winced as they closed them tightly around his wrists.

His shoulder throbbed as they hauled him upright, pushed him out the door, and mirandized him.

They dragged him down the dimly lit hall that smelled of tobacco, urine, and whiskey.

John tried to fight the panic churning in his stomach. He had never been arrested before, though his uncle said there could be that possibility. As they shoved him into the rear seat, John wondered if he should call his mom or his uncle. His mom would be more helpful getting him out, but his uncle would understand why he was in trouble.

In the end, he didn't call either of them. He would wait to see how complicated this whole thing got. He didn't want to worry either of them unnecessarily.

CHAPTER 9

Hank's phone rang. He saw it was from the station and excused himself to go into the front room. Darcy wanted to follow him, but Abby shook her head slightly.

Uh-oh, Darcy thought. Abby knew her too well. In moments, Hank was off the call and grabbing his coat.

"Sorry I have to run, Abby. Pot roast was great. Thanks for having me."

Darcy shot out of her seat. "What's up? Is there an emergency? Can I come with you?"

"Just an arrest, no, and no. I'll call you when I am done. Thanks again, Abby." He was out the door in a rush.

Darcy sank back down in her seat. "Well, that was fun. I wonder what the arrest was about."

"Probably just routine, Darcy. Don't get in a flap about it." Abby said. She began clearing the table, and Barton jumped up to help.

"I guess I'll take Mac and go home. Your kitchen is only big enough for two. Thanks for dinner." Darcy scooped Mac up and left. In the cool corridor she smirked, thinking of Abby and Barton alone and unbuffered.

By the time she reached her apartment and turned on the police scanner, the arrest and any talk of it was off the air.

"Damn," she said. Mac, who had jumped onto her bed, jumped off, reacting to her tone, and ran back into the front room.

"Not you this time, buster," she laughed at Mac's inquisitive head tilt and clear brown eyes. "It is quite possible the arrest had nothing to do with my investigation," she continued to talk to Mac, who now joined her on the sofa.

"But if it wasn't connected, why did Hank run out so fast? And why wouldn't he just tell me what the call was about?" Darcy scratched Mac behind the ears and the spoiled dog rolled onto his back to invite more attention to his belly.

"Abby has totally ruined you. You think you're almost human, don't you?"

Mac scampered into her lap and snuggled, letting her pet him. Darcy found it soothing and almost dozed off, but her cell phone's ringing made her jump up to scrounge it out of her purse.

"Hello?"

"Hi. You sound groggy and breathless. Should I be worried?"

"Hank. What are you doing?"

"Calling to give you a tip. We just arrested John Blue Feather for the murder of Latham Kellogg."

"Are you sure?"

"We generally try to base our arrests on evidence."

"No need for sarcasm, Nelson. I was asking for amplification, as in based on *what* evidence?"

"I'm not laying out our case for you, Ms. Moreland. This is a courtesy call, as in based on *courtesy*."

Darcy ran her hand through her hair in frustration. When their official paths crossed, she always got prickly with him, and he turned ultra-formal on her.

"Hank, I'm sorry. I appreciate you thinking of me and calling with the tip. May I ask if John will be available for me to talk to any time tomorrow?"

"I doubt it. He'll have to be arraigned and then, if bail is set— which isn't exactly a slam-dunk—he might be out by late afternoon. I wouldn't save any airtime for it."

"Will you let me know?"

"If I can." Hank was quiet for a moment. "You want me to come over so we can make up?"

Darcy laughed. "Straightforward as usual, Nelson, but I think I'll pass for tonight. I'm tired and tomorrow is shaping up to be quite interesting. Besides, it wasn't that big of a fight."

"I'm pretty sure I can escalate the argument with very little effort."

"Hmm. G'night Hank." Darcy tried to swallow a yawn. "I'll see you tomorrow."

In minutes, Darcy snuggled into bed with Mac by her side.

Her ringtone jangled through her dream .She sat up and snatched the phone from her bedside.

"For heaven's sake, Hank. No means no."

There was silence on the other end.

"Hank?"

"No, Ms. Moreland. It is Mary Blue Feather. I apologize for calling so late in the evening, but I need your help. I called the station and Wendy gave me your cell number after I convinced her that it was information about the case you were working on."

"No offense, but shouldn't you be calling a lawyer?"

Silence again.

"You know about John being arrested."

Mary said it as a statement, and Darcy didn't feel she had to reveal where she had received the information. "Yes, I know."

"This is going to sound like a biased mother, but John is innocent."

"Ma'am, I'm not the one you have to convince."

"Please call me Mary as you did earlier today, and you are wrong, Darcy. You are exactly who I must convince."

"Ma'am—"

"Mary." she interrupted. "I won't try to argue my case with you tonight, but if I could meet you tomorrow at your office, I think I can give you background about why they suspect John."

Darcy was conflicted. On the one hand, she felt the pull of loyalty to Hank and the police. Hank was right when he said they didn't just arrest people off the street without evidence. On the other hand, as an investigative reporter she would like some background on John Blue Feather.

"Darcy? I could meet you somewhere else if you'd like."

After a long soul-searching silence, Darcy relented, "That might be best, Mary. How about we meet in the coffee shop at the Prairie, about nine?"

"Thank you so much. I really appreciate this, Darcy."

"I've only agreed to listen."

"Yes, of course. I'll see you tomorrow morning." Mary clicked off.

Darcy flopped on her bed and pulled her pillow over her face.

By 8:45 the next morning, she had already been to the office to brief Zach about the arrest and Mary Blue Feather's call, driven to the coffee shop, and ordered a medium latte. She was waiting at a table by the window when she saw Mary Blue Feather come around the corner to the glass doors.

Darcy studied Mary Blue Feather from a distance. Her black hair was scraped tightly into a knot at the back of her head. She was, as Darcy's mother would say, built on the sturdy side. Maybe five feet tall without her sensible one-inch pumps. Her long coat was wrapped around her Native American roots. The trading blankets had been used a century ago to bribe her people from their land. Darcy appreciated the irony of it.

Mary entered the coffee shop with a burst of freezing wind. She nodded to Darcy and stepped up to the counter to place her order.

As Mary walked toward the table, Darcy looked at her face. Must not have gotten get much sleep last night, Darcy thought, if the dark circles under her eyes were any clue.

"Thank you again for agreeing to meet with me," Mary said as she slipped off her coat and sat.

"I hope you don't mind if I tape our conversation for my notes." Darcy placed the slim silver recorder on the table between them. "I promise not to use anything you tell me without your express permission."

"That's fine. I don't know exactly how to begin."

"Well, let's begin with where we left off yesterday. Did you talk to John about the protest?"

"I tried to call him. I left a message, but he didn't return my call. Nothing strange about that. He knows I'm not totally sympathetic with his activism, so he often avoids me." Mary ducked her head as if embarrassed to have to share the rift with her son with a comparative stranger.

The waitress brought their orders, so the women stopped talking. Darcy watched the young girl go back to her counter before she began again.

"Does he contact you when he isn't so involved?" Darcy asked. "I don't mean when he was younger, but there must be sometimes when he would reach out to you. I don't call my mom if I'm stressed or angry about anything. You know how mothers are." Darcy managed a short, self-deprecating laugh and Mary joined her.

"Yes, I am familiar with the mother phenomenon. Your point is, since he didn't call me back, he must have been involved in something. Is that it, Darcy?"

Darcy stirred her latte then looked up. "It's a reasonable theory, isn't it?"

Mary took a sip of her plain, black coffee, and said, "I suppose it is. He may well be involved in something, but I am certain it isn't murder."

"Have you talked to him yet?"

"No. They wouldn't let me." Mary rummaged in her purse and found a small business card stuck in her wallet. She slid it toward Darcy.

"I hired a lawyer who is meeting with him right now since he is scheduled to be arraigned this afternoon."

Darcy looked at the card. *Darren Kincade, Esq. Criminal Defense, Family Law, Divorce*, it read. Darcy slid the card back.

"I remember yesterday you said I would have to go on blind trust with you since I didn't know you yet. I'm asking for the same consideration, Darcy. You must take it on blind trust I know my boy and I know he is incapable of murder."

"Mary," Darcy grasped Mary's hand, "you wouldn't be the first mother to have complete faith in her son and be disappointed."

Mary raised her dark brown eyes to Darcy's. Tears welled, but Mary willed them away. She squeezed Darcy's hand briefly before letting go.

"You're probably right. I am not so naïve as to believe that John would never kill. He comes from warrior blood, you know."

Darcy blinked, then looked around the shop. "I'm not sure that fact ought to be bandied around."

Mary laughed. "The operative word is warrior. He would fight back if he had to. They often recruit our people for war. But John would never kill anyone because they did not agree with him. That is not the way of the warrior."

"Are you sure the old rules still apply?" Darcy didn't know if John was a murderer, but she wanted to help him. For his mother's sake, if nothing else.

"The old ways are the only thing John would follow. It has become his way of life."

Darcy realized she did not know what the old ways were. "Why don't you tell me a little about John? How old is he?" Darcy asked.

"John is twenty-three this last September. He thinks he's full grown, but . . ."

"You don't?"

"A young man doesn't mature for a long time. Women mature faster. We must because we have the children."

"Is John married?"

"No. I wish he were, but no." Mary sipped her coffee and her eyes drifted past Darcy to the street beyond. "I married John's father when I was just out of college. He was four years older than I. Impressive for a young woman."

"What happened?"

"He went to work on the rigs. Fell to his death. I was left to raise John by myself. I was luckier than most. I had an education and got a job with the state."

"John was raised in Cheyenne?" Darcy thought it might help with a jury if they thought he was local.

"In the sense that he was born and raised here, yes. He was born

Arapaho on both sides. I'm sure Stuart Johnson told you I sent him to live with my brother during the summers when John was in his early teens."

"I think he mentioned something about it," Darcy hedged.

"Don't worry about being diplomatic, Darcy. Stuart was furious with me. We have been, well, I guess you could call us friends, for a long time. John and Stuart got along great until John started seeing him as the enemy."

"Your brother influenced him?" Darcy sipped her latte but didn't taste it.

"Stuart calls it radicalizing him, but yes, John is passionate and committed. I wanted him to have access to his heritage and now . . . now I'm not so sure." Mary dug a tissue from her purse and blotted her damp eyes.

"What do you want me to do, Mary?"

"I just thought . . . I thought since you seemed to want more than just the surface details, the reason for the bison head and the arrow and Native American issues, you'd . . . you'd dig a little deeper for John."

"I'll do what I can." Darcy clicked off the recorder. She hadn't received much useful for the story, but she was committed to helping this woman if she could.

Back at the office, Darcy found a yellow sticky note on top of a pile of her papers. It simply said, Zach.

"'What new hell is this?'" she said to the empty office, quoting Dorothy Parker.

She scrounged in her desk drawer for a Snickers bar she had hidden away. She opened it up and took a large bite, then carefully wrapped the rest to save for later.

She was still licking her lips free of any recalcitrant chocolate when she knocked on the window beside Zach's open door.

"Hi, Boss. You needed me?"

"Yeah." Zach glanced up from the pile of papers on his desk. "Come in and close the door, please."

Uh oh, Darcy thought. It was never good when Zach wanted the door closed.

Darcy closed the door but did not sit. She gathered from Zach's tone this was going to be a formal meeting.

"Ah, for heaven's sake, Darcy. Sit down. You act like I'm the principal or something."

Darcy sat. "Well, Zach . . . you're not sounding friendly."

"It isn't friendly at that, come to think of it." Zach stood up from behind his desk and sat on the edge closest to Darcy. He had closed their physical distance, and now he was taller and glaring down at her.

"I thought I told you to work with Adkins—"

"Zach, listen I tried—be fair."

"Being fair is above my pay grade. Let me explain this to you again. Uncle Arnie wants his nephew to collaborate with you. Uncle Arnie owns the station. Therefore, you will do what he wants. Questions?"

"Yeah. I'm not sure how to get Adkins to listen to me. I just had to grovel to our local FBI agent about Adkins' lack of due deference," Darcy could see Zach was unmoved. "I'll continue to do my best, Boss." Darcy stood. "Where is he?"

"Last I saw, he was in post-production with Netters."

"On my way." Darcy left Zach's office.

When she got to post-production, Netters was editing some snippets of video while Adkins was sitting on the counter that ran around the circumference of the room. He was throwing wads of paper into the wastepaper basket and judging by the clutter, not doing it very well.

"Adkins. Where have you been?" She thought she would start on the offensive.

Adkins dropped to his feet and began picking up the stray lumps of paper and throwing them away properly.

"I couldn't find you," Adkins explained in a rush, "so I came in to help Bill here . . . "

His explanation dribbled off when Netters glared at him, then at Darcy and went back to work.

"Hey. Don't blame me." Darcy tried to remove herself from Netter's list. "I can't watch him all the time."

"Get him out of here," Netter replied without looking up from the monitor.

"Okay. I'm going to do a stand-up about the arrest made regarding the Latham Kellogg murder in front of the station. Want to come?"

Netters looked at her, then Adkins. "Keep him away from me," he said quietly.

"Absolutely," Darcy promised. "Okay gang let's go. I need to stop by my office to get my coat, but I'll meet you at the van."

By the time she got to the van, Netters was at the wheel and Adkins was in the back with the equipment. Just as she opened the passenger's side door, she heard Netters growl, "You touch anything back there and Uncle Arnie will be short a nephew."

"Damn, Bill. Ya don't need to drudge on me like that. We're all part of the team, aren't we, Darc?" Adkins whined.

Darcy turned in her seat and tried to edit what she really wanted to say into something more . . . professional.

"Tell you what, Adkins. You can call me Moreland or Darcy, but I don't respond well to nicknames."

"But Bill always calls you—"

"And he," she nodded in Netter's direction, "likes to be called Netters, not Bill. Am I making myself clear?"

"Yeah sure, Darc . . . y." Adkins finished just in time. "Got it."

They pulled up in front of the jail and Darcy jumped out.

"Set up in front of the jail entry. I'll go get the details and meet you," she said to Netters.

He didn't move.

"What?" she asked.

Netters flicked his head in Adkins' direction.

"Oh. Yeah. Right. Adkins, you're with me."

As they made their way into the jail, Darcy said softly, "Let me do the talking. Just watch and learn."

Adkins draped his arm across her shoulders. "I understand you have to talk to me like that in front of the camera guy, but come on Dar . . ."

Darcy spun out from under his arm and whipped around to face him. Gone was the desire to be professional.

"You touch me again without my permission or call me Darc one more time and I will not be responsible for what happens." She looked directly into his suddenly pale face.

"Aw c'mon—"

"Don't test me, Adkins. You're supposed to be learning to be a good reporter. First lesson. Learn when to shut up!"

By now, they had reached the reception area. Darcy put her professional mask back on.

"Hello. I am Darcy Moreland from Channel 23 News. I was wondering if I could get a little more specific information about the arrest made last night in the Latham Kellogg case." Darcy laid her ID on the desk.

The young officer at the desk checked her ID, then raised a questioning brow in Adkins' direction.

"Oh, he's with me," Darcy explained.

Now both brows shot up.

"Not *with* me . . . I mean, he's an intern. Learning the ropes."

"I'll take this, Donnelly." Hank appeared from nowhere and steered Darcy away from the desk. "What do you need?"

"I'd really like an interview with the accused."

"Not a chance. What else?"

"Could I talk to the arresting officers?"

"Nope."

"Well, why don't you just give me what you think I deserve then?"

"There are laws against that in at least 20 states, babe."

"This must be my day for telling men off—" Darcy began with some heat.

"You can have the mug shots." Hank looked at Adkins. "Send him to get a copy from Donnelly."

Darcy turned and faced Adkins. "You heard the man. Make sure they're as clear a copy as you can get."

Hank and Darcy both watched him cross to the reception area.

"I heard you met with Blue Feather's mother this morning," Hank said.

"Are you following me?"

"Small town. People talk. You weren't exactly hiding at the coffee shop."

"True. So what?"

"Mothers are biased when it comes to their sons."

"Hmmm. I wonder what your mother would tell me."

Hank winced at the thought. "Nothing good, probably."

"I need to put that on my bucket list."

"Here's the generic press release. Don't editorialize."

"Thanks for the release . . . and please don't tell me how to do my job." She turned and walked out the door. Adkins followed holding the mug shots.

Hank stood to the side so he could watch her. Even through the plate-glass window, he could catch phrases from the release.

John Blue Feather . . . arrested . . . Wyoming Hotel . . . for the murder of Latham Kellogg . . . member of the Arapaho . . .

Ah hell, he thought. There she goes, giving more details than were included in the official press packet. He should have known better. He went back to his office.

CHAPTER 10

AFTER THE STAND-UP, DARCY, NETTERS, AND ADKINS returned to the station. Netters disappeared instantly, but Adkins stuck with her like a hot fudge lava cake.

"Hey Adkins, why don't you go to the postproduction room and watch Netters edit the piece? Editing is almost as important as the stand-up itself, you know."

"Netters doesn't like me," Adkins answered, sounding petulant.

"He doesn't have to like you to teach you the fundamentals. Go on. I'll meet you there in a minute." Darcy turned down the hall toward her office. Adkins followed at her heels.

"What're you going to do?"

Darcy stopped and turned. "I am only going to make a couple of phone calls. Boring stuff."

"Uncle Ar—"

"Adkins, be very careful." Darcy's eyes narrowed.

"If I promise not to say or do anything, can I watch you?"

"I suppose if I tried to explain the difference between 'can' and 'may' it would be a waste of time," Darcy said softly, then tried to sound encouraging. "Sure, come on."

Darcy slipped behind her battered metal desk and shuffled papers, trying to find the note about John Blue Feather's lawyer. She found the number and dialed.

She got the receptionist, explained who she was, and asked him to return her call. The receptionist didn't sound hopeful, and Darcy knew hearing back from Kincade was a long shot.

"See? Boring stuff."

Adkins crossed his arms but said nothing.

Darcy raised her eyebrows in surprise. Maybe he could be trained, she thought as she dialed Mary Blue Feather's number.

They quickly passed the call through a couple of layers of state bureaucracy. Darcy doodled in the margins of her legal pad.

"This is Mary Blue Feather."

Darcy made an impulsive decision and snapped the call on speaker mode so Adkins could hear.

"Hi Mary, Darcy Moreland here. I have you on speaker. I hope that's alright."

"Uhm, I guess so." Mary's soft voice belied the certainty.

"Just an associate of mine who is helping with the story. Say hello Adkins," Darcy said, and caught Adkins' grin at the associate explanation.

"Uhm, hello." Adkins leaned into the speaker. Darcy pushed him back.

"If you trust him, I guess it would be okay."

Mary sounded absolute in her conviction, and Darcy had a powerful urge to take her off speaker. She didn't want to be responsible for Adkins' trustworthiness. God help her. Darcy closed her eyes, gritted her teeth, then decided the risk was worth it.

"I'm calling to see if you have had any luck getting John bailed out."

"Not yet, but his lawyer went down for the arraignment. He thought it best that my brother and I stay away from the courtroom right now."

"Has John said anything more about Kellogg or anything else?"

"Not to me. I don't think he has been allowed any outside communication except with his lawyer."

Darcy nodded to Adkins, trying to imply that was standard. Adkins nodded back.

"Mary, I was calling to tell you I left a message for John's lawyer to call me as soon as he can. I doubt he will unless you tell him it's okay. I promise I won't use anything he tells me unless you give me permission."

Adkins' face had the shocked look of a freshly caught fish. He kept opening and closing his mouth, but thankfully didn't say anything.

Mary was quiet for a moment. "What exactly do you want to ask him?"

"I basically want to know what the charges are. First degree, manslaughter etc. I'd also like to know what evidence the police think they have linking John to the crime."

"Darcy—"

"Mary, I know it's a lot to ask on faith, but you came to me to dig into this. The charges will be public knowledge after the arraignment, but I'd like to hear the lawyer's take on them."

There was silence on the other end, and Darcy was afraid Mary would refuse outright.

"I can suggest it, but I can't force Kincade to give you any information," Mary finally said, sounding overwhelmed.

"I understand. If you could call him and encourage him to get in touch with me, it would help a lot. You also need to reassure your son I am just looking for the truth."

"I'll try, Darcy, but you need to know my son has gone his own way for quite a while now. He doesn't usually listen to my opinions."

Darcy heard the deep sadness in Mary's voice. Her estrangement from her son was obviously a profound wound for her. Darcy wished she didn't have to expose Mary's pain to public scrutiny.

"I understand this is hard for you, Mary, but if we can't get his cooperation . . ." Darcy let the sentence hang.

"I know. I'll try." Mary clicked off.

"Way to play her, Darcy!" Adkins bounced out of his chair, raising his right hand in the air for a high five.

"Put your hand down." Darcy pushed out of her chair and advanced on him.

Adkins had the good sense to sit down, and she loomed over him.

"I'm supposed to train you. I get Uncle Arnie is watching. I get I can't bludgeon you to death without consequences . . . but don't tempt me beyond human tolerance." Adkins cringed back in his chair.

Darcy propped herself on the edge of the desk in front of him. "For your information, I was *not* playing her. Mary Blue Feather has spent a lifetime trying to straddle two worlds with as much dignity as she can muster. Now she is faced with choosing between us who she doesn't know, and her brother and son who she knows and loves. If she makes the wrong choice, she could lose everything and everyone she cares about. We are asking for an enormous leap of faith."

"Yeah, I know . . ." Adkins began. Darcy cut him off.

"No, you don't know, or your first reaction wouldn't have been a sophomoric assumption that the woman had been played."

Adkins sunk lower. Darcy acknowledged his surrender and went back around to her own seat.

"Adkins, most investigative reporting is boring—just digging for details. There's no flash or dash to it."

Adkins nodded. Sensing the crisis was over, he straightened.

Darcy continued, "You still don't have the slightest notion about how this works. Your job is to compile a grocery list of details, then take those details and put a human face on it, so it makes sense to our audience. To do that, you must have some well of humanity in you."

"Uh . . . yeah. Okay."

The boy looked puzzled. Darcy felt faintly sorry for him. He didn't seem to have the instinct or knowledge about how to observe people that is required for being a reporter. It was like he was being asked to build Trump Tower with an erector set.

"Just keep your mouth shut, your brain engaged, and it may come to you. For now, we go check Netters in editing."

CARL STEVENS HAD JUST WATCHED THE NOON BROADCAST. He could feel the sweat pooling under his arms.

Things were getting out of control. Stevens could feel the terror rising in the back of his throat. It left a sour bile residue. He took a sip of cold coffee and choked.

Sputtering, he got up from his desk, walked to the window, and rested his head on the cold glass. He looked at the street below. A scrap of paper was dancing in the gusts of wind whirling in and out of the downtown office buildings.

Someone had killed Latham Kellogg. They'd arrested some hot-headed Native American kid, but Stevens was fairly sure John Blue Feather hadn't done it.

He'd met John Blue Feather when the boy had addressed the City Council about setting aside some empty building to open a museum centering on the contribution of the Native Americans to the city's history.

Stevens had been head of the Downtown Development Organization and as he'd told Blue Feather, he had no problem with the idea of a museum, they'd just have to pay the rent on whatever building they chose. The city of Cheyenne could not bankroll such an uncertain venture.

The kid had been disappointed Stevens remembered, but not violently so. However, Stevens thought, if Blue Feather or his more aggressive friends got wind of what was really going on . . . well, everything would hit the fan, and he was damned if he was going to be the only one splattered.

He had to call Frye, the former county coroner. He'd know if anyone had been poking around.

Stevens wiped his damp forehead on the back of his sleeve, then sat behind his laptop. Scrolling through his addresses took too long and, in his nervousness, he scrolled past it a couple of times. He made a fist to control his trembling. Finally, he managed to highlight the number. It was Frye's personal number.

Stevens wiped his hand on his pant leg; the sweat from his palm was making holding his cell phone difficult.

He waited for Frye to pick up, telling himself he'd be damned he'd leave a message that could come back and hang him. He was about to hang up, when Frye answered with a gruff, "Yeah?"

"Frye? It's Carl, Carl Stevens. Have you seen the news?"

"What the hell's the matter with you?"

"I'm a little shaken. A Native American kid's been arrested for murdering Latham Kellogg."

"Ah crap."

"My sentiments exactly. I don't think the kid did it, but he hangs around with some of those AIM organization folks. I think his uncle Mike Brown is one of them."

"Ah jeez, Carl. You promised there was nothing to this. You swore no one would ever find out."

"Calm down," Carl said trying to do so himself. "Has anybody been snooping around? Anybody asking questions?"

"Hell no. I haven't even been in town. I'm at my hunting cabin outside of Encampment, just hiding out from my wife. Since I retired, she's been—"

"Okay, now pay attention Jim. We just need to make sure there's no connection among you, me, or Kellogg. I don't think the cops will question you. Why would they? But just in case keep laying low."

"Okay, but what about the . . ."

"Shut the hell up about that. I'll let you know when things have cooled down around here." Stevens glanced at the frosted window on his door. There was no one there.

"Right now, the important thing is to wait this out and not do something stupid that will call attention to us." A horrible thought flitted into Stevens' mind. "Frye, you didn't tell your wife about the money, did you?"

"Hell no. She thinks we're living off my 401K. That's a hoot."

"Good. So, we just wait until someone comes to take Kellogg's place. Got it?"

"Yeah, sure Carl."

Stevens clicked off and sank deep into his large leather chair.

Thank God, he thought. At least Frye had been gone, and there was no way to connect either of them to Kellogg.

He looked at his watch. He decided to go see Patrick Tucker, the District Attorney. Stevens thought he should tell the D.A. to speed the trial up before people started snooping around.

Stevens left by the back door on the East side and walked the two blocks rather than looking for a parking space.

It was late afternoon, and the winter shadows were drifting

across the street. The wind this afternoon was about 10 miles an hour. Mild for Cheyenne, Stevens thought. No gale force winds, but still bitterly cold. He pulled his collar up around his ears and tucked his face as far into the shelter of it as he could.

The gray skies promised more snow, and Stevens picked up his pace. He wanted to see Patrick Tucker and then go home to a warm brandy and cheerful fire.

Just as he turned the corner, he heard some angry voices carried on the wind. He squinted but could only make out a large gathering painted gray by the dim light. As he got closer, he recognized an angry contingent of AIM activists.

He could see the signs they held. Splashed in blood red paint, they all said about the same thing:

Free John Blue Feather!

One more victim of the White Man's Justice!

and

American Indian Movement!

Stevens felt like he'd been kicked in the gut. This was just the complication he had wanted to avoid.

He squirmed through the North edge of the crowd making his way to the front door of the County Courthouse. As he got closer, the mob got tighter, and Stevens had to push and lean to make any headway.

By the time he reached the relative safety of the front courtyard, he felt bruised and angry. He took it out on the two patrolmen guarding the door.

"Can't you keep this rabble back further from the building? This is untenable."

"Sorry sir, but they have a permit and . . ." the young cop trailed off. Stevens was already behind the closed door.

There were office workers peering through the windows at the demonstration. They gathered in small groups of three or four, ostensibly wandering over to the concession area for an afternoon shot of caffeine and a cookie, but clearly not interested in either.

Stevens felt his head and heart begin to throb. The cartoon

image of a thermometer rising and rising before ultimately exploding flashed through his mind. He had to get to Tucker before someone pulled this loose thread called John Blue Feather and the entire fabric of his world unraveled.

He punched the elevator five times before the doors opened and he had to step out of the way of a swarm of people. Thankfully, he was the only one going up. He used the time to breathe deeply and try to regain his calm.

By the time he got to Tucker's, the front office was empty. He knocked on Tucker's closed door.

"I told you not to bother me, damn it!"

"It's me, Tucker," Stevens said as he opened the door and peered in.

The usually dapper and unflappable Patrick Tucker looked like he'd run a marathon in his shirt sleeves. His tie was loosened, his collar unbuttoned. His abundant salt and pepper hair stood up as if he had run his hands through it several times, and his normally smooth complexion he cultivated with weekly facials was a mottled red.

"What the hell is going on downstairs?" Tucker turned on Stevens.

"Hey Patrick, back off. None of this is my fault." Knowing Tucker was even more worried than he was had comforted him. "When I got here, there was a demonstration mounted by the American Indian Movement. But you already know that."

"If they put any of this together . . . we're screwed," Tucker said.

"I don't see how they could. I just talked to Frye, and he's hiding from his wife at his cabin in Encampment. He's going to sit tight until I give him the all clear," Stevens said and sat in one of the chairs.

"I just don't know what happened. I saw that kid this morning at his arraignment. There is no way he could shoot Kellogg like that. But if he didn't, who did?" He flopped into the chair next to Stevens.

"I've got no idea. I get the sense that AIM might have gotten wind of the plan for the building. I think that's what triggered the bison head and the warning."

"Crap Carl, if they know that much, it won't be long before they put the whole thing together."

"Not if you keep your wits about you. Draw out the trial. Pull whatever attention you can away from the murder and focus on the terrorist leanings of the AIM. Convince the jury they're a danger to national security."

Tucker leaned forward. "That might just work," he considered. "There is such a thing as Limited Political Terrorism, which are acts of terrorism committed for ideological motives, but which are not part of a concerted campaign to capture control of the state."

"Great! Zero in on the checkered history of AIM and connect Blue Feather to it. Make the murder seem like the natural progression of a domestic terrorist group that is now identified and contained."

Tucker stood up and paced. "All we need to do is buy some time. The legislature will be in town next week. We just need to get someone to rubber-stamp our re-designation of the property, and we can move forward."

Stevens began to breathe easier. "Meanwhile, we need to keep AIM and Blue Feather's lawyers busy defending themselves on terrorist charges. This may work better all around. By the time the plan is publicly announced, Blue Feather and AIM will be so discredited no one will take them seriously."

"But the question remains, who killed Kellogg and why?" Tucker moved back behind his desk.

"Why don't you call Tucci and find out what's going on?" Stevens suggested.

"Because he said he didn't want us contacting him, that's why. They're pretty picky about that."

Stevens looked at his watch. "I guess I'll take off. We just follow the plan, right?" Stevens moved to the door.

Tucker straightened his tie. "We just follow the plan."

JAMES FRYE DIDN'T MUCH CARE FOR NIGHTTIME in his cabin. He could feel the darkness close in on him in a way that was more oppressive than in town. He heard critters in the dark and it made him itchy.

He poured another two fingers of Black Label into his glass

and poked at the fire in front of him. He jacked up the volume on his radio, trying to drown out the creaks and crackles he kept hearing outside.

It was probably a nocturnal animal. He was pretty sure it wasn't a skunk. He'd been sprayed once, and he'd never forget the smell.

His head bobbed as he jerked awake and then dozed off from the warmth of both the whiskey and the fire. He finally stood up shakily and tottered over to the small cot on the other side of the fire. He'd barely dropped his jeans to his ankles when the door flew open and slammed against the inner wall.

"What? What?" Frye yelled toward a bright night ops flashlight set on strobe. Frye took a step, floundered on his jeans, and fell face first to the floor.

He didn't know if he passed out for a second, but when his vision cleared, the throbbing light had stopped and settled into a bright LED glare.

Rather than risk trying to get up, Frye rolled onto his back. "My wallet's on the table there. Take whatever you need."

The light flicked in the table's direction and Frye watched as a disembodied hand reach out to flip his wallet open. The light swung back to him. He heard the man walk toward him. The light went dark just as the man hunkered next to him.

Frye's eyes wouldn't adjust to the dark coal blackness, and he became even more terrified. He smelled peppermint gum and felt the warmth of a gloved hand that ran slowly down his cheek, almost like a caress.

Then he felt something cold and metallic press into his temple. His whiskey muddled brain didn't realize it was a gun barrel until he heard the click. His scream echoed in the room briefly, even after he died.

CHAPTER 11

DARCY WAS BEAT. She could not wait to get home, kick off her heels and dive into her sweats. She had done an update on the five o'clock news, which was taped to be shown at ten, so she was done for the day.

Grabbing her laptop and large purse, she turned off the lights and closed the door. As she turned, she ran into Zach Horton. Zach reached out and steadied her.

"Easy, Darcy," he said with a chuckle.

"I'm on my way home, so—"

"Not yet. AIM is protesting the arrest of John Blue Feather in front of the county courthouse. I need you to go down and try to get a comment from the participants."

"Zach, I have some left-over pasta and a little Sangiovese I was looking forward to polishing off."

"You can do that after." Zach went back down the hall, then stopped and turned back to her. "Oh yeah, and take Adkins with you." He didn't wait for her to answer.

"I work for a tunnel-vision, newsaholic, ambition-driven jerk. It's a wonder Kelly can put up with him," Darcy muttered as she began the search for Netters and Adkins.

She finally found Netters in the editing room. He was leaning into the monitor and squinting. His Cubbies cap was resting precariously on his head, brim facing backwards and showing a frizzle of red hair Darcy knew he hated.

"Jeeze, Netters. Don't you ever go home?"

Netters jumped. "For cryin' out loud, Calamity! Don't sneak up on a guy like that."

"Sorry," she said perfunctorily. She perched her butt on the ledge by his monitor and crossed her arms.

Netters pretended to ignore her, but finally gave up.

"What?" he snapped at her.

"Horton wants us to go cover a protest at the county court-house. Some AIM demonstration."

Netters moved before her sentence was completed. He twisted his cap around, turned off his monitor, and wrenched himself into his shearling jacket. He grabbed his equipment case on the way out the door.

"I'll meet you at the van. I'm supposed to bring Adkins," she called after him.

Netters turned back to her. "Ah hell, Darcy." He looked distressed.

"I know. I don't like it any more than you do but-"

"Where are we going?" They heard the shout behind them.

Darcy whirled around to see Adkins running up the hall, yanking on his fine merino wool coat. They turned to leave without answering. Adkins trotted in their wake.

The scene at the courthouse was controlled chaos. Small pup tents were being set up on the courthouse lawn as darkness dropped the temperatures into the 20's.

Darcy scanned the scene and headed for the steps where a tall middle-aged man was having a heated conversation with one of the police officers.

"Hi. I am Darcy Moreland from Channel 23. I hate to interrupt—"

"Then don't," replied the middle-aged man without even looking at her.

Up close, Darcy could see sculpted cheekbones paired with coal black hair streaked with white and worn in a carelessly braided tail that hung down his back. He wore a leather jacket with fringe down the back of each arm and his worn jeans clung to his lean hips like a sausage casing.

"You must be Mike Brown, Mary's brother and John's uncle," Darcy said.

The man stopped haranguing the officer and turned. His eyes were a flat dark brown, almost black, as they narrowed on Darcy. The spit dried up in her mouth.

"Yeah, I'm Mike Brown. Who the hell are you, and how do you know my family?"

"I was trying to explain before. Mary called me to help John. I work for the TV station here as an investigative reporter," Darcy replied simply.

Mike Brown crossed his arms, and Darcy's lips twitched into a small grin. It was such a clichéd pose.

"You find me amusing, Ms. Moreland?" Brown asked.

"Not you exactly. Your use of stereotypical poses is amusing, though. Does that fall under the category of giving the audience what they want?"

A small chuckle rumbled from him, and he dropped his arms to his sides. Darcy released the breath she hadn't known she was holding.

"You're perceptive, but annoying. You interrupted my explanation to this young officer that we have a license to demonstrate peacefully in front of the courthouse." Brown's glare shifted from Darcy to the officer.

"Yes sir, but as I was explaining, your license doesn't allow you to camp out here." The young officer looked at Darcy for help.

"What does the license say?" Darcy asked.

Brown passed the sheet to her, and she scanned it quickly.

"Well, I'm no lawyer, but there doesn't seem to be any restriction on how or for how long they can demonstrate." Darcy glanced up at the officer. "Perhaps you should ask the city attorney and have another, more specific license drawn up."

The officer looked at the darkening sky. "Chances are pretty good he's left for today."

"Just to clarify things, officer," Mike Brown said. "I am a lawyer, and I can guarantee you won't get this license changed tonight. We might as well agree to an amicable truce for this evening."

The officer looked bleak. He checked his watch, looked over at the officer standing on the other side of the door, and shrugged.

"That settles it for now, right?" Brown was pushing, but Darcy could understand why. He wanted to make sure he got the officer to agree in front of a witness.

"I guess so . . . but no open fires." The officer wanted to keep the façade of control.

"My people know how to keep warm, Officer, but thank you for your concern." Brown turned away and took Darcy with him toward the proliferation of pup tents and Army surplus canvas. Darcy caught Netters' eye. Adkins moved toward her, and she shook her head slightly as Brown ducked into the tent and pulled Darcy in behind him.

Darcy thought the tent smelled of oil, but she was grateful it was warmer than out in the wind. Brown sat on several sleeping bags littering the tent floor like confetti.

"Sit," he patted the ground.

"Thanks." Darcy sat and looked around. "Doesn't quite have the romance of a tipi," she said.

"No, but unfortunately, I can't get my hands on 15 to 20 bison skins to make a tipi. Hell, we can't even buy them on the hoof, but Ted Turner can. This tent has its own history. In 1963, a tent like this went on a Mt. Everest ascent, weathering 60+ mph winds and temperatures reaching below -20°F. I think it can handle a Wyoming winter night."

"Hmm . . . impressive." Darcy reached into her handbag and pulled out her small tape recorder. "Do you mind?"

"No. The purpose of this demonstration is to get publicity." Brown leaned back a little and unbuttoned his jacket.

There was something compelling about Mike Brown, Darcy thought. About mid-forties, she figured. His glossy black hair was threaded with white strands, which made him look like an elder. He had the tanned skin of a man who spent most of his days outdoors. His jaw was pugnaciously square and his teeth white and even.

"You look a little like a travel poster for the New West," Darcy said, trying to ease into the interview.

"I'm not sure whether to be insulted or not. I get that perception is more important than truth in your field, Ms. Moreland, but we aren't from central casting and the issues we believe in are serious."

"Now I don't know whether to be insulted or not." Darcy rose to her knees above him. "The issues are evidently serious enough that your nephew is cooling his heels in jail and his mother, your sister, is beside herself with worry. I don't think either of those issues is trivial."

Brown closed his eyes and a pained look flitted across it. "Sorry. I am more used to being belligerent and rude to Federal Agents."

"Like Stuart Johnson?" Darcy asked.

Brown's eyebrows raised just a fraction. "Especially Johnson."

"Mary doesn't mind him," Darcy said, more to watch Brown's reaction.

He didn't disappoint. A red tinge infused the sharp planes of his face and his eyes glittered like obsidian.

"Johnson just hangs around Mary to get to me. I hate that he uses her like that."

"I've talked to both of them, and I didn't get that impression. I think they are genuine friends." Darcy had no idea why she felt the need to justify some relationship between two people she hardly knew.

Brown surged to his feet in one fluid motion and snapped, "Get out."

"Okay, but I'm the only one here with a TV crew. Not sure your protest will make good radio." Darcy stood up, plopped her recorder into her purse, and yanked it onto her shoulder.

Brown stopped her just as she was ducking out through the tent flap.

"You're right. The protest is more important than anything else. Where do you want to shoot this?" Brown asked.

"Let us do a sweep shot of the tents and then I'd like to shoot an interview with you back here," Darcy said.

Brown backed into the tent, and Darcy went to tell Netters the plan.

With a light bar attached to his camera, Netters made quick work of "the tenting at the courthouse" shot. Darcy, Netters, and Adkins squeezed into the confines of the tent.

"Who is he?" Brown asked, pointing to Adkins.

"He's an intern helping me with the story," Darcy said.

Brown nodded. "Let's get going. The guys who are supposed to share this tent are freezing out there."

Brown sat once more on the tent floor and crossed his legs. Darcy and Adkins followed suit while Netters crouched to get the shot.

"Test?' Netters asked.

"'Take care of luxuries, and the necessities will take care of themselves,' Dorothy Parker," Darcy said into the mic.

"Got it." Netters widened his stance and aimed the camera.

Darcy spoke into the mic.

I am here with Mike Brown of the Arapaho tribe, a member of AIM, the American Indian Movement, and the uncle of John Blue Feather, arrested last evening in connection with the death of Latham Kellogg. What is the purpose of this protest, Mr. Brown?

We are demanding justice for John Blue Feather who stands accused of a murder he did not commit. It is simply another example of the tyranny of this government.

Isn't it common practice for people accused of crimes to claim to be innocent?

John is only implicated because he's an active member of AIM and we have been exercising our rights to determine the use of the old Thompson's Furniture building.

Is AIM accepting responsibility for the bison head and the warning?

We neither confirm nor deny.

How is it you feel you have a right to the building, Mr. Brown? Does AIM own it?

No. They stole it from us like the land it sits on.

So, your animosity stems from old grievances like the Fort Laramie Treaty.

Surprised you know about that, but no. Our grievances stem from more recent abuses of power.

Such as what, Mr. Brown?

We will submit a manifesto at John's trial, which will detail the graft and greed of the governing bodies of not only this city, but this state as well.

Sounds like a sweeping condemnation. Could you give us any details?

No. Although AIM had no part in the murder of Latham Kellogg, we won't let it stop us from continuing to protest the flagrant abuse of the white man's government.

Darcy gave Netters the sign to cut and dropped the mic to her lap.

"Okay, Mr. Brown, you got that little commercial for free. Even when we edit it down, and rest assured we will, you'll still get your sound bites. In exchange, I want some actual information. I can keep it off-the-record, if necessary, but I need to know what your strategy is. I promised Mary I'd try to help."

"Off the record?" Brown's left eyebrow shot to his hairline. He glanced in Adkins' direction.

"Ignore him," Darcy responded. "Tell me what I want to know, or we'll reduce coverage of your little picnic to a five second blip."

"You have a nasty little attitude when crossed. I like that." Brown grinned.

Darcy tried to clamp down on her impatience. "Look Mr. Brown, we're on the same side here—"

"Oh, I doubt that."

"I mean insofar as I want John to get a fair trial. If he's innocent, I want him set free."

"As do I," Brown agreed. "I doubt, however, the Federal Government shares our goals. They have arraigned John on charges of murder perpetrated while engaging in acts of terrorism under the USA Patriot Act."

"Are you serious?" Darcy looked at Netters.

Netters had drawn closer and hunkered down at Darcy's side. He shook his head, implying he did not get it either.

"How can they possibly make this about terrorism?" Darcy leaned in.

"Under the Patriot Act any action designed to intimidate or coerce a civilian population, is dangerous to human life in violation of the criminal laws of a state or the United States or influences the policy of a government by intimidation or coercion can be designated as terrorism."

"By that rule, they might designate anyone who protests against the government as a terrorist."

"Slippery slope, ain't it?"

"But why would they want to do such a thing? Isn't murder enough of a charge?"

"Good question. What might the D.A. be trying to hide? Why the smoke screen?"

"I'm not much on conspiracy theories," Darcy said.

"But I am," Netters interrupted. "What do you think they're trying to hide?"

"We think they're trying to get control of the land the store stands on. We know Latham Kellogg was snooping around at the capitol, digging into state and federal law as it pertains to Native American rights. We just don't know what he found out. We knew enough to launch the protest with the bison head to scare them into slipping up."

Brown turned his attention to Netters, and Darcy studied him. He looked like a kid who was describing a high school prank instead of a middle-aged activist.

"So, you admit you planted the bison head?" Darcy asked.

"Sure," Brown answered, then grinned. "Off the record."

"Are you kidding me?" Darcy jumped to her feet.

Brown rose also but had to stoop due to the slope of the tent. "You offered 'off the record' before we began this conversation."

"He's right, Darcy. You did promise," Adkins chimed in.

Darcy and Netters transferred their attention to him. "Be quiet, Adkins," they said in unison, as if they had practiced it.

Adkins' face screwed up, and he looked like he was going to counter with something acidic but changed his mind.

"You think the FBI has tied John to the protest and an implied threat? You think they're going to prosecute him in Federal court?" Darcy followed Brown as he ducked out of the tent.

He turned to her. "Yes, in a nutshell. That's what I think. If it were just the bison head incident, we could probably get it transferred to tribal court since no property was damaged. But it's not. And now Stuart Johnson cannot wait to grab a juicy case to discredit AIM. What better way than by tying it to the Patriot Act?"

"I think you're wrong about Stuart Johnson, Mr. Brown," Darcy said.

"Yeah. You would." Mike Brown turned and walked into the middle of the improvised campground.

BACK AT THE STATION, DARCY AND NETTERS reduced the report down to the bare bones interview spliced onto some pictures of the tent city. They were so busy, they did not notice Adkins had not followed them into the editing bay.

Adkins was next door, downloading the section of Brown's admission of AIM involvement from his phone video. Once he had it downloaded, he edited Darcy out and darkened Brown's profile, so he was unrecognizable. He used a mask over the audio and fiddled with it until Mike Brown sounded like a robot.

"This is too cool," he whispered to himself.

Next, he dubbed in his own voice asking the questions Darcy had asked. Darcy may have promised the information was off the record, but he had not. He felt a slight tug of conscience and then squashed it. This was a cutthroat business and if he ever hoped to go play with the big boys in the larger market areas, he had to be ruthless.

By the time Adkins had finished, it sounded like he had gotten an exclusive interview with an active member of the American Indian Movement who admitted the group tried to intimidate Latham Kellogg.

He made a quick call to Uncle Arnie and told him of the report. Then he took the saved interview on a thumb drive and uploaded it to a file transfer protocol site for downloading by the station for use on the air. He would let Uncle Arnie run interference for him on that end.

As for the rest of his evening, he bought some beer and KFC. He planned to go home and watch his exclusive report on the 10 o'clock news. Zach would have to take him seriously after this, he thought.

CHAPTER 12

Detective Hank Nelson hung up the phone after talking to the Carbon County Sheriff. They had found the body of James Frye earlier that day in a small cabin near Encampment. Seems a drinking buddy had wandered in to visit Frye and found him dead with two bullet holes in the temple.

Hank leaned back in his leather chair, ignoring the aggrieved creaking of the wood frame as it tilted back.

An ache began at the middle of his forehead and radiated outward. He rubbed the pain on the side of his head reflexively and closed his eyes, trying to think.

Two shots to the temple . . . execution style. Again. What the hell was going on? First Latham Kellogg, now James Frye. The difference here was Hank knew Frye. Didn't like him much but knew him.

James Frye had been the county coroner when Hank first joined the force. In Hank's opinion, Frye played a little fast and loose with bodies he was obligated to process. Hank never caught him doing anything illegal per say, but the coroner was always playing the angles. Hank wouldn't put it past him to take a kickback from the funeral homes. Frye wouldn't be the first.

Hank also didn't like Frye's callous disregard for the dignity of the deceased, particularly if they were poor and homeless. He'd been on sites several times when Frye had said things that were insensitive about the dead.

"Ah shit," Hank said with a sigh. "Doesn't matter now, anyway. Guy's gone." He rubbed the back of his neck where the ache from his temples had migrated.

He picked up his phone and dialed Darcy's number. She answered on the second ring.

Hank heard some rustling noises and guessed she'd retrieved her phone from under her lunch or something. He surveyed his clutter and decided not to tease her about it.

"Hank?"

"Yeah. I was going to ask if you wanted to have dinner tonight, but you don't sound happy to hear from me."

"Uh, sorry. Distracted and discouraged. I can't find a way to get John Blue Feather out on bail. Any ideas?"

"Be patient and let the justice system function. It usually works." Hank sorted a couple of reports into stacks.

"Spoken like a biased practitioner of the justice system. Even you have to admit you guys get it wrong sometimes."

"I'm in enforcement, not justice. I don't have to admit anything, but for your information, some recent developments have come to light that may go a long way towards helping your friend."

There was a slight pause, more rustling, and a soft click before Darcy spoke.

"What exactly might those be?"

"Turn off your recorder." He waited for the click.

"Okay. Not taping. So . . .?"

"Got a call that James Frye's body was found this morning in Encampment. The cause of death appears to be identical to Kellogg's wounds."

"That's great . . . uh I mean . . ."

"I know what you mean, but for now it changes nothing."

"You can't be serious!"

He could tell Darcy was trying hard to control a shriek and choking on it.

"I am serious. We have no time of death. The body is being sent to Loveland for examination by the Medical Examiner. Until he determines cause and time of death and ballistics examines the bullets, your friend John Blue Feather is staying put."

"That's absurd! John's been in jail. How could he possibly—"

Hank said slowly, enunciating each word, "We don't know how long Frye has been dead."

"Don't patronize me, Nelson. Did they find a gun?"

"No."

Silence for a beat, then, "Do you still want to have dinner?"

"I don't think so. You've got your teeth clamped so hard around this case; I don't think we'd do anything but argue." He clicked off.

Hank tossed his phone onto the littered surface of his desk. Lord that woman could turn him seven ways to Sunday. He thought she'd be happy that John Blue Feather stood a good chance of being exonerated. Instead, she was still irritated about his being in jail.

He was eager to find the killer. Multiple murders were rare in Wyoming. There was the occasional "act of passion" usually centering on women or drugs or both, but he couldn't remember the last time he'd had to investigate two murders, likely committed by the same person.

He didn't like the feeling. It gave him the creeps, like watching a film when the music gets weird. You know something bad is going to happen, you just don't know what. He was out of ideas.

Hank slipped the report on the Kellogg murder out of its folder. He read the report about the wounds and the weapon used. If Frye's murder matched, it meant there was a connection between the two men how and why?

It had to have something to do with the building and that consortium Kellogg had mentioned. Sometimes a consortium was a collection of people looking for an investment opportunity, but sometimes it could be something more sinister. Two murders slapped this into the sinister column in Hank's book.

Hank liked to build a case like a wall, one brick at a time. He told himself to slow down and wait for the information from the Frye murder investigation. No point in trying to build a wall without all the bricks and mortar.

DARCY LOOKED AT HER CELL. SHE could not believe Hank had hung up on her. She had half a mind to call him back and cuss him out.

She would *have* to have half a mind to do that. If her relationship with Hank had taught her nothing else, it had taught her the man was as unmovable as a concrete pillar when he wanted to be. She realized she was also unmovable in her own way. No wonder they argued.

She knew it was better to let some time pass. The next occasion she talked to him, she would pretend nothing had happened. It annoyed her down to the bottom of her Irish soul not to attack head on and in full voice, but Hank was immune to her temper. She would wait until she could reason with him.

Darcy picked up her phone and dialed Abby's number. By God and greyhound, she thought, having dinner with Hank was not her only option.

"Hi Abbs," she began without preamble, "I thought I might pick up some rotisserie chicken at the store and bring it home for dinner. What do you think?"

There was an uncharacteristic silence on the other end.

"Uhm. Well . . ." Abby stammered.

"Something wrong?" Darcy asked.

"No. I mean yes. I mean, not wrong exactly. But I have plans, Darcy. Barton is taking me to a Japanese restaurant in Fort Collins this evening."

"Oh," Darcy said.

"Do you want to come along?" Abby asked.

"No. Don't be ridiculous. I'll pick up Mac about five-thirty if that's early enough."

"Perfect. Barton isn't picking me until six. It will give us a little time to get caught up."

"Okay. See you soon." Darcy hung up and put her phone down.

Since when had she become so dependent on Hank and Abby? She stuffed papers and her laptop into her bag in a flurry. She had always prided herself on being independent and here she was feeling at sixes and sevens because she didn't have any plans for a Friday night.

By the time she picked up the chicken and a little chocolate ice cream, she convinced herself that an evening at home with her dog and her 19-inch flat screen was going to be fun.

Rather than drag the chicken into Abby's, driving Mac nuts and taking a chance on melting the ice cream, she dumped her stuff in the oven and freezer respectively, then bounced down the stairs to Abby's. True to form, the door was unlocked.

"Abbs," she hollered, "it's just me."

"Be out in a minute," Abby shouted back from the bedroom.

Mac was dancing around her feet, and it surprised Darcy. His exuberance went a long way towards soothing her feeling of abandonment. She stooped to scoop him up and plopped him into her lap as she sat in her accustomed place on the flowered settee.

Darcy snuggled and scratched Mac. Abby swished into the room.

"Wow, Abby. You look great," Darcy said.

Abby smoothed her hands down a subtly blue green nubby-wool pencil skirt, topped with a perfectly matched cashmere sweater.

"Do you think so?" Abby twirled once and then sat across from Darcy.

"Is that new? I don't think I've ever seen it before."

"Brand new. I was just waiting for an excuse to wear it."

"Dr. Barton is a lucky man," Darcy said.

"Enough. What's new with your investigation? I feel like I haven't talked to you in days."

Darcy filled her in about Mary Blue Feather, the arrest of John Blue Feather, and ended with the information about James Frye. Abby was pensive. She twirled her pearl necklace around her finger and back again.

"What does Hank think?" Abby asked when Darcy had finished.

"He thinks they can't let John go until the COD and TOD are established."

"Cause and time?" Abby clarified.

"Exactly, even though Hank can see John isn't involved in either murder. He's just being stubborn about that."

"Darcy, he has to follow protocol. I'm sure he wants to do right by John when he can."

Darcy answered with an unladylike snort just as the doorbell trilled.

Abby rose to go to the door, primping slightly at the mirror. She opened the door and let Dr. Barton in.

"You look like a spot of spring on this dreary winter's day, Abigail," Barton said as he took both of Abby's hands in his.

Abby tugged one of her hands free, but Barton clung to the other. "Darcy stopped by to get Mac and fill me in on the investigation so far," Abby said.

"Fascinating." Barton moved into the living room, relinquishing Abby's hand reluctantly as she sat in her favorite chair. Barton sat on the arm.

Darcy rose, tucking Mac under her arm. "Don't let me keep you guys. I was on my way out."

Barton rose from his perch on Abby's chair with old world grace. "Please don't let me interrupt. I'm interested as well."

Darcy's eyes darted to Abby, who nodded, and she dropped back into the settee. Mac, bored with all the talk, leaped off the furniture and curled up by the hissing radiator.

It took only moments to fill Barton in. He made interested noises throughout the narration, but when she told him of James Frye's body being found, Barton's eyes grew round with surprise.

"And he had the same wounds as this Kellogg fellow, you say?" He had scooted so far forward on the arm, Darcy was afraid he would fall.

"Hank said they sounded similar, but he's withholding judgment until the Medical Examiner makes a determination."

"Quite right. It wouldn't do to go rabbiting off without certified facts," Barton nodded.

Darcy sat tight-lipped and Abby jumped in, "Our Darcy is concerned about John Blue Feather and she's a little put out with Hank for being slow to release him."

"Oh," Barton said.

"Well now, everyone is up to date." Darcy rose. "I think I'll take my dog and go hunker down for the evening. You guys have fun." She plucked Mac up and swept out of the door before Abby and

Barton could say goodbye.

"Sometimes Darcy moves so fast she makes me breathless." Abby picked up her coat from the back of her chair.

Barton took her coat and helped her put it on, lingering behind her long enough to whisper in her ear, "You make me breathless without moving an inch."

DARCY SAT CROSS-LEGGED on the large sheepskin rug she had splurged on at a summer sale with just such an evening in mind. The carcass of the chicken looked mangled sitting in its juices on the middle of her large yellow ware platter. Mac had eaten his fill and slept on the oversized brown couch while Darcy ran through the channels on the remote.

"Not much of interest, Mac. I'm not a fan of reality TV." She knew her dog wasn't listening, but she wanted some human sound, even if she had to make it herself. She was lonely.

The snow falling softly outside her window was lit delicately by the streetlamp. She thought it looked like a movie set. She took a deep sip of her wine and almost choked when her doorbell rang.

"Wonder who that is," she said as she raced Mac to the door. She took a moment to peek through the Judas hole.

Hank stood there with a bottle of wine in his hand and a silly grin on his face. Darcy couldn't help but laugh.

"I thought you didn't want to see me tonight." She swung the door open, plopping one hand on her hip.

Hank took a moment to look at her. Her hair pulled into a loose ponytail with tendrils escaping down her cheeks, she looked positively charming. She had on a short pink t-shirt that brushed the bottom of her last rib, but did nothing to hide her navel, which peaked enticingly above the gray sweatpants riding precariously low on her hips. The outfit ended with her feet encased in fuzzy pink house socks.

Hank thought it was an enchanting mix of hoyden and temptress made even more alluring because it was unintended.

"I bring wine and good news. They released John Blue Feather on bail this evening and have reduced the charges to malicious vandalism. Happy?"

Darcy hugged him while simultaneously snagging the wine from his hand. "Ecstatic. Here," she handed him a glass after he took off his coat, "I have a bottle working."

Hank eyed the chicken and the soft rug on the floor. He sat on the chair and began tugging off his boots.

"For heaven's sake. Here. Pour yourself some wine and I'll get the boots."

She straddled his outstretched leg, tugging the boot off, then repeated the motion with his other foot.

Hank sank to the rug and pulled her into his lap. He kissed her.

Darcy pushed away and sat up, facing him. "Hey, just because you brought wine doesn't …"

Hank pulled her close. "And good news. Don't forget the good news." Darcy melted into his arms.

CHAPTER 13

THE NEXT MORNING CAME AS A COMPLETE SURPRISE to Darcy. She cautiously opened one eye to glare at the cold winter light streaming into her bedroom. She closed it again quickly, praying the dull ache that was making her ears ring would go away.

Cautiously, she patted the mattress next to her. Based on a fuzzy memory of hot sex and good wine, she assumed Hank was next to her. If not, it would have been an extraordinary dream. She slapped a hard muscled arm and risked opening her eye to a tiny slit once more.

"Not a dream," she mumbled half into the pillow.

"That hurt," Hank joked.

He sat up and swung his legs off the bed, treating Darcy to the sight of a wide shouldered back tapering to a trim waist and tight backside.

"I didn't say you weren't dreamy. I was simply remarking that you were not a figment of my imagination. This is a good thing." She indulged herself by running her palm up his back.

Hank turned and kissed her deeply. "Good morning," he said in a whisper.

"Hmmm." She stretched luxuriously, popping several vertebrae back into alignment. "That felt more like good night. It was a good night, wasn't it, Hank?"

"The best. Want me to jog your memory?" Hank nuzzled her neck.

Darcy pushed him away. "Coffee. I need coffee . . ."

Hank stood to pull his shorts and jeans on. He left his jeans unbuttoned a little at the waist. Darcy giggled.

"What?" Hank sounded incensed.

"Nothing. I just noticed you are wearing the red chili peppers shorts I gave you. Appropriate."

"Thanks." Hank sank onto the bed again and looked at her expectantly.

"I said I need coffee." Darcy tucked and rolled off the other side of the bed.

She grabbed his denim shirt off the floor and pulled it on as she padded barefoot to the kitchen.

Darcy opened the small freezer compartment in her ancient refrigerator, then cussed professionally when she found a mere dusting of coffee grounds at the bottom of the bag.

Hank leaned against the doorway with his arms crossed over his chest. He had the gall to flash his perfectly aligned, dazzlingly white smile in her direction.

Darcy scowled. "Amused? You're amused?"

"Slightly. You look tempting in my shirt."

She threw the offending bag away. "Since you think this is funny, why don't you go get some coffee? A latte preferably, and another bag of ground coffee for later."

"Why don't we go together, and I'll buy you breakfast?"

"Works for me."

Darcy sashayed past him, flinging his shirt off in his general direction.

Within ten minutes, she was dressed in her sweats, with polished teeth and face, and a ponytail ruthlessly pulled through the back of a pink baseball cap.

"Want to check with Abbs and see if she wants any?" Darcy asked as she secured the leash to Mac's collar.

"Fine, but I draw the line at buying a cappuccino for fuzzy face there." Hank shrugged into his leather bomber jacket.

"You're a riot, Nelson." Darcy wiggled into her ski jacket and tied a thick scarf around her neck. "Dang! By the time I bundle up to go out, I'm too tired to go anywhere."

"Stop whining," Hank said as he scooped Mac up and pushed Darcy through the door.

They clambered down the stairs and stopped at Abby's door. Darcy banged on the door more for form's sake, but when she tried to open it, trusting it would be unlocked as usual, it did not give.

"That's strange," she said. She banged some more on the door, then listened for any movement. She could hear a slight rustling, and she could swear she heard voices whispering. She glanced at Hank, who seemed engrossed with scratching Mac's neck.

"Abby! Abby!" she shouted through the door. "It's Darcy. Are you okay?"

The lock clicked open, and Abby's rumpled, sleep-creased head peered out.

"Huh? Why are you making that racket?"

"Are you okay? Your door was locked."

"I'm fine and I'm going back to bed."

Abby tried to close the door, but Darcy pushed a little to open it wider. Beyond Abby, a disheveled Barton was trying to zip up his slacks on the run.

Darcy's eyes popped open, and she looked from Abby to Barton. She opened her mouth, but nothing would come out.

Hank dropped Mac to the floor and snagged Darcy's arm, trying to pull her away.

"Sorry, Abby. We're going for coffee. You want anything?" Hank jerked Darcy behind him.

Abby tried to smooth her hair but gave it up. "No. No, thank you. We're fine." She looked behind her. "Aren't we fine?" Her question hung in the air wistfully.

"I wouldn't say no to a small Cinnamon Dolce Latte. Would you like a Dark Cherry Mocha, Abigail?"

Abby blushed and by then Barton was at the door with his arm slung across her shoulders.

"I'd settle for a black hole to crawl into," Abby muttered.

"Don't be silly," Barton said. "We're all adults here. No need for any awkward uneasiness, is there?" Barton's soft green eyes looked from Darcy to Hank, daring them to disagree.

"No problem here," Hank answered for both of them and guided Darcy out the front door of the building before she could react.

The cold hit her like a slap, and she shook her head to clear it.

"Are they . . .? Did they . . .?" she sputtered, climbing up into Hank's truck.

"Most likely," Hank said as he tossed Mac onto her lap and slammed the door. He laughed when he caught sight of Darcy's face. She looked like she had been pole-axed.

"Good God!" Abby slumped in her favorite chair with her head in her hands.

Barton hunkered down beside her. "Abigail. What is the matter?" He kept patting her knee ineffectually.

Abby looked up and tears swam in her eyes. "Did you see her face? She knows!" This last statement was a wail.

"Knows what? That we slept together?"

Barton was totally perplexed. It had been a long time since he had cared what people thought of his infrequent forays into what used to be called promiscuity. He liked to think he was careful and discriminating, but he knew he had the heart of a romantic.

Abigail's distress, however, sucked the joy right out of his marrow. He had no wish ever to hurt her.

"Abigail, please don't cry. Is it being with me? Are you embarrassed of me?" He was pretty sure that wasn't it, but he had to ask.

Abby gazed at him, her watery eyes glistening with unshed tears. "Don't be an idiot. I am embarrassed about me. I hate to be an old fool, but worse, I hate being caught at it."

Barton's face lit up, and he chuckled in both humor and relief. "Well, hell if that's all—"

"All? You dim-witted Lothario, Darcy, was a student of mine. She looked up to me. I was a role model of dignity and decorum, and now look!" Abby wiped her eyes with the back of her hand.

"Doesn't Darcy have a healthy sex life?" Barton prodded.

Exasperated, Abby glared at him. "Of course she does. She's young."

"I'm pretty sure I've seen every inch of you—"

"Oh God, don't remind me." Abby dropped her head into her hands.

"My point is I didn't see a 'Use By' date stamped on your butt."

Abby giggled, then laughed, then cried, and then laughed again.

CARL STEVENS LOOKED AT THE GLOSSY SURFACE of his desk, piled high with file folders and scraps of paper. He was shredding as much evidence as he could. He was terrified.

James Frye's body had been found shot like Latham Kellogg's . . . two in the head. His stomach roiled. He knew who was responsible, and it wasn't John Blue Feather. He had left messages at all the contact numbers he had, but no calls had been returned and he was panicking.

He heard his phone buzz and thrashed around to find it under the piles of paper on his desk. He took a deep breath to steady himself.

"Stevens here."

"Your security has been breached."

The curt statement was even more terrifying, delivered in a raspy whisper.

"I don't think is has," Stevens tried to argue, but even he could hear the quiver in his denial.

"We don't pay you to think. I presume you got the message we left."

"You mean . . . you . . . did that too?"

"Shut up! Are you a moron? Your office could be bugged. Get in touch with that State Senator . . . what's his name?"

"You mean Mitchell? Paul Mitchell on the Native American Affairs Committee?"

"Yeah. Call him and that worthless D.A. Patrick Tucker. Tell them we are done screwing around. Convince them to do what we paid them for or you're next."

The phone went dead, and Stevens felt his stomach drop to his feet. He leaned forward, almost in half and silently repeated the mantra, "Breathe . . . Breathe." His head spun, and he swallowed convulsively as bile rose to the back of his throat.

He sat up and grabbed his phone, scanning through the contacts he had on speed dial. The D.A. Patrick Tucker picked up almost on the first ring.

Stevens didn't even identify himself. "I just got a call. I need to know what they originally told you to do for them."

"Uhm . . . nothing specific. Just to create a favorable legal climate. They didn't get specific until this Kellogg thing."

"It's worse than just Kellogg. They've eliminated Frye too. Sheriff found him up in his cabin in Encampment."

"Oh shit. Why? What did he know?"

"You don't need that information, but this screws up the trial for John Blue Feather. He was in jail at the time of Frye's murder."

"Not necessarily. He could be guilty of Kellogg's murder and not Frye's or Frye's could've happened before Kellogg's."

"Reasoned like a half-brained D.A." Stevens got up and paced. "Don't you get it? They want it shut down and shut down now before it gets public and messy. They aren't happy."

"What the hell do you want me to do? I have no control over what the police do. If they don't charge him, I can't try him."

"Fine. I'll just tell them you're useless to them now, like Frye and Kellogg." Stevens hung up and threw his phone down.

He opened the large desk drawer and pulled out some Black Label. Not bothering with a glass, he took a long swig straight from the bottle. The fiery liquid burned all the way down. He shook his head to clear it.

Bolstered, he reached for the phone again.

WYOMING STATE SENATOR AND PARTNER in the law firm of Mitchell, Mayhew, and Burns, Paul Mitchell oozed charm as he held out his gold pen with its Waterford cut crystal capstone to Margaret Bingham. The pen had been an anniversary gift from Mitchell's very Irish wife, Katie.

The marriage had foundered, but the pen was impressive, and

he was determined to impress Margaret Bingham, the soon to be a widow of Harold Bingham.

"Are you sure this is the right thing to do?" Margaret's lightly powdered brow wrinkled as far as her botoxed brow could manage.

"Absolutely. I had our C.P.A. look it over carefully." He reached across the desk and twitched the paper a little to facilitate signing.

"But his children will be upset," Margaret persisted.

"They are all grown now and have lives of their own," Mitchell deepened his voice and softened it. He had a gift for soothing nervous witnesses and apprehensive clients. "I think the new provision for them is generous, yet still leaves you with enough to live comfortably. I am sure Harold would approve."

Margaret sent him a hesitant look but accepted the pen. She laboriously scrawled her signature where the little sticky arrows indicated, then handed Mitchell's pen back.

"Very good. Now let me run this out to Connie in the front and she will make a copy for you to take home. We'll keep the original on file for you here." Mitchell scuttled out.

Margaret barely had time to appreciate the luxurious art in Mitchell's office before he was back.

"I am so glad we got your authorization so we can take care of some of these pesky details for you. You have enough to handle right now." Mitchell helped her into her heavy camelhair coat and propelled her gently towards the door.

Margaret stopped short before entering the reception area and turned to him. "I don't want Harold to think I've been picking over his bones before he dies. It feels . . . I don't know . . . somehow ghoulish."

Mitchell's hand at her elbow snaked forward to hold her cold, thin-boned hand and he gave it a reassuring squeeze. "Now Margaret. May I call you Margaret?" He arched an eyebrow as if waiting for her consent. She nodded slightly, and he continued. "Harold would want nothing more than the smooth transition of control of his estate. If he were able, I'm sure he would tell you the same thing."

"But . . ." Margaret began again.

"Margaret, you must listen to me carefully. I know this is a trying time for you, but you need to trust me and my firm to look after your best interests." Mitchell was damn sure he did not want to see one of his most lucrative client's assets divvied up among the three children who no longer even lived in the state.

Margaret turned to him, eyes wide and brimming with unshed tears. "If you think it is for the best," she said softly.

"It is," he replied with characteristic confidence.

"And you'll explain all that irrevocable trust stuff to the children?" she persisted.

"Of course I will Margaret." He moved her closer to the door of his cavernous office. Mentally, he cursed again his hubristic impulse of choosing the largest space. It made it difficult to get rid of clients quickly.

His phone rang imperiously, and it gave him an excuse to leave Margaret at his door.

"So sorry. If you need anything Margaret, be sure to call me." He gave her a quick, impersonal hug, and dashed back behind his desk, simultaneously lifting the receiver.

"Mitchell," he said into the phone and perfunctorily waved a perfunctory goodbye to Margaret.

He listened to Stevens ramble on in a panic for a moment, then put him on hold. Then, he closed his door, pushed the intercom button, and said he didn't want to be disturbed.

Clicking back on with Stevens, he took control of the conversation. "Calm down. You don't know they're responsible for the two murders, no matter what they've implied. Why would they kill Kellogg? Wasn't he their own man?"

"Because," Carl Stevens snarled, "he wasn't getting the job done, and he knew too much. Kind of like you and me, huh Mitchell?"

"But why would they kill Frye? He wasn't even the coroner anymore."

"Frye could incriminate them and testify to their manipulated designation of the remains. They accomplished that little hat trick through you, Mitchell, if I recall."

"Grab hold of your cojones, Stevens, and stop babbling. What exactly did they say?" Mitchell began scribbling some notes to himself.

"The guy said our security had been breached and I should call you and Patrick Tucker and make this go away, or we'd all be eliminated. He didn't say so, but I got the impression if we didn't get control of this thing, they'd cover their tracks and disappear."

"Guy? What guy? Didn't you get a name?"

"No," Stevens admitted faintly.

"Then he could be anyone," Mitchell pointed out. "A reporter sniffing around or the FBI, for that matter."

"No. He asked if I had gotten his message earlier."

"What message?"

"They . . . ah . . . they . . ."

"Spit it out Stevens." Paul Mitchell was losing any semblance of patience.

"They killed my dog. I thought it was some kids in the neighborhood who were ticked off because I voted against improvements for the skate park . . ."

"They what?"

"Slit his throat and left him to bleed to death on my front porch. I barely had time to call animal control to dispose of the body and hose the porch down before my wife and kids came home. I told the kids a truck hit Jake. God, it was awful." His voice quivered again, and he took another swig of whisky.

"Okay seriously, calm down," Mitchell said again. He wrote Kellogg, Frye, and Jake on a page, connecting them with arrows.

"Even if they don't kill us, we've got to make sure they don't leave. We have to follow through. I was counting on investing. It is the only way I can pay for my kid's college," Stevens continued.

"Sending your kids to school is the least of my worries. Can Tucker pressure the cops into uncovering Kellogg's murderer quickly? Or perhaps we can implicate one of those transients who hang around the shelter?"

"I could ask, but that might not be easy . . .

"None of this is easy. Call one of your contacts and ask for the gun. Let me know when you get it."

"But that's—" Stevens had been about to say illegal. Even he understood the incongruity. "Yeah. Okay, I'll be in touch."

"Stupid son of a bitch!" Mitchell exploded when he hung up. He tore his notes into tiny fragments, dropped them into his wastebasket, and then kicked it across the room. It clattered against the wall.

Connie Tibbets opened the door a crack. "Is everything alright, Mr. Mitchell?"

"Yeah. Sorry Connie. I was just pacing trying to figure something out, and I tripped on the wastebasket."

Connie looked at the grey broadloom carpet and saw bits of yellow paper strewn over the floor. "I'll just pick that up." She rushed in and was on her knees, picking up the basket and the paper.

Mitchell's lawyer's mind played through the dilemma. If he made too much of an issue about it, she would remember it later. She would recall he seemed upset about something. He decided to finesse.

"Thanks, Connie. Clumsy of me. I just wasn't watching where I was going." He laughed, and she joined him as she set the basket back by his desk.

"It's all cleaned up now, no harm done." She left the office, closing the door daintily behind her.

"If only things were always that uncomplicated," he said to himself.

CHAPTER 14

IT WAS AMAZING TO DARCY HOW EASILY MOLLIFIED she could be with a sweet latté and a pumpkin muffin. Just the smells filling the cab of Hank's truck went a long way to overcoming her initial shock that Abby McNeil had a sex life.

Nope, she thought as she pressed her palm over her twitching eye. Maybe not yet.

Hank wisely said nothing as he helped Darcy jump down to the icy sidewalk. He reached in and snagged the bag of muffins, handing it to Darcy as he grabbed the carriers holding various coffee concoctions.

They picked their way up the treacherously icy front steps.

"I should call the management company and complain," Darcy said.

"Uhm hum," Hank agreed.

"Would you do it? It would have more punch coming from a police detective."

Hank swung one of the heavy doors with the oval beveled glass wide to let Darcy pass. "Should I say my name or just that I'm a detective?"

"Huh?" Darcy rubbed her cold red nose with her gloved hand.

"If I just say I'm a detective, they'll want to know if there is a special department that checks on icy steps. If I say my name, they'll want to confirm that I am a tenant."

"You're just being difficult," Darcy said as she paused in front of Abby's door.

"You started it." Hank knocked sharply.

Darcy could think of nothing to say.

Abby was dressed for the day in faded blue jeans and a muted pink sweater. Darcy noticed she had also put on a little lip-gloss and mascara. Small pearl studs graced her earlobes.

"Come in, come in. Barton will be out in a moment. I put some dishes out on the table for our little impromptu feast." Abby gestured to the sun-dappled table with its embroidered white cloth.

Darcy could tell Abbs was not near as blasé about this as she wanted them to believe.

Barton entered from the bedroom, buttoning the cuff of his blue long-sleeved shirt. His dampened hair gave evidence of a quick shower, and his eyes were sparkling with good humor.

Hank held out a chair for Darcy. She sat and watched as Abby placed the muffins on small plates and passed them around. Hank read the descriptions on the cups and distributed the coffee.

"This is a pleasant way to begin a Saturday," Barton offered. His conversational foray was greeted with grunts and hmms.

Giving up any pretense of good manners or finesse, Darcy dove right in. "Barton, what are you doing?"

"You mean besides eating breakfast?"

"Ah yes, I presume you mean to ask what my intentions regarding Abigail are?"

Darcy nodded and did not take her eyes off of him, though she was aware Abby had gasped and Hank had exclaimed, "Darcy!"

Barton said plainly, "My intentions are none of your business."

Darcy was so shocked she could only sputter for a second, though Hank's chuckle of surprised amusement was not lost on her.

Abby placed her hand tenderly on Barton's arm and said, "Thank you."

"Wait a second!" Darcy finally found her voice. "I am just looking out for a friend. I love Abby and I don't want to see her hurt."

Barton rounded on her. "That you assume I would hurt Abigail is insulting to me. That you would assume Abigail wants you to look after her is insulting to her."

Darcy glanced at Abby and then Hank, looking for some support, but got none.

"I am just concerned—"

"You are intrusive, and I have just the type of eccentric kind of manners which allow me to say so."

Darcy could not put together any cogent argument.

"Darcy," Barton continued a little more gently, "I know that your job requires that you be intrusive when you investigate, but those are not qualities which work well in personal relationships. If she chooses, Abigail is always free to share whatever confidences she wants with you, but I will not be badgered, and I will not allow you to badger her."

"Couldn't be clearer," Hank agreed. "Butter?" he offered to Darcy. He put the dish down but looked sublimely unruffled.

After the meal, Barton and Hank cleaned up most of the dishes. Darcy was picking her muffin apart with the precision of a dissection. Abby had retreated into the television room as a distraction. She selected an early morning news-magazine show aired on both Saturday and Sunday mornings. Usually, it was a compilation of stories and features from the week.

They passed the job of anchoring the dreaded weekend show around so that nobody had to do it every weekend. This week, Cary Morrison had pulled the duty.

Darcy watched half-heartedly as she ate muffin crumbs from her plate.

"Is her hair really red or does she dye it?" Abby asked.

"Now who's being nosy and intrusive?"

Abby turned to her, stricken. "Oh Darcy, don't—"

"I'm sorry, Abbs. I didn't mean that. I guess Barton scraped a little too close to the bone. Nothing that won't heal."

Out of the corner of her eye, she saw video of her interview with Mike Brown at the AIM demonstration . . . but something was off about it.

"Abbs, turn it up."

Darcy identified the voice of Mike Brown, though he was blacked out. He was answering a question Darcy remembered Netters had asked about why Kellogg's consortium was interested in the building.

They are trying to get control of the land that the store is on. We know Kellogg was snooping around at the capitol, digging into state and federal law as it pertains to Native American rights. We just don't know what he found out. The bison head was used to scare them into slipping up.

"Oh my God Abbs! That wasn't from the original interview. That was later when we were talking to him off the record!"

Darcy leaned closer to the TV. Barton and Hank squeezed in and were watching as well.

The camera caught an out-of-focus head shot of Adkins.

So, there you have it, folks. In my exclusive interview, a representative of the American Indian Movement has admitted responsibility for the bison head mystery. The same representative categorically denied any involvement of his organization in the death of Latham Kellogg. We will continue our investigation into that mystery as well. This is Bryce Adkins reporting for Channel 23.

"Oh no! No, no, no!" Darcy was up and pacing, holding her head in her hands. "Damn that little squint! How in the hell could he do it? I don't mean ethically; the guy is a moral midget. But how did he film Mike Brown and Netters without me noticing?"

Hank handed her a glass of water and pushed her onto the settee.

"Does Adkins have a cell phone?" Hank was hunkered at her side.

"Oh shit! Shit, shit, shit! That dirty little squint . . . uh sorry Barton."

"No need to apologize to me." Barton took a sip of his coffee. "Should I be offended for you, Abigail?"

"Oh, stuff it, Barton! This is serious. Darcy's credibility and journalistic integrity are on the line and you're poking fun." Abby's ice-blue eyes flashed.

"Quite right, my dear. Sorry Darcy."

"No problem, except now you will all have to testify at my trial." Darcy leaped up and dashed to the door, grabbing her coat on the way.

Hank was faster. He reached above her and slammed the door shut. Darcy spun around, ready for battle.

Hank's voice softened to a low rumble, more startling than a shout. "I'm not the enemy here . . . yet. You are not going anywhere. You are going to sit down and call your boss and tell him what Adkins has done. Clear?"

"Hank is right, Darcy," Abby said. "Going off in a temper to find Adkins and claw his eyes out—although certainly not without appeal—would only land you in jail, and Hank would have to put you there. He'd be desolate."

Darcy fished her phone from her bag. She turned her back to the living room and dialed Zach's personal number.

Before she opened her mouth, Zach was talking. She tried to listen to what he was saying, but the words jumbled in her head like Scrabble letters, and she could not make them align.

When Zach finally took a breath, she said, "So what you're saying is you can't do anything about this?"

She wanted to sound appalled, or at the very least offended, but it was like a blow to the solar plexus. It knocked the wind out of her. Zach was her bastion of journalistic honor.

"Sure," she said. She clicked off at the tail end of his glum apology.

She flopped onto a hard-backed chair by the table and stared out at the pearl gray sky beyond.

Hank slipped into a chair across from her and took her hands. "What did he say?"

"He said Adkins had cleared it with his uncle first. Zach hadn't even been in the loop. I could hear how ticked he was. That should help, but it doesn't. Arnold Christenson's fair-haired nephew is being reassigned as a full-time reporter. He impressed Uncle Arnie with his spunk and initiative." This last statement dripped with acid.

"Oh, Darcy," Abby moved instantly to her side, "I am so sorry. Do you think the story will do any actual damage?"

Darcy's whiskey-colored eyes focused on Abby for a moment, then widened. "Oh my God! I need to call Mike Brown. He'll think I sold him out . . ."

Hank stood and held her coat out for her. "He's probably still in front of the courthouse. With any luck, we can talk to him before he sees the report."

Abby and Barton watched them slam out the door. Barton was smiling.

"What?" Abby demanded.

"I just thought you were magnificent, pugnaciously defending your young." He lifted his coffee to her.

"Oh, shut up, you old fool!" she said, but she was pleased.

Hank and Darcy arrived in time to see the last of the tents folded into the back of Mike Brown's dusty brown pickup.

Hank had barely stopped before Darcy slammed out. She looked around franticly for Mike and then spotted him at the same moment he saw her. She stopped and watched him advance on her with the shoulder-down stride that screamed brawler.

"Before you go off half-cocked, Mike, hear me out."

"Like hell I will. 'Off the record.' I trusted you because my sister did. Now look." He gestured at the group straggling off.

By now, Hank had joined them, but he hung back, watching.

"I know it looks like we tricked you, but it was a stupid intern who taped you after our interview. He's the station owner's nephew and—"

"Leave us the hell alone." He strode past her and got into his truck.

Darcy followed. She knocked on the window until he rolled it down.

"What?"

"How can I fix this?" Darcy asked, shivering in the icy wind.

"You can't. Stuart Johnson wants me to come in for questioning. Do you know what kind of trouble John and the AIM organization are in? The FBI makes it a point to eliminate domestic terrorists, and they're not too picky about how they do it. If I fail to show, it's just another nail in the case they're trying to build."

"Domestic terrorist? You didn't detonate a bomb or anything, and depending on where you got the bison—"

"It was one of mine. I slaughtered it for food for the grade school on the rez. So what? Johnson has been waiting for years to find a charge that will slap me into a federal prison. You just handed me to him wrapped up in a bow of video tape. I gotta go." Brown zipped the window up and pulled away.

"Damn that snot-nosed little shit!" Darcy kicked a chunk of ice in the road.

"Not that watching you cuss like a drunken cowboy isn't amusing, but if we're going to fix this, we need to get ahold of Stuart Johnson before Brown goes in. There's enough bad blood between them. It might not matter that what AIM intended was just a protest." Hank steered her across the slick street to his truck.

Once they were safely out of the wind, Hank started the truck and turned up the heat. "I'll try a professional courtesy ploy, but I can't guarantee it will work." He tapped punched in the number for the FBI.

"Do you have his private number?"

"No, but they can patch me through. Uh yes. This is Detective Hank Nelson of the Cheyenne Police Department, and I was calling Agent Stuart Johnson about a joint case we are coordinating. Yes, I'll hold."

"Hank, thanks for trying, but this is my mess and I need to clean it up."

"Hi Stuart. This is Hank Nelson from CPD. Sorry to bother you at home. I have a friend who would like to talk to you about the protest at the Thompson's store. No, not Mary. Darcy Moreland, the journalist from Channel 23 News. Could we meet you somewhere?

Great. Thanks. We'll be right over." He clicked off and tossed his phone into the cupholder on the dash.

"What am I supposed to say? Oops, I work with idiots?"

"I don't know, but you don't have much time to figure it out. We're here." Hank parked in front of the Cracked Cup, one of many coffee shops that had popped up downtown. Darcy wasn't quite over her amazement that she could get anywhere in 5 to 15 minutes in Cheyenne.

Darcy could see Agent Johnson sitting by the window. She and Hank slid into the seats across from him.

Darcy took a deep breath and said, "I assume you've seen the morning report."

"You mean Adkins' exclusive?"

Darcy clenched her teeth to keep from saying several exceptionally unprofessional words. She managed a curt, "Yes."

"I did." Agent Stuart Johnson enjoyed watching Darcy Moreland struggle for control.

Darcy explained her interview with Michael Brown and her later off-the-record conversation that Adkins had taped on his phone and re-edited. In the end, all it boiled down to was, "Oops, I work with idiots."

"Adkins' report gave a slanted perspective of Michael Brown's intentions," Hank offered.

"I thought so too. That's why I asked Mr. Brown to come in Monday, to talk. There's no love lost between us, as you know Ms. Moreland, but I think they manipulated his position."

"He's convinced you're just waiting to convict him of domestic terrorism and send him off to federal prison," Darcy said.

"I have no intention of doing anything like that, but Michael Brown knows more than he's saying, and I think he can help clear up some other parts of this investigation."

"I know I have no right to ask, but could you share any information you find that's not classified?" Darcy asked.

DARREN KINCADE, JOHN BLUE FEATHER'S LAWYER, was meeting with him at his mother's small brick bungalow on the Avenues.

"Here's how this falls out. If they can connect you to AIM, they will charge you with domestic terrorism. That can bring federal penalties."

"But Darren, are you sure they'll go that far? If it had been some high school prank—" Mary twisted a large turquoise and sliver ring on her finger.

"The FBI doesn't think anything AIM is involved with is a prank. John, is there any way they can tie you to this?"

"Well, yeah. The bison head belonged to my Uncle Mike. It was his idea to stir things up a little. He called it, 'lifting the stone.' You know, like when you lift a stone and all the bugs scurry out from under it?" John took a deep sip of the tea his mother had made for him.

"Yeah, I get the imagery, but what did you do exactly?"

John looked at his mother, who nodded imperceptibly, then back to Johnson. "I helped transport the bison head from my uncle's ranch on the reservation and I helped place it in front of Thompson's store."

"Is that all?"

"Yes, that was all we did. Uncle Mike had a buddy who had copies of the old newspaper and we bought the old arrow from a junk man on Lincolnway."

"We?" Mary jumped in. "As in Mike and you?"

John looked confused. He did not like the pinched look his mother was giving him. "Yeah. I even remember the guy joking about selling us our own artifacts. Uncle Mike said later he wanted to punch the guy out . . . but he didn't, Mom. Honest."

Mary ignored John and turned back to the lawyer. "I wonder why the guy hasn't come forward."

"Probably because the major thrust of the investigation and media interest was on the murder of Latham Kellogg. Once this goes to trial as a case of domestic terrorism, I bet the pawn shop owner will jump at the chance for his fifteen minutes of fame." Darren Kincade threw his pencil down in disgust.

"I don't get what the big deal is?" John paced the small living room crammed full of furniture and family treasures. "All we did was plant a bison head with a newspaper and arrow. We didn't damage anything."

"Latham Kellogg is dead."

"Yeah, but *we* didn't kill him." John rounded on his lawyer. "Aren't you supposed to be on my side?"

"Can you prove you didn't?"

"Well, no . . . but they can't prove we did." John perched on the arm of his mother's chair.

"Let me explain how these things work. They will establish that you, your Uncle Mike, and several others are active in an AIM organization, right?" He arched a questioning brow at the boy.

"Yeah, but—"

"That you all engaged in domestic terrorism designed to incite fear and confusion and that your machinations culminated in the murder of Latham Kellogg," Kincade continued.

"That's nuts! Nobody from AIM killed Kellogg."

"You aren't listening to me. All the FBI has to prove is that you are involved with AIM. There are files full of details about AIM protests and takeovers. They can use the tape of your uncle saying Kellogg was looking into state and federal law as it affects Native American land rights. It is not a large reach to characterize the protest as a possible prologue to an AIM takeover. This is implying the tribes on the Wind River reservation might have a claim on it. The Federal Prosecutor could phone this one in."

"How does all this connect Mike and John to murder?" Mary asked. Her voice cracked, and John rubbed her shoulder to soothe her.

"It doesn't. It doesn't need to. It connected them to AIM. The bison head and the arrow are perceived as a threat. A threat carried out through the murder of Latham Kellogg."

"But that's ridiculous!" Mary stood. "All of this is circumstantial evidence."

"There are men doing time in Federal prisons on a lot less."

CHAPTER 15

Anthony Triolo and Vincent Stefano Sassano did not belong in Wyoming. Both were born and bred in New Jersey and had only recently moved to Las Vegas, which was tolerable . . . but Wyoming?

Triolo aimed his 22-caliber pistol at a knothole across the room and squeezed off a shot.

Sassano jumped, then yelled, "Put that damn gun away, you little guinea shit!"

"Ah Vince, I'm just practicing." He caressed the blue barrel.

"Practice outside."

"Are you loopy? It's sub-zero outside. My *balls* will freeze up and fall off."

"What's the diff? You ain't using them, anyway."

Triolo turned around to face his partner across the scarred table. "Yo, Vince. How long are we going to be here?"

"Don't know. What do you do that's so important?"

"Seriously Vince, I think Shelly likes me."

"She's a Keno Girl, you jerk. She's paid to like everybody who bets."

"I know that, but she likes me special." Triolo emptied the bullets onto the table and disassembled the gun.

"Don't you ever do anything besides shoot that damn gun and clean it?" Vince asked in disgust.

He was tired of this job too, but he and Tony were young soldiers trying to be made. Vince's dad had been connected and now it was his turn.

He reached up to touch the heavy silver cross his mom had given to him at his Confirmation at St. Dominic's. His mom wasn't ecstatic about his career path. She yelled at him, claiming that "Giovanna Sassano did not raise her only son to be a two-bit thug." They never spoke of it again. The only time Vince felt guilty about what he did was when he thought about his mom.

"Ya think they'll let us go back to Vegas soon? This Davey Crockett shit is wearing on my nerves," Triolo asked and looked around at the crude log cabin they were using to lay low.

"Yeah, I think they'll let us come back . . . if we don't screw up." Vince was skimming the article about the hit they'd done on Frye. "We shoulda done a message kill on Frye. Stupid weasel tried to shake us down."

"Boss wanted it quick, clean, and anonymous. Besides, who would get the message in wilderness Wyoming? Bunch of cowboys and Native Americans," Triolo said and spit.

Vince's phone vibrated, and the two stared at it like it was a snake. Finally, Vince's hand shot out and grabbed it.

"Yeah Boss," he said into the phone, then listened to the instructions. Vince scribbled notes to himself in the margins of the newspaper. After a while, he said, "Got it," and clicked off.

"What?" Triolo asked.

"Got another job," was all Vince said as he jerked on his heavy wool coat. He ripped off the page of the paper with the notes and walked out the door. Triolo followed.

THE WEEKEND SLID BY QUICKLY FOR ADKINS. His uncle invited him to the house for Sunday dinner and sang his praises throughout the pot roast, right up to the bread pudding.

By Monday morning, he was looking forward to going to the station and strutted into the newsroom with a huge grin on his face.

"Hi Wendy." He leaned against the office manager's counter. "Did you see my report on Saturday and Sunday?"

The usually perky blond looked at Adkins with contempt. "If you have any desire to continue to live with all your parts still attached, you'd better stay as far away from Zach and Darcy as possible. Canada sounds good. Now go." Wendy turned away.

Stung, but refusing to take it personally, Adkins believed that the animosity was just petty jealousy. Not everybody can be a rainmaker, he thought.

He was wondering if it would be too soon to apply to the larger Denver market. They would probably appreciate his style down there. He'd wait awhile and put together more videos. The one he shot with the phone was blurry, but now thanks to his promotion, he would get a regular cameraman assigned to him. He thought about requesting Netters, then laughed at the thought of how ticked off that would make him.

Lost in thought, he rounded the corner by the editing bays and collided with Zach.

Glaring, Zach ordered, "My office. Now," and left Adkins standing alone in the hallway.

When he had gathered his wits, he looked around to see if anyone else heard the order. He shouted, "On it, Boss," to save face and strode confidently to the third door on the right. Once at the door, he wiped his suddenly damp hands on his pants.

Adkins knocked on the doorframe. Zach did not look up from the papers spread out on his credenza behind his desk as Adkins entered. "Sit."

Adkins slipped cautiously into a chair in front of Zach's large desk. While he waited, he glanced at the pictures and degrees hung on the wall.

One showed Zach standing with the governor and another with the Wyoming legislative contingent. A third picture caught him by surprise. Zach was standing with one of the Thunderbird pilots in front of the jets.

"Damn, Zach. Did you get to go up in one of those Thunderbird planes?"

Zach turned around and stared at Adkins until he squirmed. "Yes, I did, and the fact that you have been here for ten months and have never noticed that picture before speaks to your finely honed observation skills."

Adkins was not so oblivious that he missed the sarcasm. "Look, I can tell you are upset—" he began.

"Upset? You think I am upset because you pirated a video from this station and presented it as your own? You think I am upset because you aired a segment that was off-the-record, compromising the journalistic integrity of not only Darcy Moreland, but this entire station?"

"I know I colored a little outside the lines—"

"Adkins, this isn't kindergarten. You're playing fast and loose with people's lives."

"He was just an old Native American," Adkins said.

Zach paused, and the knuckles of his fists turned white. Adkins should have been warned by the crimson flush that rose from the collar of Zach's pristine blue shirt.

Finally, Zach said softly, "If you ever do anything like this again, you're fired. Am I making myself clear, Adkins?"

"I don't think Uncle Arnie—"

"You *don't* think. That is the problem. I may have to keep you this time, but I don't have to like it." Zach scribbled something on a memo sheet and tossed it to Adkins.

It was a story assignment on the new waste treatment plant outside of town.

Adkins wanted to argue about the assignment, but Zach's eyes dared him to. Thinking discretion the better part of valor, he rose.

"On it, Boss," he said, wanting to sound confident.

DARCY SPENT THAT MORNING DOING DAMAGE CONTROL. Her first call was to Mary. She didn't get through right way but left a message. She wouldn't blame Mary if she didn't return the call. In one major screw up, she had sold both Mary's son and brother out.

She threw her pencil down on her desk, but it didn't help. When the phone rang, she was so frustrated and angry she didn't notice who was calling.

"Darcy Moreland," she said. She listened while Mary asked her to meet with her and Stuart Johnson at a downtown pizza place at noon. Darcy agreed instantly.

She didn't care what Mary asked her to do to fix this. She'd do it. Which brought her mind back to Adkins.

"You look pleased. What are you thinking about?" Netters flung his long, ungainly body into a wooden chair next to her and perched there like a bird on a wire.

"I was thinking of what I'd like to do to him." She didn't have to specify who him was.

"I don't know, maybe hanging him by his tongue?"

"I like it. Call me when you've got a venue."

"Get in line. He asked me to do the video on a story Zach assigned him this morning about the new waste management plant." Netters let out a chuckle, then forced his face to look sincere. "I told him I already had an assignment, but I'd be really interested to see his interview."

Darcy laughed aloud. "Zach must be *really* ticked if he gave him that. Who did he go out with?"

"That new kid, Chris Budgely. You know, the one with all the pimples."

"Now there's a pair to draw to. I'm going to meet Mary Blue Feather and Stuart Johnson for lunch and see if I can smooth things over."

"Yeah, well, good luck with that." Netters rose. "I'm going to hang out in the editing bay. If you need me, just call."

"Will do."

Noon arrived slower than normal. Darcy dithered about what she would say and how she would say it. There was no way she could undo Mike's public confession. Mary had trusted her, and because of that trust, Mike had agreed to the interview.

She dropped her head into her folded arms. What a mess.

When it was time to leave, she thought about calling to cancel, but recognized that would be cowardly and she was not a coward.

When she got to Pantano's, the air was redolent with warm yeasty smells mixed with garlic and oregano. The scent soothed her frazzled nerves. She chose a table tucked into a far corner. One perk of being the first to arrive.

Mary and Stuart were on time. They entered, saw Darcy, and came over. No warm hugs nor effusive greetings. Mary sat across from her and began yanking off her gloves. Stuart slipped his overcoat off and laid it on the spare chair.

Darcy cleared her throat with a soft cough then dove right in.

"Mary, I know you're angry and I am, too."

"I don't think our anger is comparable, do you, Darcy? They may send my son and brother to jail. How about that little snitch from your office? Anything happen to him?"

Darcy felt embarrassed. She had never wanted to lie so badly in all her life, but she was determined to earn Mary's trust again.

"His uncle, who owns the station, promoted him to full reporter status," Darcy admitted.

"Figures," Mary said tersely.

"Is that all?" Stuart asked.

Darcy answered, "Well, Zach sent him out to do a story on the new waste management plant with a grass-green videographer. Not exactly a plum gig."

"Well, that's something anyway," Stuart conceded.

"Mary, listen. Zach and I are both livid, but we don't own the station. I know it's a cold comfort, but guys like Adkins will trip on their own ego soon enough," Darcy said.

Before Mary could respond, the waiter came to take their order. Darcy wasn't hungry but she ordered a small tomato and basil pizza. She was hoping sharing a meal with Mary and Stuart would somehow show her goodwill.

When the waiter left, Mary said, "I trusted you and you were ... not careful."

Hard to argue with the truth. "Mary, I had no idea that Adkins was smart enough to do something like this. What I am guilty of is underestimating his capacity for insensitivity and his utter lack of ethics. It won't happen again, but I understand that hardly helps now."

Mary's tear-swollen eyes flicked to Stuart, who squeezed her hand, then turned back to Darcy. "I've talked to my bosses, and they're okay with Mike and John coping a plea of guilty for vandalism and malicious mischief. They'll probably get a fine. Mike may do a little jail time because of his checkered record, but I think John's lawyer can deal it down to probation."

"I am so relieved; I can actually breathe."

"Not so fast," Mary interrupted. "We would like you to put some pressure on the D.A. to agree to the lesser charges. He seems unwilling to consider it even though the Bureau is okay with it."

"I'd be happy to try. One question though—why is the FBI being so accommodating?"

Now it was Stuart's turn to look embarrassed. The bleak look he shot Mary was telling. "To tell the truth, we've never been fans of AIM, but we'd rather not waste time and money on penny-ante protests. We'll wait for them to commit something more than vandalism. If we can connect AIM to Kellogg's death, for instance . . ." He dribbled off when he saw Mary's tight jaw and narrowed eyes.

"So, you want me to do a sidebar that the FBI will call it vandalism, but Patrick Tucker is stonewalling, is that right?"

"Pretty much." Stuart looked relieved.

"Okay. I'll try to get an on-camera statement from D.A. Tucker this afternoon. If luck is with us, you'll see it on the five o'clock." Darcy got up to leave. She looked down at Mary. "Thanks for giving me the chance to make this right."

Mary merely nodded, but Darcy was encouraged.

ADKINS WAS FREEZING. The Chevy van Zach assigned him was the oldest on the lot. He knew Zach was pissed off but figured he would get over it. This tuna can on wheels with no heat in the middle of winter sucked.

"Man, what did you do to draw this bucket of bolts?" Chris Budgely asked as he tugged his threadbare surplus Navy pea coat tighter around his doughboy body.

"I showed some initiative and ruffled some feathers. It's mostly professional jealousy."

"Yeah, I figured. Where are we going?"

"To the new solid waste dump treatment plant to do a feature on it." Adkins could barely push the syllables through his clenched teeth.

Budgely wisely left him alone.

About ten miles out, a black SUV with heavily tinted windows passed them slowly and then suddenly swerved right in front of them, screeching to a stop.

"What the fuck!" Adkins shouted as he tried to brake and careened the van into the burrow.

"Shit," Budgely swore as the van rested precariously nose down in the ditch.

The driver's door wrenched open with a screech, revealing two black-clad men, their faces covered with ski masks. The shorter of the two held a gun rock steady, aimed at Adkins' head.

"Oh my God! Oh my God! Oh my God!" Budgely started screaming.

"Shut your friend up or I will," the man with the gun growled.

Adkins couldn't shut Budgely up. He was frozen in shock and so terrified he thought he might have wet himself but was too scared to look down to see. Budgely had no trouble choking back his screams, though his face turned from red to purple with the effort and he couldn't stop a soft sob.

"We're looking for Adkins."

"Him! That's him. I don't hardly know him." Budgely kept pointing at Adkins as if the more he gestured, the more he'd be believed.

Adkins finally found his voice. "Shut up, you worthless piece of shit."

The taller man jerked Adkins from the van and yanked his arms behind his back, securing them with a nylon-cable zip tie. Adkins screamed in pain as the sharp tie cut into his wrists.

"For God's sake, call the police," Adkins shouted at Budgely, who pulled out his cell.

"Throw it out the window or lose the hand," the gunman said.

"Ah man!" Budgely said. "I just got this." He threw it out the window, watching as it landed on a soot-covered snowdrift and skittered off out of sight.

"Now get the hell out of here." The gunman slammed the driver's door shut. Budgely scooted to the driver's side and gunned the engine, trying to rock back and forth to get on the road.

The gunman prodded Adkins towards the back of the SUV, opened the door, and pushed him into the flat cargo area. He landed hard on his shoulder and shrieked. The taller man secured his ankles with another cable tie, tossed Adkins' legs in like so much dirty laundry, and slammed the door shut.

Adkins wrenched himself up into a sitting position, hoping he could keep track of where they were taking him. His hopes were shattered when the gunman leaned into the back and forced his eyes closed with duct tape.

"Please. Please don't hurt me," he pleaded. "I'll do whatever you want."

The men laughed. "Yeah, we know you will," said the man who was now tapping his mouth shut.

The SUV lurched back onto the road. Adkins toppled into a heap in the back. For several miles, he heard the whir of the tires on highway pavement, but then they turned off onto what he could only suspect was a rutted gravel road judging by the way he began bouncing around on the hard floor.

Adkins knew Wyoming was full of back roads that crisscrossed thousands of miles, leading to nowhere. He whimpered.

"Can't you shut him up?" the driver shouted.

"Sure," the gunman opened the glove compartment and took out a syringe. He held it steady as he drew in clear liquid from a small bottle.

"A little Bobzo for Bozo," he said and tossed the small bottle back.

Kneeling on the seat, he pulled Adkins close and tore his shirt down, exposing his shoulder. He waited for the road to smooth a little, then injected the tranquilizer.

By the time he threw the used needle out the window and replaced the syringe, Adkins was slumped over and quiet.

"Where the hell did you get Benzodiazepine?"

"I used to date a girl who worked in a pharmacy, and she'd give me all the tranqs that were past their expiration date. I told her it was for my Nona, who couldn't afford the drugs."

"Tony, you're a real piece of work."

"Ain't I just?" Tony laughed.

CHAPTER 16

Pete Loman, Wyoming State Senator, scanned the statement he intended to make in front of the Indian Affairs Committee he chaired.

He checked for any hint of the benign neglect that had characterized his dealings with the Shoshoni and Arapaho tribes for the past thirty years. He needed to tread carefully here. In the past, the approach he often took was treating Native Americans as if they were large children in need of guidance.

That had eventually put his ass in the grinder. The Governor and the ranking US Senator had failed to stonewall the Arapaho Tribe from entering a gaming compact with the State. The tribe hired a lawyer to push a case in the US District Court through, claiming that the State failed to negotiate in good faith with the tribe.

Then the bottom fell out of Loman's bucket. Damn career politicians, he thought. He'd hitched his wagon to their grossly oversimplified WASP mentality. Everyone had fled the scene, leaving him to pick up the pieces.

Here he was five years later, placating the Native American Affairs Committee members who had long memories and being forced to smile every time those sons of bitches reminded him that the Northern Arapaho Tribe was the first ever to get the right to self-regulate class III gaming—a right which they planned to keep.

They ran the Casino, they got the revenues, and the state got nothing. But Pete Loman wasn't out yet. Not by a long shot.

He couldn't count the number of pow-wows he'd attended, the never-ending tribal council meetings. Hell, he'd even showed up for the ribbon cutting ceremony for the casino on the rez. By the time he was through groveling, the tribe had given a large contribution to his reelection fund, and he was secure again for another four years.

Better than that, he thought as he swung his feet up onto the mirror-polished desk at his law firm, Loman, Loman, and Pollock, was the fact that he was now in the perfect position to get something back after all that humiliation.

The Wyoming Legislature was designed to be a part-time job. They met for 40 days on average, then went home to their day jobs and constituents, who let them know for the remaining 325 days exactly how they thought they were doing.

Loman hungered for a full-time government job with all the perks and the potential for a lifetime away from his home state. To do that, he needed a deep war chest. He had his eye on Washington D.C., and it was finally looking like a real possibility.

Nothing better screw this up, he thought. He was out of time and patience, and he had new friends to impress.

DARCY SAT IN D.A. PATRICK TUCKER'S OUTER OFFICE waiting for him to "work her in" for a short Q-and-A. Netters sat across from her in a duplicate wooden armchair with his feet cradling his camera.

Darcy looked at her watch. She was running perilously close to not getting this done before airtime. She eyed the receptionist.

"Do you think he'll be much longer?" she asked the twenty-something with improbable sable-colored hair.

"I don't really know." The receptionist scratched her head with the eraser end of the pencil she'd been chewing. "I can ask him."

"That would be great," Darcy said. "We'd really like to get his comment on the FBI's position before we go on air. It looks better for him that way. Otherwise, it looks like he's trying to avoid us."

"I'm sure he wouldn't want that." The girl scrambled from her chair. "Just let me remind him you are on a deadline . . . uhm that is what you call it . . . a deadline?"

"Among other things," Netters spouted off. Darcy shot him a quelling look, but he went back to reading an ancient copy of *Time*.

The girl opened the door a crack and leaned in. From her perspective, Darcy could see into Tucker's office. He was on the phone, and he looked harassed and angry.

"What?" he exploded when he noticed the girl.

"I'm sorry sir, but the people from the TV station are on a deadline and would like to get your comment." She lowered her voice to a stage whisper, "She said you don't want to look like you're avoiding them."

"I'll be out in a minute," Tucker snapped at her.

"Yes, sir," she said as she closed the door softly. She turned to Darcy and Netters, smiled, then sat behind her desk once more.

Moments later, Patrick Tucker emerged from his office, straightening his tie.

"Hello. Ms. Moreland, isn't it? How can I help you?"

"We'd like to get your comment on the latest development in the *United States v. Brown and Blue Feather* case, sir." Darcy turned her body slightly so Tucker would move with her and not be aware Netters was getting in place to shoot video.

"What development would that be, Ms. Moreland?"

"We've learned from the Federal Bureau of Investigation that they will agree to a reduction of charges from terrorism to vandalism. What is your position?" She shoved the microphone, which had magically appeared in her hand, under his chin.

Tucker took a moment to look down and then back up at Darcy as if to say, "Nice trick."

"We are still studying the situation as it applies to this case, Ms. Moreland. Since it is a local jurisdiction issue, you can understand why we don't always agree with the FBI's assessment."

"When do you think you might decide? Will they release the defendants on bail?"

"This case is not as simple as it may seem on the surface," Tucker said, then looked at his watch. "Terribly sorry, but I am due in court."

"Shall I just say you had no comment?" Darcy said to Tucker's back.

He swiveled toward her, and the icy glint in his eye flashed momentarily before it vanished. He stretched his face into a professional, practiced smirk and took a step toward Darcy. Darcy held her ground, but Tucker's sudden malevolence unnerved her.

"Why would you want to imply this office has anything but the safety of our citizens as its goal?"

"Because it seems a little like overkill to try these men as terrorists for leaving a bison head in front of a storefront." She held out the mic again.

"We believe AIM to be an American terrorist organization," Tucker said, as if Darcy was too stupid to know that.

"One man's terrorist is another man's revolutionary, as they say. Whatever the goals of the American Indian Movement, the fact remains the bison head belonged to Mike Brown and although John Blue Feather helped place it, they did no permanent damage to any person or property."

"Who are you, Ms. Moreland? You sound like their defense attorney."

"I'm just a journalist trying to get to the facts of the case," Darcy replied. She could see by the grim set of his mouth the interview was over.

Tucker nodded, then turned and left without another word.

"Hmm," Darcy said as she handed the mic to Netters to put away, "I think I pissed him off."

"I noticed. Good job, Calamity."

Darcy linked her arm through Netters', and they left the building.

A LITTLE BEFORE FOUR O'CLOCK, ABBY AND BARTON bustled into her apartment after an afternoon spent at the State Library. They had been trying to find information on Wyoming law and the Archaeological Resource Protection Act.

"I don't quite see how the law pertains here. Maybe I'm just dense," Abby said as she unwound her long, multicolored scarf and pulled off her gloves, stuffing them into her pockets.

Barton slipped up behind her on the pretense of helping her take off her coat. He tugged it off, but not before he kissed her neck in several places.

Abby giggled and stepped away, swatting at him ineffectually. "Stop that now. We must get these files organized for Darcy to look at tonight."

She picked up the folder of xeroxed copies they had made from several sources and spread them out across the top of her dining room table.

"You sort them, and I'll get the teapot going," she said as she scurried into her tiny kitchen.

Barton hung up his coat and scarf on the hall tree next to Abby's and for a fleeting moment thought of how nice the coats looked hanging companionably like that. He chuckled at his own flight of fancy, then seated himself at the table and began to read and highlight passages.

"You know, there could be a connection between the Native American bones and Frye's murder." He raised his voice a little so Abby could hear him in the kitchen.

"What made you think of that?" Abby asked, bringing in a plate of cookies and napkins.

"See here," Barton pointed, and she leaned over his shoulder.

If the remains are inadvertently extracted, then a consultation is necessary. If the remains covered by the law are discovered, the project will be stopped for 30 days.

"But we don't know when the bones were discovered, do we?" Abby sat next to him and looked at the highlighted section.

"I think we do. See, I copied an old coroner's report on some remains unearthed when the Thompson's store was expanding its basement storage area. Look who signed the report."

Abby took out her reading glasses and looked closely at the

signature. "Okay. James Frye checked out the bones. So, he made a mistake."

"Look at the determination," Barton prompted.

"Mixture of large and small animal bones, consistent with an abandoned campsite," Abby read. "Well, that doesn't seem right. If you're a county coroner, shouldn't you be able to distinguish between human and animal bones?" She crinkled her brow.

"You'd think. I'd lay a dollar to a donut Frye took a bribe either from old man Thompson or Terry Anderson—he was the contractor on this job—to falsify the report about the bones so they wouldn't have to stop the project for 30 days."

"That is suspicious, but circumstantial. You couldn't prove he took money unless you have access to his bank files."

"True. But it got me to thinking . . ."

The shrill whistle of the teapot interrupted their conversation. She jumped up. "Hold that thought. I'll be right back."

He sifted through the pages until he found what he was looking for. Abby returned with a tray carrying a gold teapot and two small teacups and saucers with gold rims.

"We'll let the tea steep for a little while before I pour. Now, what were you saying?"

"I was just saying it got me thinking. Frye's recent retirement was a little precipitous," Barton said.

"Come to think of it, it seemed abrupt, but I think I remember reading he retired for health reasons."

"Maybe it's just as simple as he knew where the bodies were buried. Ironic, yes? But what if he came into a large sum of money so he could suddenly afford to retire?"

"Why would you think that?" Abby poured the light brown liquid into the white cups and the air became redolent with the scent of Orange Pekoe.

"Because of this." Barton handed her another report.

Abby read silently for a moment, then looked at Barton over her readers and the paper. Her eyes widened and her mouth formed a slight "o."

"Just so." Barton nodded and sipped his tea.

"But why would he go back and amend the report to reflect that the remains were that of a Native American woman and child? Why not just lose the bones?" Abby offered Barton a cookie and took one for herself.

"Here," Barton said, and passed her another page.

"Is this what you were doing while I was copying dry as dust statutes?" Abby's voice held an edge to it.

"I just had a hunch. It could've been nothing. It still might *be* nothing, but it is an interesting bit of nothing." He chomped down on the oatmeal raisin cookie. They were his favorites.

Abby went back to reading. "This says Pete Loman was charging Anderson construction with failing to inform the tribe and authorities about human remains found at the site. Why would he care?"

"Partly because he is chairman of the Native American Affairs Committee, though I haven't noticed him kicking up much dust in that capacity."

"Then why . . .?"

"Look at the part about it coming to his attention through Laramie County Coroner, James Frye, that the bones were Native American, but he had received undue pressure from the contractor to identify the bones too quickly. He admits to making a mistake." Baton sipped his tea and his soft green eyes twinkled.

"Sounds like a case of closing the barn door after the cows escaped. The construction was completed, and old man Thompson sold the store."

"Look down a little further where Loman petitions the court to acknowledge the desecration of a Native American burial site. He suggests reparations be made to the Northern Arapaho Tribe in the form of declaring Thompson's store Indian land."

"That makes no sense. Why would they even want it? It's clear across the state from their reservation land. And who would pay Frye to change his determination? What for? And why would someone kill him because of it?"

"It is a mystery wrapped in an enigma, but I bet if we keep digging and Darcy keeps digging, we'll figure it out."

"I can't wait for Darcy to get home," she said. "Maybe I should invite Hank too, unofficially. If there is a connection, I bet he'd want to know."

"Commendable impulse, Abigail. I think it's our civic duty to keep Detective Nelson informed of our investigation." Barton took another cookie.

ADKINS FELT THE SWEAT TRICKLE DOWN HIS FOREHEAD, off his nose, and plop onto the SUV's floor. He tried to make his terrified brain focus on the tickling sensation so he wouldn't be able to think of anything else. He fervently wished he were back in that freezing piece of tin the station had given him.

The SUV bounced in and out of ruts, jarring his hipbones, but he couldn't lie on his back because of his arms, and he couldn't scoot up enough to sit.

With his mouth taped shut, all he could do was moan. He went in and out of consciousness, fighting to remain awake.

By the time they jerked him out of the back of the SUV and cut the cable tie at his feet, there was no feeling in them. He was aware they were dragging him somewhere.

"Damn dead weight," Sassano grunted as he and Triolo pulled Adkins across the threshold of the cabin.

"I don't know why the boss didn't just let us pop him. Even knocked out, he's a whiney jerk," Triolo said.

"You're too quick to pop someone, Tony. There are other considerations here," Sassano said and flopped Adkins onto the bed in the back room. He took out his knife and sliced through the cable tie on Adkins' arms.

Adkins curled up in a fetal position on the bed.

"Think we should take the tape off?" Tony asked.

"Probably. It will mean we'll have to wear those ski masks whenever we come into this room, though." Vince pulled out a chain, attached it to Adkins' ankle, and locked the other end to the bed.

"Another good reason to pop him," Tony grumbled. He bent over the bed and took perverse pleasure in ripping the duct tape off Adkins' eyes and mouth.

Adkins yowled in pain but didn't open his now lash-less eyes. He curled into an even tighter ball.

"Let's leave him alone. I gotta call the boss and let him know we got him. You put the lock on his door, okay?"

Vince left the room and Tony followed. They closed the door and Tony opened the bag from the hardware store. He easily attached a hasp and padlock to the outer door.

When he finished, he sat and waited for Vince to finish the call. Tony threw some more wood in the fireplace and poked at it to take the chill off the room.

He looked up when Vince came and sat down.

"What'd the boss say?"

"Just to keep him here until he calls us. Then we can let him go." Vince leaned back on the old couch and plopped his feet on the ancient coffee table.

"Why can't we just kill him and ditch the body in the woods?" Tony asked.

"Because the bodies are piling up, and this *jerk* has an uncle who owns the TV station. The boss doesn't want to antagonize the local press if he can help it."

"Are we going to at least ask for a ransom?"

"No. Boss just wants to stop the reporter here from stirring up the waters. When he gives us the go ahead, we're supposed to dump him."

BUDGELY PULLED INTO THE STATION'S PARKING LOT. He turned off the engine and sat there, trying to make his hands stop shaking.

He kept replaying the attack over in his mind. It was like trying to tell someone about a dream. He couldn't keep the details straight. He was sick to his stomach.

Budgely ran into the station after getting out of the van. He slammed the front door hard behind him. Wendy looked up and was going to yell at him when she noticed how pale he looked. She zipped around the corner of the counter.

"What the hell happened?" she pushed right into Budgely's face.

"They t . . . took him," he stammered out.

"Who took him? Who is him?"

"Adkins. They took Adkins. Call the police. They had guns. I couldn't do anything to help him." Budgely fell heavily into the first available chair and dropped his head into his hands.

Zach came running out of his office. "What is going on out here?"

"He says someone kidnapped Adkins. He said they had guns," Wendy answered.

"Call the police. Ask for Detective Nelson," Zach snapped orders, then crouched in front of Budgely. "What happened? Did they say anything?"

Budgely just shook his head. His face was the color of wallpaper paste, and Zach knew he was close to passing out. He took hold of Budgely's head and forced it down between his knees.

"Take it easy. Just breathe deeply and try to remember as many details as you can," Zach said. "Did you get a good look at them?"

"No. I mean yes, but they had ski masks on and I . . ." he looked up at Zach and his eyes filled with tears.

"Put your head down."

Damn! Zach thought. Who the hell would want Adkins and what was he going to tell Uncle Arnie?

CHAPTER 17

Darcy and Netters blew into the station in a flurry of wind and snow pellets. They were cold but so energized about their story on the D.A.'s odd reluctance to change the Brown/Blue Feather plea that they did not notice the small crowd in the entryway.

Darcy noticed Zach first, hunkered in front of a young man who had his head in his hands. Zach was speaking softly to him. Darcy looked around, then sidled up to Wendy.

"What gives?" she asked in a whisper.

"Someone kidnapped Adkins," Wendy replied.

"You're kidding! Who's the kid?"

"That's Chris Budgely. He's new and was assigned to Adkins as a videographer. Two thugs in ski masks snatched Adkins but let Budgely go."

"Do they want money?" Darcy kept staring at Zach who was still trying to coax information from Budgely.

"Don't know. If they do, we haven't heard yet."

The station's phone trilled, disrupting the highly charged atmosphere. Several people jumped and everyone looked at Wendy, who ran back behind the counter to answer it.

"KCWY Channel 23 News, how may I help you?"

Wendy, praying it wasn't the kidnappers, went almost as white as Budgely.

"Yes, sir. He is here right now. Oh? Yes sir. I will connect you. Please hold." Wendy's light brown eyes rolled just slightly, a hangover from her adolescence.

"Zach, it's Mr. Christenson. He wants to talk to you privately. I'll connect him to your office phone."

"Thanks, Wendy. Can you get Chris here some coffee?"

"Sure can," Wendy said.

All eyes followed Zach down the narrow hall toward the production area of the studio. He disappeared into his office and closed the door.

Moments later, muffled conversation drifted up the hall. No one could hear what Zach was saying, but there was no mistaking he was angry. Everyone in the lobby held their breath and strained to listen.

Zach came down the hall. His face looked stressed and pale to Darcy.

"What's up, Boss? Did they ask for a ransom?" she asked.

"Something like that. Chris, stay put. The police are coming and will want to talk to you. Everybody else, there will be an emergency production meeting for all staff in fifteen minutes. Attendance required, no exceptions. Wendy, tell on-air-talent we'll run the promo loop for that cooking thing." Zach turned and left before anyone could ask questions.

"Well, that was strange," Darcy said as she looked at Zach's closed office door. "I don't think I ever remember having an emergency production meeting that was mandatory."

"This sounds serious. I think I'll go get a Red Bull," Netters said and drifted off.

Within moments, Wendy had made an announcement reaching every corner of the building except the studio, where a live broadcast was in progress. She called the booth director's number and gave him the news about the meeting and Zach's order for the fill loop.

Fifteen minutes later, everyone at the station was crowded into the small conference room. Darcy and Netters sat on the floor by the door. When Zach strode in, he almost smacked them with the door. Ordinarily, he would have made a joke about it, but not today.

"Not good," Netters observed.

Darcy watched Zach move to the head of the scarred oak table. She worried about her friend as he pinched the bridge of his nose. She knew he only did that when he was furious or when he had a raging headache. She was hoping for the headache.

"Thank you all for being prompt," Zach began. "I don't know how many of you have heard the news that Adkins has been kidnapped." He waited for people to gasp and comment, then plunged ahead.

"There have been no ransom demands, per se. Mr. Christenson called earlier and informed me that the kidnappers have contacted him. They have demanded that all investigative reporting concerning the Thompson Furniture store, the Brown and Blue Feather case, and any discussions of AIM protests cease and desist. They assured Mr. Christenson that Adkins will remain alive so long as we met these demands."

"So that leaves us with reporting the lineup for the Frontier Day's Night Show and the high schools' game scores," Darcy said.

"I think you've grasped the concept, Darcy. We can also report on the weather and the Dow Jones."

Darcy watched a muscle twitch on the right side of Zach's jaw.

"But Zach, they can't dictate what we report."

"Mr. Christenson owns this station and Adkins is his sister's son. I think he can and will dictate what we can report."

"But Zach—" Darcy argued, but Zach stopped her with a look.

"If there is anyone besides Ms. Moreland who has questions, I'll try to answer them."

Netters tapped out the last few drops of Red Bull into his mouth and then pinned Zach with a glare. "So how long do we have to barter our journalistic integrity for the life of that little squint?"

"Mr. Christenson will let us know when our deal with the devil is done. In the meantime, we will do whatever we can to assure the safe return of one of our staff members. Questions?"

"What do we tell people when they ask why we're not report-ing the news anymore?" Cary Morrison, the evening news anchor, asked as she flicked an imaginary crumb from the lapel of her navy-blue blazer.

"Any and all of you are free to investigate opportunities with other news organizations. I wish you wouldn't because I think we have a great team here, but I will understand if you feel you must." Zach waited for any other questions. When there were none, he headed for the door. "Moreland and Netters, my office. Now," he ground out on his way past.

Darcy and Netters exchanged worried glances, but then scram-bled to follow Zach down the hall. As soon as they came through the door and closed it behind them, Zach looked at them and flopped into his chair.

"I know this sucks and I know you're crazy mad . . . and hon-estly so am I. But we can't do anything that will jeopardize his life regardless of how we feel about him."

"I could," Netters said.

"Shut up, Netters," Darcy poked him. "You can't even kill a moth that flies into the newsroom. Who do you think you're kidding?"

"But I wouldn't have to kill him. Someone else would. I think it's perfect."

"As appealing as the fantasy of Adkins on the edge of a cliff is, I don't think any of us could really bring ourselves to push him off." Zach leaned back in his chair, looking weary.

Netters opened his mouth to argue, but Darcy poked him again.

"Listen," Darcy began. "We must be rattling some cages with our investigation if they took a high-risk move like kidnapping. Isn't there any way to continue digging?"

"I don't see how, Darcy," Zach said.

"Zach, we just talked to the District Attorney. He wants to ram the trial of Brown and Blue Feather through as fast as he can. When I asked him if the FBI agreeing to a lesser charge didn't influence him, he fobbed me off with some political claptrap about local jurisdiction. I know he's dirty somehow. I just need a little more time to connect the dots."

Zach sat up quickly. "No, Darcy, and that's an order. If they're willing to hold Adkins to control what we report, they'll have no problem killing you or anyone else who doesn't follow their demands. Adkins is only valuable to them because he's Christenson's Achilles' heel."

Hank Nelson slipped in without knocking just in time to hear Darcy's impassioned plea and Zach's order. But as much as he enjoyed watching Darcy with the bit between her teeth, Zach was dead on.

"Zach is right, Darcy," Hank said. "Holding the nephew of the owner only works if people at the station obey him. You go against Christenson, Adkins dies, and someone is free to focus on you and Bill, since you guys are the ones stirring the pot."

"Why are you here?" Darcy asked.

"I'm here with the guys to question Budgely," Hank said. "I get a little itchy when you're even close to trouble. Calamity isn't just a nickname with you, it's an occupational hazard."

Netters snorted, then tried to choke back his laughter when Darcy swung on him.

"Yuk it up you two. We are knee deep in some kind of conspiracy that involves murder, vandalism, AIM, the District Attorney, and only heaven knows what else. We can't even investigate because they've kidnapped Adkins."

Hank's face sobered. "Darcy, be patient. We'll figure out how to get Adkins back."

"I'm still a little foggy on why," Netters said.

"Because kidnapping spooks the citizens when people are yanked off the streets and makes them doubt their police force."

"Okay, I'll buy that," Netters relented.

"Where's the guarantee someone else doesn't get yanked off the streets or killed? Maybe it will be Netters or me next."

"True enough, which brings me to my other reason for being here. Zach, can I have temporary use of Darcy and Bill to aid in this investigation? We could use their expertise."

Zach's face lit up. "Of course, Detective. I would be happy to lend them to you."

"Cute Nelson, but it won't work. You don't want our 'expertise'. You want us in protective custody?"

"Not precisely, but I do want you both where we can see and protect you. You are the most visible common denominator in this story."

"Are we bait, Hank?" Darcy asked him.

Hank paused a fraction of a second too long.

"We are. You're using us for bait." Darcy stood now with her hands on her hips.

"Awesome," Netters said from his corner.

"Not awesome, you idiot. Protective custody isn't as fun as it sounds. It means you have someone always dogging your steps." She looked at Hank. "And being bait can get you killed."

"Awesome," Netters repeated. "Can I have that cute redhead from homicide? Tessler, I think her name is."

"Get a grip, Netters. This isn't e-harmony.com, is it Detective?"

"No," Hank shot a conspiratorial look at both Netters and Zach, "but it could be. I've asked to be your cop. Do you mind?"

"My cop? Like my date?"

"If you like."

"I don't like. I'm an investigative reporter and I intend to continue to investigate." She paused and glared daggers at both Zach and Hank. "I'm pretty sure my journalism credentials are sufficient to contribute to the newspaper." She strode to the door, but Hank stepped in front of her.

"Okay, I tried doing this the nice way. Now we'll do it my way." He clicked his phone on. "This is Detective Nelson. I want Officer Jody Tessler to be placed on protective custody duty. Have her meet us at the Algonquin Apartment building on 18th. Apartment 201. No uniform." He hung up.

"Awesome," Netters said and scrambled to stand.

"We'll meet you there, Bill. Bring whatever notes or film you have and whatever portable unit you'll need to view it."

Netters moved through the door, and Darcy followed him. Hank grabbed her upper arm and turned her toward him. "Get your laptop and notes. We'll set up at your place until we can find a better situation."

"Who do you think you're giving orders to?" Darcy stood her ground.

"Darcy, cooperate with me and you can continue to investigate till your little black heart is satisfied. Cross me and I'll put you in jail."

She eyed him closely. He would arrest her. He would make up some charge that would take her forever to unwind. The rigid set of his jaw and the ice blue of his eyes told her there was no hope.

"Yes, sir." She barely stopped herself from giving a military salute and spun away from his grip.

Hank watched her storm down the hall.

"She'll get over it once her Irish has cooled," Zach said.

"Is it ever cool? It's been my experience that it's always right under the surface."

"You're probably right, but the good news is, she doesn't hold a grudge."

Zach laughed at Hank's bleak look, and they walked to the front lobby together.

BARTON GENTLY WORKED THE CORK OUT OF A BOTTLE of Merlot and poured two glasses. He looked at Abigail as he came back into the living room and couldn't resist the glow that worked up to his face from his heart.

She was the most delightful lady he had ever met. She was sitting in her chair, engrossed in reading the files. The late afternoon sun glinted off her soft silver blond hair and almost created a halo.

"What are you smiling at, you old fool?" Abby looked over her readers at him.

Barton handed her the wine. "You look positively beatific in the sunshine, Abigail." He sat across from her and the pile of files on the coffee table.

"Don't be absurd. I am far from a saint. Do you suffer from short-term memory loss?"

"Be at ease, Abigail. I never forget a thing." He took pity on her and changed the subject. "I think we've sorted these files into reasonable order. When does Darcy come home?"

"She usually stays until after the five o'clock news, but that varies depending on what she's working on. I'll try her cell." Abby dialed Darcy's number, but it went to voice mail.

"Oh well," Abby said as she hung up. "She never listens to messages anyway, but she'll see I called."

Barton looked at his watch. "I think I'll throw a big salad together if that's okay. As it is, we have enough spaghetti and meatballs to float a large boat."

"That's okay. It will freeze if we don't eat it all."

A loud knock on the door startled them both. Mac bounded up from his favorite patch of sun and began barking furiously at the door.

Abby rose. "Get Mac, will you? Sometimes he thinks he's a Doberman."

She waited until Barton had scooped Mac up before she opened the door. Darcy swept in.

"Sorry about knocking and scaring you and Mac." She took Mac from Barton, then flopped onto the couch. "I'm evidently leading a parade. Come on in everybody."

Abby stood back and greeted Hank. "Oh good. We were going to call you. Oh, and Mr. Netters. Here, you can put your things down over by the door." She started to shut the door, but Hank stopped her.

"Can we leave this open for a little while? We're expecting another officer. Netters, you watch for Tessler."

"On it," Netters replied, pulled a dining room chair around, and sat facing the door.

"Well, this is quite the group," Abby said and slipped into her favorite overstuffed chair.

Hank stood behind Darcy and, just to irritate her, he placed his hands gently on her shoulders. She tried to shake him off but failed.

"Sorry for the intrusion, Abby. It's my fault. I'm placing Darcy and Bill in protective custody until an emergency is resolved," Hank said.

"What emergency? Darcy, are you alright?"

Barton sat on the arm of her chair and dropped his arm across her shoulders in silent support.

"I'm fine, but Adkins got kidnapped and Hank thinks Netters and I are targets too. Hence the protective custody." She glared at the space behind her.

Abby glanced at Netters still watching the door like a cat at a mouse hole.

"Bill doesn't seem to mind," she commented.

"Why would he? Mr. Accommodating back there assigned a cute little officer named Jody Tessler to be Netter's companion. He's thrilled."

"Who did they assign for you?"

"I assigned myself, Abby," Hank said. "My theory is they will both look less official if they are seen with members of the opposite sex. You know, less threatening."

"Oh. I see," Abby said.

"And we aren't allowed to broadcast any results of our investigation until they return Adkins," Darcy added. "It's a condition of his ransom."

"Well, that's a shame. Barton and I went to the State Library and found some files that are, at the very least, interesting." Abby gestured to the papers on the coffee table.

Darcy leaned over and plucked the top file. She scanned it. "This is an old coroner's report Frye signed. He identified the bones as animal remains."

She handed the copy to Hank, forgetting she was still angry with him. Hank scanned the report and sat down next to Darcy.

"And this says there's a rule that construction would have had to been delayed if they found human remains. Do you suppose they coerced Frye into misidentifying the bones?"

"Stranger things have happened," Hank said as he picked up another file.

"Barton and I think he got paid to re-evaluate the bones and declare them human and Native American later because he retired so abruptly. We just can't figure out why the re-evaluation," Abby said.

"Then there's this about Pete Loman suing the construction company for not informing the tribe." Barton handed another slip to Darcy.

"Hank, look at this. State Senator Pete Loman suggests that the store be given to the Arapahos in reparation for disturbing a burial site."

"Curiouser and curiouser, as they say in Wonderland."

Everyone was silent as they read through the pile of files, so when Netters shot out of his chair and flung the door wide, he startled everyone.

"Hi Officer Tessler. We're all in here. Come on in."

Jody Tessler's bright green eyes grew large with surprise. She cautiously peeked into the room and was visibly relieved to see Detective Nelson.

"Oh, thank God, Detective. I was afraid I'd blown my cover already."

"Let me take your coat," Netters offered moments before he slipped it off and away. He quickly pulled out another chair for her and placed it next to his.

"I'm Bill Netters and you're my custodian," he said with a huge grin.

Jody looked from Netters to Hank, who nodded. The silence was heavy.

"How would everyone like spaghetti and meatballs?" Abby asked and amid a spattering of, "Sure," "That would be great," and "If it wouldn't be a bother," Abby and Barton disappeared into the kitchen.

CHAPTER 18

STUART JOHNSON FINISHED HIS NOTES on the briefing Edwin Taylor, the FBI Special Agent in charge, had just given. The kidnapping of a local hotshot reporter was high on the Chief's concerns.

Johnson found himself in the awkward position of explaining Adkins' involvement in the Brown/Blue Feather case and summarizing the phone call he'd received from CPD Detective Hank Nelson about the kidnapper's demands.

The Chief ordered Johnson to contact Mary Blue Feather, John Blue Feather, and Mike Brown to warn them about the potential danger and offer protection.

He called Mike Brown first, since he was bound to be the most belligerent. When Brown answered, Johnson identified himself.

"Yeah, Johnson. What do you want?"

"There has been a kidnapping—"

"Mary?" Brown snapped.

"No. Adkins. The guy who played the incriminating tape of you on TV."

"And I should care about that little jerk because . . ."

"Because the station was told to stop all investigations surrounding your case or the disposition of Thompson's Furniture Store. Do you know why they might do this?"

"You accusing me, Johnson?"

"No. If I thought you had anything to do with this, I'd have already arrested you."

"It wouldn't be the first time the FBI got it wrong."

Johnson could feel his neck tighten. "Listen Brown, it would be in your best interest to tell us whatever you know about the Thompson store and who all is involved. I am authorized to give you protection."

Johnson could hear the deep, hearty laughter and knew Mike Brown would tell him nothing.

"Well, if you change your mind, you know where to find me."

The laughter stopped abruptly. "Stay away from me and mine, Johnson. I don't want you sniffing around my sister. I really don't want you convincing my nephew to count on the Federal Government for anything. I'll take care of them."

"Yeah. You've been doing a real skillful job so far. How'd little Johnny like jail? I'm guessing Mary was just ecstatic to see both her brother and her son locked up."

"I'm warning you, Johnson—"

"And I'm warning you. I am following this investigation wherever it leads. If it leads to your front door, I will put you away. If you seriously gave a damn about your family, you'd stop dragging them down with you."

The line went dead.

That went well, Johnson thought.

He dialed the Wyoming State Tourism office and asked to speak to Mary Blue Feather. When she came on the call, Johnson felt a decided chill on the line.

"Yes Stuart. What do you want?"

"That's just what your brother asked when I called him. You guys need some new dialogue." There was no response. "Look Mary, this is an official call. They have kidnapped that young reporter from Channel 23—"

"Darcy?" Mary sounded alarmed.

"No, that intern guy, Adkins. Anyway, my department chief wanted me to call and warn you, Mike, and John. I can offer protection. Predictably, Mike refused, but I was hoping you and John would take me up on it. We don't know who the kidnappers are, but they have demanded Channel 23 stop their investigative stories on the AIM demonstrations as well as your brother and son."

Mary didn't say anything for a heartbeat. Stuart felt a hollow ache, as if it were the ghost pain of an old wound. Mary would always see him as the enemy of her people and especially of her family. She would never consent to any relationship she saw as being essentially a conflict of loyalties.

"Thank you, Stuart," Mary said finally. "I'll warn John to be watchful."

"What about you? Can I provide you with protection?"

"I don't think so, no. I'm not affiliated with AIM."

"Mary, that's not the point," Stuart said, struggling to keep his frustration out of his voice. "We don't know who might be in danger or used as leverage."

"I will be careful as well."

Johnson hated the defeated tone in her voice. It hurt that she didn't see his concern for her as personal rather than official.

"Enough. I'm putting an agent on you." He winced, hearing his sharp tone, but refused to mollify it.

"Well, Stuart," the sharp spine was back in her voice, "I guess you can waste taxpayer's money any way you wish. Just don't expect me to make it easy." She hung up.

Johnson rubbed his chin as if she'd actually hit him. "At least she's not meek and docile anymore," he said to himself.

WYOMING STATE SENATOR SHOULDN'T HAVE TO put up with this shit, Pete Loman thought, but he didn't hang up the phone. The voice at first hadn't sounded familiar, but the caller was assertive and took Loman's lack of response as encouraging. Loman felt a chill of recognition. This guy was a corporate lawyer Loman had met at a conference.

"Look, I'm aware your client is not happy with the way things are playing out in the press here, but frankly, he has only himself and his people to blame. Wyoming isn't a frontier state anymore.

We don't tie up our horses on Main Street, and we especially don't litter the place with dead bodies."

Loman could barely breathe.

"Mr. Loman—"

"Senator," Loman corrected.

"Of course, Senator," the lawyer quickly agreed with an unctuous tone that made Loman bristle.

"Don't patronize me. If your client wants his plans to go through, he's got to knock off all the heavy-handed nonsense."

"People here cling to the fiction that they still have a say in their government. It wouldn't be wise to disillusion them right now."

"Senator Loman, my client is concerned about the timeline. He wants negotiations with both the Arapaho Tribal Council and the State Legislature to reach an amicable conclusion as quickly as possible."

"Really? I figured I'd just sit around till spring." Loman laced his sarcasm with as much contempt as he could muster. "I don't know what you Ivy-League types do, but out here we practice law. There are steps to go through."

After a loaded pause, the lawyer said, "I am aware procedures must be followed, but I am tasked by my client to inquire what exactly has been accomplished and what still needs to be done."

"Tell your *client*—" Loman stressed the word to imply he was tired of playing the anonymity game. By God, when he came through for this guy, he would demand names, "—that I've sued the construction company and asked for the court to recognize the desecration of a Native American burial site."

"And how is that going?"

"Well, a little slower now that the body of former County Coroner James Frye has been found dead in a cabin up by Encampment." Loman waited for a reaction. The silence on the other end was thick.

"How unfortunate," the lawyer finally said. "Hunting accident?"

"Don't get cute. They murdered him execution style, just like Latham Kellogg. He was supposed to be my prime witness. Now we've got nothing but a revised report."

"That should be enough."

"Not with bodies dropping all over the place. The carnage is beginning to stink, and the stench is causing questions. All the questions make discretion dicey. Do you get it?" Senator Loman wanted to reach through the phone line and choke this son-of-a-bitch till his tongue lolled out of his mouth.

Again, silence. "My client has taken steps to quiet the questions, but you should know it doesn't buy us much time."

"What steps?"

"If I told you, you would be required to tell the police about this conversation. That would lead to your arrest and disbarment, assuming you lived that long. Do *you* get it?"

The Senator felt the shock like a fist to his gut. He slipped the phone back into its cradle and wiped nervous sweat from his hands onto his precisely creased trousers.

Adkins had never been so miserable in his whole young life. At first, when he'd heard the thugs leave the room they had stashed him in, he felt weak with relief. He had been certain they were going to kill him.

He unfolded his legs slowly, wondering if they still worked. Except for a screaming soreness that dissolved when he worked his legs back and forth as he sat on the edge of the bed, his legs worked fine.

He rolled off the smelly, uncovered mattress and crossed close to the door, careful to drag his chained ankle slowly. He held his breath, terrified the men beyond the door would come back in.

He listened to their conversation and was elated to hear they had no orders to kill him . . . yet. He was afraid the smart one wouldn't be able to control the reckless one. That was how he thought of them now.

Adkins rubbed his arms, trying to sooth the bone-deep chill which had seeped into every crevice of his body. In his low-level panic mode, Adkins thought he could see his breath, and he shivered. His stomach gurgled, partly from the tacos he'd had for lunch and partly from terror.

How long were they going to keep him locked up in this freezing cabin? They were probably going to starve him to death.

Oh my God, he thought. I don't have the skill set for this. I don't *do* deprivation!

Why was this happening to him? Why not Darcy? She had started this entire investigation in the first place.

His thoughts piled up like the contents of a compost heap. No garbage was too miserable to be excluded. He kept turning the refuse of his mind repeatedly, trying to find an angle as he paced a short trail back and forth in the tiny room.

Maybe, he thought, he could convince them Darcy was to blame, and he was the only one who could control her. If they wanted to shut down the investigation, he was the man to do it.

Shuffling over to the door, he knocked loudly on the weathered boards and then soothed his scraped knuckles by blowing on them as he waited for a response.

"Hello?" he called, then waited.

"What?" came the listless response.

"Can I talk to you guys?" Adkins asked, almost pleading.

"No. Shut the hell up."

Although the words were harsh, their tone was without heat, so he tried again.

"I couldn't help but overhear you talking about your boss wanting to shut down my investigation . . ." He stopped, half-fearful of reprisals for listening at the door.

"Yeah, well, mission accomplished," Tony got up and wandered toward the door.

Adkins could hear the change in volume and felt encouraged. "Yes, for now, but what about Darcy Moreland? Do you have a plan to stop her? She's a loose cannon, you know. I don't think she'll care if you kill me."

"I'm beginning to feel the same way," Tony said.

Adkins felt fear clamp his belly and tighten his neck, but he took a deep breath and plunged on. "Okay. You don't know me, and you don't know her, but take my word for it. Even Zach Horton, our station manager, can't stop her. She's treacherous and persistent.

I've seen her work stories before. She chews on them till all the details come out. She's even got an in with the police. She's the lover of a detective there."

A deep silence finally broke. "So, what's your point?" Adkins identified the smart one's voice.

"My point is, if you let me out of here, I can go back and keep her from digging up any more about you guys. My uncle owns the station, so I have clout." Adkins hoped the smart one could connect the dots.

He heard soft mumblings far away from the door, but he couldn't make out any distinct words. Adkins waited. He felt his insides turn to water.

"Look," he continued, shouting now. "You don't need to hold me. You've made your point. You can obviously pick up anyone anytime. Everybody got that message . . . except Darcy. She's bull-headed if you know what I mean."

No response from the other side of the door had Adkins breaking out into a clammy sweat, even though the temperature of the room was chilly.

Vince and Tony moved as far away from the door as possible.

Tony was almost excited by the option. "Hey, Vince. Let's call the boss. This sounds perfect! We wouldn't have to babysit this jerk for God knows how long."

"The boss said to hold him," Vince said.

"Yeah, but the boss hasn't heard about this Darcy he talks about."

"Like we should take the word of a jerk like him. This woman, Darcy, is obviously an enemy of that little squint." Vince went back to the hard-bottomed chair, snugged up to the table, and laid out his cards for solitaire.

Tony followed him. "Listen, I don't think the boss will care about her love life, but what if what he says is true and she keeps digging?"

"You think that little squint could keep her in line if her boss can't? Besides, if what he says is true about her detective boyfriend, why would we want to step into that pile of shit?"

"That's the point," Tony said, elated Vince was at least listening. "The little pisser would be responsible. Don't ya see? This way, no one pokes around looking for the pisser, and we still get a clamp-down on the bad press. If he screws up, I shoot him."

Vince looked at Tony. Truth be told, the guy creeped him out. His eyes were squinty and so dark they were almost black. Vince sometimes thought his eyes looked dead. The only time Vince could remember Tony smiling was when he talked about screwing or killing, the only things he cared about.

"Look Tony," he began, "I don't like this job any more than you do—"

"I liked the shooting part, but this waiting is a pain in the ass. I have talent. It's wasted here." Tony wiped a sheen of oily sweat from his forehead. "Jesus, I hate this. If you sit close to that fire, your balls roast and your butt freezes. I don't belong here. I belong in Vegas."

"You belong where the boss says you belong."

"Shows how much you know, you *leccaculo*."

"Butt kisser?" Vince shot up so fast his chair crashed backwards.

Tony looked into Vince's narrowed eyes and backed away. "Easy Sassano. I was only joking." His back jolted hard on the rough log surface of the wall.

Vince froze with his arm raised and his fist clenched. He vibrated with restrained rage. "Triolo, your sense of humor sucks. Don't call me names in English or Italian. You don't know me that well."

"Sorry. Sorry." Tony raised his hands in surrender and slipped to the side and out of range. He ran his hands through his thick, dark hair and tried to pull some air back into his now-empty lungs.

Vince walked over to his chair and set it upright with deliberate care. The adrenaline rushing through his system was making him shake.

He did not know why he was so quick-tempered lately. It was the job partly. He hadn't really thought through what it was going to entail.

His hand went to the cross his mother had given him, and he rubbed it between his thumb and finger for comfort.

He did not mind offing guys who threatened the family. That was sort of like self-defence. But those two guys they had killed weren't dangerous. They may have screwed up in some way, but overall, they seemed like pretty harmless guys.

Ah hell, he thought. Maybe he didn't understand all the twists and turns. Maybe he just wasn't cut out for this. Maybe he should go home and get a job at his Uncle Gino's garage. He rubbed at the tightness in his chest under his cross.

Vince shoved away from the table and went to one of the small windows to look out. Snow covered everything but the tops of the drifts and the edges where it met the ground were gray. Like sin taking over the soul, Sister Mary Pat used to say, nibbling away, minor sin by minor sin, until everything turned a dirty gray.

He hated being trapped in a cabin with Triolo. The guy wasn't right. He had a vital piece missing. There was no telling what he would do.

Vince felt anxious, like the guy in the circus who played around with the wild animals. It was never *if* they attacked you, but *when*. What the hell did the boss expect him to do if Tony went off the rails?

Vince glanced over at Tony, slouched by the fireplace, playing with his knife.

"What the hell, Tony," he said. "Why don't we call the boss and see if we can cut this little jerk loose?"

Tony perked up like a dog offered a chew toy. "Really, Vince?"

"Yeah, sure. Why not? We could tell him about this guy offering to make sure all the investigations stop. He might think it's a good idea."

"Yeah, and maybe we could get out of this bullshit state. You think he'd let us come back to Vegas?" Tony had picked up Vince's cell and brought it to him. "You call. He likes you best."

"Jesus, Tony. Grow up. We just work for the guy," he said but took the phone anyway.

He turned the phone on speaker so Tony could hear, too. They did not have to wait long to be connected. It took even less time to explain what Adkins had said.

"Okay. You can cut him loose but keep tabs to make sure he's telling the truth. Any more diggin' around and I want it stopped. You get me?"

"Yes, sir," said Vince.

"So, Boss," Tony leaned over the phone eagerly, "if this Darcy something or other doesn't stop digging around, can I take her out?"

Vince waited nervously, hoping the boss would rein Tony in. The main reason he'd agreed to approach the boss with this idea was he was terrified Tony would go berserk and kill the guy in the back room before he could stop him.

"Just make sure no more exposés hit the air or print. I want this shut down tight until we get the authorisation. Is that clear? Screw this down tight and screw it down quietly. *Comprensione per?*"

"Yeah Boss," Tony answered. "We understand."

"*Merda!*" Vince muttered.

CHAPTER 19

A BBY'S LIVING ROOM FELT LIKE A SAUNA. There were too many bodies packed into a small space. The combination of snow-dampened coats hanging on the hall tree and over the backs of chairs coupled with the hiss and spurt of the radiators vainly trying to keep the 30-degree wintry wind out raised the collective humidity.

Barton sat on the small settee across from Abby and next to Jody. He cradled a snifter of brandy, warming it in his hands.

Hank, sipping straight coffee, took the other armchair and watched Darcy resting crossed legged on the flowered carpet at Abby's feet. She was blowing into a huge mug that said *Get Your Kicks on Route 66*, trying to cool her Bailey's spiked coco.

Darcy's face glowed with a flattering rosiness, and she looked about 14. Hank felt an all too familiar twist around his heart. He didn't know if it was because of his personal feelings for her or because she was in danger. Probably both.

Hank studied Jody Tessler too. She was the one unknown in the room. She was as fresh-faced as Darcy, but her green eyes were focused as she assessed everyone in the room. He noticed Jody sipped Orange Pekoe from a dainty flowered cup and watched as she swatted Netters' wandering hand away when it landed on her shoulder without losing a drop of tea. She'd do, he thought.

Netters, momentarily discouraged, resettled on the arm of the settee above Jody.

"So, what's the plan?" he asked, looking at Hank.

"Officer Tessler will pose as your girlfriend—"

"That's not going to work if she won't let me touch her even casually," Netters burst forth, then clamped his mouth shut, embarrassed he'd revealed so much.

"She's not obliged to in private, Bill." Hank tried to be gentle, recognizing the symptoms of a full-on crush. "She will, in public, give every appearance of being attracted to you, but her job is to protect you. It would be . . . unwise to distract her. Do you understand?"

"Yeah," Netters sounded sullen, then brightened. "Where are we going to sleep?"

Officer Tessler rolled her eyes and then shot Hank a pleading look.

"Do you have a room at your place to put her up in? She'll need enough room for personal privacy. Can you provide that?"

"Yeah. My apartment isn't grand or anything—"

"I'd settle for reasonably rodent and bug-free," Jody said, then glanced anxiously in Hank's direction.

"Officer Tessler will do her job no matter what the conditions are," Hank gently warned the new officer, "but I'd appreciate it if you could make her feel as comfortable as you can." Hank took another sip of coffee.

"Oh sure, Hank. No problem." Hank was grateful Officer Tessler's back was to Netters.

"And where are *you* going to sleep?" Darcy asked, already knowing the answer.

She really enjoyed making him squirm, Hank thought. He was predictable. She knew it, and he hated it. He was never comfortable when his personal and professional life overlapped.

"We could stay at my place," he offered.

"I don't think so," Darcy said. "Try again."

"Then I guess I'm waiting for a gracious invitation from you."

"You want gracious?"

"If you can manage it." He loved to see her bristle. It made him chuckle.

"You can save your charm-school humor for someone who's impressed." She loved the twinkle in his eye, though she would never let him know it.

"I'll just go home and pack a toothbrush," Hank said as he followed her to the kitchen. He stood behind her at the sink as she rinsed out her cup, resting his hands on her shoulders. He felt her tense under his palms and then relax. His finger ran up the side of her neck, gently rubbing the tension away. He grinned when she shivered.

"Cut that out," she swatted at his hand and spun around to face him.

Hank didn't step back. Instead, he stepped forward and bracketed her with his arms. "I know it annoys you to have round-the-clock protection, even if it *is* me—"

"*Especially* if it is you," Darcy couldn't help interrupting.

"Alright, especially if it's me." Hank stooped lower, kissed her softly, then whispered, "So much for token resistance. Now shut up and listen."

Darcy blinked, shocked as much by the kiss as the command.

"You and I will be joined at the hip until we find Adkins and arrest his kidnappers. Is that clear?"

"I can't have you dogging my steps while I investigate this story. You have cop written all over you. No one will talk to me if you're hanging around," Darcy said.

"You'd be surprised how ordinary I can look if I try. You can introduce me as a colleague—"

"A colleague? Are you crazed?"

"Okay, then introduce me as your over-protective significant other, which is closer to the truth."

Darcy pushed him away with both hands, but Hank caught her wrists and pulled her close.

"Listen to me carefully, Darcy. I will try to accommodate you as much as I can, but I will not allow you to go your own stubborn way. These guys are dangerous."

"Allow? Allow!" Darcy sputtered.

Hank sucked in a lung full of air. "Okay, poor choice of words, but however you want to dress it up, I want your word you won't go anywhere without me or Officer Tessler."

"For heaven's sake, Darcy," Abby said from her chair, "just be grateful for the protection and do what Hank asks."

Hank watched the fight drain out of her. "Stay here while I run home and get some things," he said, and turned to Officer Tessler. "I'm leaving you in charge." He slanted his eyes to Darcy and then back. "Don't put up with any nonsense from her.

"I've got my stun gun, sir," Tessler offered.

"Really? Can I see it?" Netters began patting Tessler around the circumference of her utility belt.

She slapped his hands away. "Knock it off! What part of 'I am armed' confused you?"

"Try to catch Officer Tessler up while I'm gone, guys," Hank said as he slipped into his jacket and left.

By nine o'clock, Jody Tessler knew more than she wanted to about bison heads, the American Indian Movement, Mike Brown, Mary & John Blue Feather, FBI Agent Stuart Johnson, District Attorney Patrick Tucker, Senator Pete Loman, Former County Corner James Frye, Latham Kellogg . . . and William Tecumseh Netters.

She felt like her brain was swathed in five layers of cotton batting. And yet he was still talking.

"Darcy and I went to Tucker's office to get an on-air explanation, and Darcy shoved the mic right into his face. I thought the guy was going to have a heart attack. He didn't have any explanation about why he was going ahead with prosecuting Mike Brown and John Blue Feather for terrorism. We think it is either to garner press—this *is* an election year—or more likely he was bought off by whoever wants this investigation stifled."

Netters finally sank back into the soft cushions of the chair Hank had relinquished. He looked at the little group still assembled with a satisfied grin.

"Did I miss anything?" he asked.

"William, I think that is the most I've ever heard you say in all the time I've known you," Abby said. "Are you ill?"

"No, just trying to be thorough."

"That you were my boy." Barton rose slowly, babying his right knee which seemed to delight in making him feel old by throbbing all winter. "I think it's time to call it a night. Officer Tessler looks like she's getting a headache."

"You can say that again," Jody said under her breath and glanced at Netters. Louder she said, "I hate to impose, but I'm supposed to keep both Darcy and Billy here . . ." she fought back an unprofessional grimace, ". . . under my protection until Detective Nelson returns."

"Quite right, my dear. Quite right." Barton began picking up cups and glasses and trundled off to the kitchen.

"Are you okay, Darcy? You've hardly said a word all night except to fight with Hank," Abby said.

"Fine. I'm fine. It's just been a busy day and now this kidnapping thing. I never liked Adkins, but I wouldn't wish this on him. Do you think he'll be safe? I mean those guys are probably responsible for Kellogg's death and maybe Frye's as well."

"We are giving it the highest priority level, Ms. Moreland. I'm sure something will break in the case soon," Jody said.

Darcy factored in how young and new to the police force Jody was. "I'm sure you're right."

Darren Kincade watched the snowy sleet slither down the window, leaving small slug-like trails on the foggy glass, and waited for his clients, Mike Brown and John Blue Feather, to show up.

The waitress came by again to top off his already scalding coffee and he placed his hand over his cup in mute refusal.

She looked momentarily startled and her light brown eyes blinked, then widened in surprise. This place catered to the guys from the railroad, anyone who was looking for a warm, cheap place out of the weather, and, later in the evening, the drunks. Almost no one refused refills. She cracked her gum, then shot him her 100-watt smile.

"Okay. But if ya need anything, just holler," she said, and walked off.

Kincade looked at his notes on the long, yellow pad and shook his head. There were so many layers to this case he wasn't getting.

He might be a young lawyer, but he wasn't stupid, he thought. The US Attorney had filed charges earlier today. Kincade had been assured by the FBI agent he was going to suggest the terrorism charges be dropped, but Patrick Tucker had done a 180 and filed under the Homeland Security law dealing with potential threats.

What the hell was going on? Kincade griped silently. Mike Brown was an aging activist and Kincade could sort of understand why everyone would breathe easier if he was in prison, but John had no record and was being railroaded.

Kincade felt the Wimpy Burger he'd had for lunch knot in his stomach.

Calm down, he told himself. *'Law had to be approached unemotionally for it to function,'* he parroted one of his law professors in his head.

But damn it, he had gone into law to make a difference. All he was doing now was running around roadblocks.

He had no patience with the convoluted practices of the courts. He almost wished for the old Common Law system. The accused gave their side of the story and the village voted. It was a lot less messy.

He drew more boxes in the margin of his notepad, coloring them in until they were black squares and looked like a chessboard.

"Sorry to have kept you waiting." John Blue Feather slipped into a seat opposite Kincade. "I made the mistake of telling my uncle we were meeting. He wants you to represent me exclusively. He said he'd get a Public Defender for himself. Can you call him? He wouldn't listen to me." John's cheeks were red from the cold, and he unwound three loops of his long, multicolored muffler.

Catching Kincade's interested look, he laughed. "My mom knit it for me. She thinks if I have a long one, I'll have to wind it around my neck at least once. She worries."

Kincade motioned the waitress over. "Coffee?"

"Sure," John said.

"Can you bring my friend a cup, too?" Kincade asked.

"Uh huh," she said and grabbed a cup from the adjoining table, filled it, and put it in front of John with a flirty grin and another snap of her gum.

Once John's cup was filled and Kincade's topped off, she sashayed back behind the counter, humming a disjointed tune.

"I think your uncle is being wise to separate your cases." Kincade's words were direct, but his soft, gray eyes were sympathetic.

"Darren, I won't do that. It would be like turning my back on him." John turned the warm cup in his hands.

"John, I understand, but you must face reality. Your uncle has belonged to radical groups for years and participated in who knows what."

"They never proved anything," John said with more volume than he intended. He looked around at the empty tables surrounding them and slunk down a little in his chair.

"The FBI has him on a watch list. That alone could prejudice the judge and jury, and he knows it. You are young and have no previous run-ins with the law. Your uncle knows that if you separate the cases, you'll probably get a slap on the wrist and probation."

"But they want to try him as a terrorist," John said.

"Well, he is by the loose logic of 'whoever isn't with me is against me.' It doesn't matter. What your uncle sees as justice, the FBI sees as terrorism." Kincade stirred his coffee and watched the steam rise from the cup.

"I get that. It's not like I haven't been raised hearing these arguments all my life. My mom is of the, 'let's just all try to get along' school, while my uncle is of the 'bomb them if they can't take a joke' school." After a brief beat, John looked up at Kincade, terrified.

"Lawyer client privilege," Kincade reassured him. "Don't worry."

John laughed humourlessly. "Yeah. Paranoia is my middle name."

"You've got a better right to paranoia than most, I would think. But John, for our purposes, we'll need to subscribe to your mother's point of view. It will go down easier if we present your case as petty vandalism and you as a young, impressionable kid unduly influenced by a radical uncle. Not too farfetched, as far as I can tell."

John's square jaw jutted out as if unconsciously waiting for someone to clip it, and his brown eyes flashed obsidian. "I won't do that. I am not a kid, and my uncle didn't unduly influence me. Hell, I had to beg him to let me come along."

"If he is and has been the most constant male influence in your life, we could make a case you were coerced unconsciously."

"Nice psychobabble, but if I agree to separate my case from my uncle's," John's eyes flashed with challenge, "and I'm not saying I will."

"Understood," Kincade agreed softly.

"*If* I do, I want to be charged with what I actually did. I don't want to be charged for my political intentions, and I don't want there to be any mention of my uncle or AIM or anything else."

"Well, I'm not going to bring it up, but you can be damned sure the US Attorney won't be as nice."

"What's up with him? I can't figure his agenda."

"Me neither," Kincade admitted. "Unless he wants your uncle buried deep in some Federal prison for a long time. It feels slimy to me, but then I'm new to the law. He probably sees you as unavoidable collateral damage."

"Well, that's flattering." John leaned back in the vinyl covered chair.

"What was the reason for the bison head? What the hell were you protesting?"

John flushed. He laughed with a self-deprecating shake of his head; Kincade found reassuring. "To tell the truth, I'm uncertain myself. My uncle talks philosophically and politically at the same time. Most of his arguments I've heard most of my life. 'The White Man has stolen our land and our pride . . .' or variations of that theme."

"So, what about Thompson's Furniture Store? What kept him from—" Kincade stopped himself before he said something un-PC.

John quirked into an amused smirk. "Going on the warpath?" he supplied the ending to Kincade's statement.

"I guess. It just seems so unconnected."

"I heard it has something to do with a consortium trying to turn the store into a casino."

Kincade let loose a slow, low whistle. "I wish them luck getting that through the state legislature. Those hypocrites have vetoed any gambling scheme that has ever come across their desks."

"Yeah, only the Arapahos and later the Shoshone have been able to circumvent the state statutes outlawing gambling," John said softly, folding and unfolding the soggy cocktail napkin without looking up. "It was a fluke that the legislature voted on a bill that gave the Native American exception to the gambling laws."

"Your uncle thought the consortium was trying to use your tribe to get around the state law? How?"

John looked up and took a sip of coffee. "I don't really know. I'm not even certain my uncle knows. He just said it didn't smell right and if history could be believed, somehow our people were about to be screwed again."

"The point of the bison head was to scare the consortium off?"

"My uncle said the protest would give notice that the consortium was trying to manipulate the Arapaho people. My uncle wanted a place at the table. He wanted to know what they intended, and he wanted to protect our people. He thought if he became a thorn in their side, they might consult with him. Now it may just get him prison time." John paused for a moment. "I heard Agent Johnson told Tucker not to bother with terrorist charges. That true?"

"Yes. But Tucker can do what he wants. Good to have Johnson on your side, though."

"Yeah. Johnson went to bat for us because he likes my mother." John laughed at the shocked look on Kincade's face. "Yup. That's us. A house divided. My uncle's an AIM terrorist and my mom's dating the enemy."

"But that doesn't explain why Tucker wants your uncle far, far away in a federal prison. Makes you wonder why, huh?"

CHAPTER 20

HANK GRABBED THE SMALL LEATHER FLIGHT BAG out of his truck and trudged back up the icy steps of the Algonquin. He knew Darcy wouldn't give him any more trouble tonight about being guarded 24/7, but he also knew her well enough to know her cooperative mood wouldn't last.

The first time someone refused to talk to her or got uneasy with him in the room, she would do her damndest to cut him loose.

Well, she could try, Hank thought, gripping his case a little tighter as he clattered through the large front doors.

He knocked on Abby's door, but then pushed into the room. Abby and Barton were in the kitchen, washing cups and spoons while Darcy sat curled up in Abby's favorite chair.

"Hi Hank," Netters waved halfheartedly from his perch on the settee, then slanted his gaze longingly toward the back of Jody Tessler who was staring out the window.

"Officer Tessler, I assume you have made certain the street exit is clear?" Hank confirmed.

Jody turned to face him. "Yes, sir. I've also checked the alleyway twice. Nothing suspicious to report."

"Good. Why don't you let Bill take you to his home and get settled in? We'll meet back here tomorrow morning. Then he raised his voice a little to alert Abby. "If that's okay with you, Abby."

Abby bustled out of the kitchen, wiping suds from her hands onto her apron.

"Of course it's alright. I'll have Barton go to the bakery and get some of those wonderful sticky buns. We'll have a breakfast party. Won't that be fun?"

Darcy uncurled from the chair and walked over to Abby. "Thanks for doing this," she pecked Abby on the cheek. "I know this is disruptive."

"Don't be silly, Darcy. I love being included in the excitement and truly, if there is ever anything I can do to keep you and Bill safe, I'm happy to do it."

Darcy patted Abby on the back and headed for the door. Jody Tessler followed Darcy and Hank out, then turned at the doorway.

"Come on, Billy. Let's get going."

"It's Bill or Netters. Never Billy. Got it?"

"Sure," Jody said as Netters pushed past her into the front foyer.

Jody raised an eyebrow and flashed an impish grin in Darcy's direction. Hank and Darcy watched them plunge into the blustery weather before they mounted the stairs to Darcy's apartment.

"I like your little Officer Tessler," Darcy said.

"She's not mine, but yeah, I think she can handle our tall friend there."

Entering Darcy's apartment first, Hank dropped his bag silently on the sofa, gestured to Darcy to hang back, and checked the bedroom, kitchen, and bath.

"All clear," he said, coming into the living room again.

"Gee, thanks, Hank." Darcy batted her eyes at him as she swooped past toward the bedroom.

"Sarcasm is not attractive, Darcy," he said as he trailed after her.

"And yet you followed me in here," Darcy said. She toed off her shoes and nudged them into the closet.

Darcy unbuttoned her blouse, but Hank grabbed the back of her shirt and pulled her onto the bed. He covered her with his body and braceleted her wrists above her head in one smooth shift.

Leaning into her, he kissed her deeply, reveling in the soft huff of Darcy's surprised breath. Tangling his tongue with hers, he thought he could almost taste the tang of sass, which was so much a part of her.

He heard Darcy suck in a deep gasp, then released a long-contented breath.

"I love the way you smell like Chanel and taste like sin," he whispered.

Darcy scrambled out from under Hank and rose to her knees, bracketing his hips. She lowered herself and gently bumped the hard bulge of his erection.

"If you want to park this thing, cowboy," she wriggled her bottom suggestively and laughed when he moaned, "you need to show me a little more respect."

"I can show you as little respect as you'd like. But right now, I am protecting you, and I can't do that when you keep turning me on." Hank flipped her onto her back again.

"Well, that's a damn shame. I was hoping this could be a little more fun," Darcy said. "Now what, cowboy? Want to play some cards? They do that in all the cop shows."

"Your eyes look like a good Irish whiskey . . . all golden brown and shining. I never get tired of looking into them." He leaned forward, kissing her softly.

Darcy groaned in frustration. "I was hoping for a sex slave, and instead I got a really cute roommate." She dropped her forearm across her eyes to ward off the glare of the single, bare lightbulb hanging from her bedroom ceiling.

She pushed off the bed, lunged across the floor, and grabbed her fluffy pink robe from the back of the door.

Hank crossed his hands behind his head and tried to remind himself that he was trying to keep her safe. Cold comfort when she looked so hot.

A large clang from the kitchen had him up and out one-legged-hopping into his jeans as he headed for the kitchen.

When he got there, Darcy was crouched on the floor.

"Get down, you idiot. They're down there watching."

Hank stooped and crab-walked over to her.

"Who is 'they'?"

"I don't know . . . a couple of guys. They're watching my windows. I came out to get some wine and glanced down at the street. They definitely want me to see them. They're deliberately standing under the streetlamp."

Hank rose cautiously to peek over the sink and through the window below. He saw two guys, bundled into heavy ranch coats, standing on the corner. One was smoking and staring up at Darcy's window. From the distance, he could not get much of a sense of them except, like Darcy, he was sure they were not from here.

"Yeah, you're right. I think they're just trying to scare you." Hank said.

"Mission accomplished." Darcy was sitting on the floor with her back resting on the under-sink cupboard. Her knees were up, and her feet were crossed at the ankle. She cradled a brown bottle of wine in her lap. She kept rubbing its neck between her hands.

Hank plucked the bottle from her, then stood. He lounged in front of the window for a long second and then sauntered to the left to find two glasses. Walking past the window once more, he stepped up to the counter, still making sure part of him was visible from the street.

Darcy tugged franticly at his leg. "What the hell do you think you're doing?"

"Making sure they see you're not alone." He poured the wine, then pulled her to stand by him at the window. "Now take the wine and look happy to have me half-naked in your kitchen."

Darcy took the glass and sipped. Her eyes shifted out the window, but she was careful not to turn her head. "Okay. So how long do we stand here performing like bears in the circus?"

"Until they understand I'm here for the night." Hank slipped an arm over her shoulder and led her back to the bedroom. He deliberately turned off the kitchen light and turned on the bedroom light so the men could track their moves.

Once in the bedroom, Hank sat and pulled on his boots. Darcy didn't get concerned until he strapped on his weapon harness.

"You are not leaving me," she said as she perched on the foot of the bed.

"Not yet."

"Well, that's reassuring."

Hank's brain registered the sarcasm, but he was in full-on cop mode, so lover mode had to stand down. He plucked his phone off the dresser and called for backup. Turning out the light, he checked to see if the men were still there by looking through a small slit in the window-shade.

"Are you going out there?"

"Not until backup gets here. My job is to stay with you and keep you safe. Those guys haven't technically done anything wrong yet, but the local patrol has orders to roust any loiterers in the area. If they go easily, we stay put."

"But what if they are the guys who took Adkins? Shouldn't you at least question them?" Darcy gulped a little wine to wet her dry throat.

"Darcy don't go seeing monsters around every corner. We'll check them out if we can, but for now we do things by the book."

Darcy fell silent, but her brain was going at warp speed. "Shit!"

"What?" Hank spun away from the window.

"If they are the kidnappers, where is Adkins? He may already be dead. Or, consistent with what I know of his character, thrown me under the bus to save his own skin. Either way, God bless his soul."

Hank laughed. He couldn't help himself. "Did you just go from two guys loitering outside to Adkins being dead or a traitor? And then you bless him? What's that about?"

"It's a mom-ism. If you say or think a bad thought about someone, you say a blessing. He's going to need a blessing if he turned traitor. I'll skin him alive and use his hide as a raincoat." She got up and started pacing.

"Note to self. Don't make Darcy angry." He looked out again. "Backup's here. They're checking ID's. If they are Adkins' kidnappers, their identification is probably bogus, but we'll get a good look at them."

Darcy stopped pacing. She stood with her hands on her hips and glared at Hank's back. "Is that all you're going to do?"

"Yes, for now. If you want to do something, call Abby and tell her about the men. Tell her to make sure she's locked her door."

"Big help," she said, but picked up her phone and called Abby. "Hi. Make sure you lock the door. Detective Nelson is hovering by the window and told me to call. There are two guys hanging out under the streetlamp. Apparently, all a CPD Detective is good for is to observe and advise. Yeah. All part of your tax dollars at work."

He watched her click off and toss the phone back on the bed.

"I don't think I'll ever get used to calling Abby and having Barton answer the phone." She flopped onto her back.

"You don't share well with others, do you?"

She propped herself up on her elbows, affording him a tempting view of cleavage to compliment the flash of thigh exposed by the short robe.

"What do you mean?"

"Nothing sinister. Just an observation. You treat Abby like she's staff. She watches your dog, cooks for you, and even helps you with your hare-brained investigations, but heaven help her if she wants a life of her own."

Darcy sat all the way up, shoved her hair out of her face, and tucked it behind her ears with a ruthless jerk.

"That's a horrible thing to say, and totally not true. I worry about Abby getting involved with Barton is all. What if he breaks her heart?"

"Abby's a big girl. It's a little insulting you think she can't manage her own love life."

"I don't want to even know she *has* a love life. She was my English teacher, for heaven's sake."

"Does that automatically negate her having a relationship with a man?"

"Oh, stop talking and do your job. What are they doing now?" Darcy got up from the bed to peer out the side of the shade. "They're leaving. Your cops aren't trying to stop them, and they are getting away. Do something." She smacked his arm with her fist.

Hank ignored her and answered his phone.

"Got it. Good job. See if you can roust that young videographer from the station and compare notes. Have Tanner get back to me as soon as he finds anything out." Hank clicked off.

"What was that all about?" Darcy planted herself in front of Hank. "And who is Tanner?"

"The patrol questioned him and showed them a picture of Adkins. Got a couple of good thumbprints on the photo. Turner is our lab guy who is going to figure out if they are in the system or not."

"Oh."

"Yeah, oh. Get dressed. I may have to take you down to the station with me."

"Okay, but you don't have to get all bossy all of a sudden." Darcy walked to her closet.

"That's what we cops do when we're doing our job. We boss people around." Hank laughed at her exasperated grunt.

TRIOLO AND SASSANO HUDDLED IN THEIR RENTED black SUV and jacked the heat on full.

"Do you think they made us?" Triolo blew on his ungloved hands.

"I'm pretty sure they know we're not tourists. The guy at the window was probably her cop boyfriend. He probably arranged for the patrol to hassle us. So, the pisser looks to be right about the boyfriend, at least."

"So, can we let him go, Vince? We could move into town and keep track of him. Stay at a place that has heat, eat at places that don't serve fries with everything."

"I guess so. Let's go get the little jerk." Vince dropped the SUV into gear. "Make sure we're not being followed."

Just to be safe, they took the Happy Jack Road instead of the Interstate. Less traffic meant less chance of being followed without knowing it.

It was dark and cold, and the two-lane highway was covered with black ice that tricked the eye into believing the roadway was dry only to trap your wheels in uncontrolled swerves and gut-wrenching spinouts. Vince hated driving it. He hated feeling out of control. At least with Tony turned around watching for a tail he was quiet for a change.

Trouble with these open spaces, Vince thought, was that it gave a man too much room to think. He preferred the New Jersey crowding of industrial parks against housing projects. And the sky seemed lower back home, more cozy-like. He'd be glad to move out of the cabin into an actual room with sheets and maid service.

He hoped the little jerk didn't give them any trouble. He would let Tony scare him good before they let him go. Make sure he knew they were watching him, expecting him to control the little lady he worked with.

When this was over, he was going to spend a week in a sauna sweating out all the cold and bad food. Couldn't find a decent Italian meal in the entire state, he thought as he turned off the highway and bounced along the rutted backroad.

CHAPTER 21

ADKINS HUNCHED CLOSE TO THE WOOD STOVE. He was cocooned beneath as many blankets as he could pull off the three beds and was sipping one of the Coors Light he'd found in a cooler.

He was feeling smug. *The boys,* as he had started to call them in his mind, were off on a fact-finding mission to see if what he had told them was the truth about Darcy. He was not sure how things were going at the station, but he was pretty sure Darcy would eventually do something. She was like a crazed junkyard dog when she was on a story.

He was as good as out of here, and the bonus was he could tell everyone what to do and they would have to do it. It was like having the mob on his side. He had no idea why *the boys* were so rabid about burying the story, and he truthfully had zero interest in finding out.

He wiped his runny nose on the sleeve of his now grimy sweater. He didn't care. When he got home, he was going to burn these clothes. He had inadvertently peed himself when *the boys* had kidnapped him, and although the stain had dried, he was feeling sticky and smelling ripe.

He passed the time thinking of what he would do when he got back home. Even Zach couldn't cross him now. The mob was controlling the news cycle. He amused himself by making lists in his head. He was certain Uncle Arnie would insist on implementing whatever he suggested. Adkins could be the new anchor and news editor, second only to Zach in power and prestige, he thought.

Yeah. He liked that just fine. He killed the beer and threw another log in the stove.

John Blue Feather hated fighting with his mom. He admired and respected her, not just because she was an elder, but also because of what she had made of herself. She lived in the white man's world and prospered. But he also admired the strength of conviction and passion his uncle Mike Brown personified.

His mom had bailed him out during her lunch hour and ordered him to move back home until they could resolve his legal issues. His lawyer, Kincade, offered to buy him lunch so they could talk over his case. Neither felt confident that it was going to go away.

He used his old key to enter his mom's house. He threw his coat on the sofa in a token symbol of rebellion, knowing full well he would hang it up in the closet before his mom got home from work. He flopped onto the sofa and his dog Toby, a shelter mutt of dubious parentage, nudged his leg and was rewarded with a lethargic ear scratch.

John was aggravated by his mother's docile approach to a life placating the white man. The warrior code his uncle espoused fit better with his own sense of justice.

He had known little about the history or culture of his people before his mom sent him to spend his summers on the Wind River Reservation in his early teens. What he learned there had made him angry. The poverty was staggering, but the apathy was worse.

His mother claimed the government duped most of his people because they did not have an education. When he was a kid, John thought it was a ploy to get him to go to school, but now he saw that it was not just the Arapaho who could be tricked. Anyone who didn't understand greed, corruption, nor how to manipulate the law was in danger of getting royally screwed. Even his Uncle Mike agreed with that.

He had enrolled in some courses at the community college, aiming for an associate degree in law enforcement. He had told his mom he would see how it went, but he secretly harbored a dream of becoming a lawyer, figuring it was better to know your enemy from the inside.

If they charged him with a felony, he could kiss that dream goodbye.

The ring of the phone reverberated through the empty house. He made a dive for it.

"Yeah?"

"Hi John Stuart. Your mother told me you'd be staying at her place until we got this thing settled."

"Yeah. I'm here. Checking up on me?" John winced at how rude and surly he sounded. His mother had not raised him to be insolent, even to the Feds. "I mean, what do you want?"

"I'd like to help you if I can," Stuart said.

John laughed. "Sorry. Old joke. One of the top ten lies. 'I'm from the Federal Government and I'm here to help you.' Ranks right up there with 'The check's in the mail.'"

Stuart was silent.

John felt his mother's spirit hovering somewhere, displeased by his hostility. "No really, sorry. It just hit me funny."

"I'm glad you can be amused when things are going so badly for you," Stuart said.

John felt a chill race down his spine. He pulled his shoulders back and sat upright, unwilling to give in to the fear munching around the corners of his consciousness like a rat with a piece of garbage.

"What have you heard?"

"That Tucker is determined to charge you as a terrorist and somehow link you to Kellogg's murder."

"That's insane!" John stood and began pacing. "What we did with that bison head was the equivalent of TP-ing a math teacher's house. Irritating and messy, but not a terrorist activity."

"I agree."

"And as for . . . Wait. What? You agree?"

"Yes. I told Tucker the FBI would be fine if he wanted to reduce the charges, but he's adamant. At first, I thought it was because your uncle was an active member of AIM, which *is* considered a terrorist group. But the closer I looked, the more it didn't wash."

"What do you mean?" John sat on the arm of the sofa.

"I mean, why would a US Attorney buck the recommendation of the FBI?"

John was quiet. His stomach tensed as he rolled the conversation around in his mind. He could not make his uncle's radical rants jibe with Johnson's obvious attempt to find answers.

"I don't have any idea why he'd do that. You have any theories?" John asked.

"I think he may have an alternative agenda. To prove it, I need your help."

"I don't know the guy. How can I help?" John picked at a small worn place on the sofa arm, making it larger.

"You can tell me what your uncle hoped to do with the demonstration."

John felt the tug of loyalties . . . ancient and familial.

"Look, I'm no friend of the AIM movement," Agent Johnson prodded, "but I would hate to see you and your uncle dragged into the system on a trumped-up charge. You can keep your uncle safe if we can figure out what is the issue here."

"What you really want to do is not piss off my mom." John was trying to find Stuart's alternate agenda.

Johnson laughed. "True enough, but not so much I would let it influence my investigation."

Tempted, John tried once more to find a chink in the agent's rationale. "Look. I can't prove we didn't kill Kellogg. I was alone in my apartment, and I don't even know where my uncle was, but I am certain he had no beef with Kellogg."

"How do you know?"

"Because Uncle Mike kept saying he was a tool . . . not literally, but like a moron. They used him to do their legal dirty work."

"Who's they?"

"I don't know. Uncle Mike said there were some deep pockets

paying to smooth the way for a casino. He said the City Council and some guy in the legislature were steam rolling the plans."

"Why did it concern your uncle?"

John paced again. He ran a frustrated hand through his hair. "I–don't–know."

"You just followed him blindly? Dropped a bison head in front of a store for the fun of it?"

"Yes. I mean, no. He's family," John said, as if that explained everything. Toby nudged his knee for reassurance. John automatically scratched him behind the ears.

"Okay. I get that. But didn't he give you some justification, some philosophy about why?"

"He said it was just another instance of the white man using power and manipulation to wring a dime out of the Native American. He said they would build the casino over the bones of our ancestors. You know, junk like that." John had to admit it sounded absurd when he said it aloud.

Agent Stuart Johnson felt the hair rise on the back of his neck. His hand drifted up to rub it unconsciously. "Maybe it's not junk, John."

"What do you mean?"

"Just a hunch. I can feel all the pieces drifting together, but I'm not there yet. I'll keep in touch." Johnson clicked off.

SEATED AT HANK'S DESK, DARCY LOOKED AT HER NOTES on her laptop. The more she ran over them in her mind, the less sense she could make of the whole mess.

A bison head dropped in front of an empty furniture store with an arrow and a clipping of an old AIM demonstration. Someone murdered Latham Kellogg, and they arrested Mike Brown and John Blue Feather on suspicion. Tucker was manic about charging them with terrorism, even though there was no proof of terrorist activity.

"What the hell am I missing?" she said loud enough that Hank leaned over her shoulder to look at her screen.

Holed up in his office waiting for reports was driving him crazy.

"You forgot to add James Frye's murder in Encampment," he supplied. "Yes, I'm still holding!" he half shouted into his phone.

"How is that connected to Kellogg?"

Hank blew out a sigh. He might as well walk it through with Darcy. Help clarify his own theories.

"Same MO, ballistics is checking the bullet, but I'm pretty sure it's from the same gun."

"But why? It makes no sense." Darcy typed in Frye's murder, then looked over her shoulder at Hank. "That would exonerate John and his uncle, right?"

"We don't know yet. We are still waiting for the TOD. For all we know, one or both of them could have done it." He spoke into the phone again, "Yeah? Well, call me back when you find something out." He clicked his phone off and tossed it on top of some file folders on his desk in disgust.

"You need to work on your people skills."

"No, I need a forensic pathologist who isn't backlogged in Colorado with a huge caseload."

"No luck getting the information from the autopsies?"

"TOD on Kellogg was ascertained at the scene, but Frye's body wasn't found right away so it requires more investigation. Ballistics is still working on identifying the ammunition found at both scenes. 'Dufus Twins' identities still haven't been confirmed with the prints they left of the photo."

"And we still don't know what the motive is . . . if there is any."

"There's always a motive," Hank said as he slipped into his heavy jacket. "Right now, I'm going to check with Carl Stevens. There's something wonky about that empty furniture building."

Darcy scrambled into her ski jacket and pulled on a hat. "Why Stevens? What does he have to do with this?"

Hank held the door open. "This is police business. You can listen, but you cannot use anything we learn until I give you the go-ahead. You clear?"

Darcy nodded. She spun around and walked backward to face Hank. "Why Stevens?"

Hank grabbed her arm and turned her back around without

missing a step. He leaned close to her ear. "Stevens is a member of the City Council who heads up the Downtown Development Committee. If anyone knows what's going on with this building, he should."

They fought through the pelting snow to reach Hank's black pickup. Darcy jumped in and waited for Hank to get in the other side.

"Why do you think something's wonky? Is that a technical term?" The corners of her mouth turned up slightly and her eyes glittered.

"Cute. They've connected both victims to the building. Kellogg because he was part of the consortium and Frye because he was the coroner when bones were found beneath the building during an earlier excavation. He first claimed they were just animal bones, but later reversed himself and said that 'after further study' the bones appeared to belong to an older Native American lady and a small male child.'"

"How did you find that out?"

"It's all a matter of public record if you know where to look. Frye retired soon after and then someone killed him. Someone has plans for that piece of real estate worth killing for." Hank pulled into a space in front of Steven's Plumbing.

"You stay behind me and try to be invisible."

Hank gave Darcy a hand as she wiggled out of her seat and jumped onto the icy street.

Once inside, he flashed his badge at the redhead behind the counter. "I would like to speak with Carl if he has a moment," Hank said as she dithered.

"Ah . . . Carl . . . I mean, Mr. Stevens is on the phone right now, but . . . I ah . . . I'd be happy to let him know you're here." She walked down the long hallway toward the back of the building.

"Do you get off on making unsuspecting females go all gooey?" Darcy asked.

Hank's grin widened, and Darcy hated that her heart fluttered a beat too. "Feeling a little green around the gills, Darcy?"

"No. Just wondered if it was an interviewing technique. They teach you that at the academy?"

"Nope. Just using what the good Lord gave me."

"Carl will see you now." Miss Redhead flashed her own high wattage grin at Hank.

"I feel like I just ducked under Harry Potter's Cloak of Invisibility," Darcy muttered on the way down the hall.

"Just the way I like it." Hank knocked perfunctorily before he pushed open the frosted glass-paned door. He flashed his badge and shook Carl Stevens' hand.

"Sit down. Can I get you a cup of coffee?" He shouted out the door, "Cindy? We need some coffee in here."

"None for me, thanks." Hank took one of the chairs in front of an old oak desk piled high with invoices and an old adding machine.

Darcy sat in the other chair and tried to get a feel for Carl Stevens from his office. Messy desk. A dusty picture in a cheap black metal frame of what she guessed was his family. Stevens was sitting next to two painfully thin blondes. Two young girls around 12 or 13 sat on stools in front of their parents. The girls looked like their mother, and all wore the phony poses of a Christmas card picture.

"Nice family," Darcy commented.

"Huh? Oh yeah." Stevens self-consciously wiped a layer of dust off the top of the frame. "Not very recent. Fact is my girls are at the University now. Just never got around to changing out the picture."

As if he had caught himself babbling, he turned to Hank. "Uhm, what can I do for you, Detective?"

"I was wondering if you knew of any plans in the works for the old Thompson's Furniture building."

Darcy watched Stevens' face lose the blotchy-red color it started with and bleach to the color of chalk.

"Uh . . . I don't quite know what you mean?" Stevens licked his liver-colored lips.

"I mean," Hank leaned in a little, "someone shot Latham Kellogg there, but before he was murdered, he said he was the representative of a consortium who now owned the building. Is that true?"

"Not precisely. No. Uh . . . the sale has not been finalized so far as I know, but they have sent good faith money to the Thompsons in Florida."

"How much good faith?" Darcy asked, ignoring Hank's knee nudge.

Stevens' watery green eyes shifted to her. "I am not privy to the amount. Ned Schuler was handling the deal."

"What outfit is he with?" Hank asked.

"Diamond Realty."

"What were the plans for the building, Mr. Stevens?" Darcy asked. "As the chairman of the Downtown Development Committee, weren't you consulted or at least informed about the plans for such a large section of downtown real estate?" She felt Hank's finger poking her in the back.

"I . . . ah . . . Cindy!" Stevens crossed to the door and flung it open to yell down the hall. "What the hell took you so long?" he asked as he took the cup from her.

"Well, I needed to open more of the Latte mix you like so well. You guys sure you don't want anything?" she asked, looking directly at Hank.

"No. We're almost done here," Hank answered. He focused again on Stevens. "Do you know what the planned use was?"

Stevens tried to buy time by blowing on his steaming cup of latte. The room fell silent apart from his asthmatic huffing over his cup. He finally gave it up.

"Truth to tell, the details are a little fuzzy. I think they have something to do with a tourist attraction. I believe I heard mention of some of the Arapahos off the Wind River Reservation, but I don't know exactly. They aren't required to go through my committee for approval, you know."

He sounded petulant to Darcy. She opened her mouth to follow up, but Hank stood, pulling her with him.

"Thank you for your time, Mr. Stevens. If you think of anything else, don't hesitate to call me." Hank handed him his card and pushed Darcy gently, but firmly, from the room.

"What's with the rush back there?" she asked once they were back in the truck. "We had him rattled."

"Yes. But there is a fine line between rattling and pushing until they run for the hills. I'd be willing to bet he's on the phone with Ned Schuler right now, warning him we're heading his way."

"Then we'd better step on it."

"No. I don't want to talk to Schuler right now." Hank pulled out his phone from the holster on his belt. "Stuart? Hank. I think you're right."

CHAPTER 22

Vince Sassano and Tony Triolo could not wait to get back to the cabin and grab their stuff. They were so anxious they dismissed the rusted out blue pickup bouncing along the rutted road behind them.

"Some old farmer guy is all," Tony said. "Doubt if he could catch us if he wanted to. He's got a load of hay in the back." Tony laughed at the thought of some jerk-hayseed causing them trouble.

"Just keep an eye on him," Vince said, cursing as they ran over another frozen rut. "God, these roads are a bitch to drive. Damned near jerked my arm out of the socket."

"Farmer boy just turned down a side road. Take it a little easy on the bumps!"

"You wanna drive?"

"Nah."

"Then shut the fuck up." Vince was nursing a small headache and this trip to town and back was stomping on his last nerve.

He finally pulled the black SUV into a clearing and up to the cabin door. Smoke billowed out of the chimney, and the glow from the windows made the place look almost friendly.

The men jumped out and slammed their doors. Vince saw Adkins pull back the curtain and peer out. Stupid jerk was going to get them caught.

He smashed through the door in time to see Adkins leap back, catch his foot on the blankets, and fall on his ass.

"What did I tell you about staying away from the windows?"

Adkins scooted on his butt as far away as he could before he bumped into a chair.

"But . . . but . . . I knew it was you guys," he said.

"How the hell did you know? It could've been some nosey hunter or farmer from around here." Vince glared down at him.

Tony pulled out his gun. "Let me pop him, Vince. Just one little pop. Teach him a lesson."

"Maybe later," Vince snarled as he wrenched Adkins from the floor and gave him a shove toward a hard wooden chair. "Now sit over there and shut up. Let's get our shit packed up."

Tony didn't need any coaxing. Even the relative rusticity of Cheyenne was better than this drafty worm-infested cabin in the backwoods of hell. He shoved his gun back into the harness he always wore.

"Right with ya."

"So, you're taking me back, right? You found out I was right about Darcy."

Vince walked over and backhanded Adkins so hard he fell off the chair. "I said, shut up."

Adkins wiped his mouth on his sleeve and saw the red bloodstain. Tears welled, but he swallowed the sob that almost escaped. He could not believe this was happening to him. He had never been so scared in all his life. He was only 23 years old. An errant thought flitted across his scrambled gray matter that if he couldn't control Darcy as promised, this wouldn't be the last blood he'd shed. He shivered uncontrollably. He scrunched into the smallest blanket he could and rested his head on his knees. He wished he knew how to pray.

WYOMING STATE SENATOR PETE LOMAN was on a conference call with City Councilman Carl Stevens and District Attorney Patrick Tucker.

"Get this straightened out and make that old degenerate in

Vegas call off his dogs. I am in sensitive negotiations here, and two murders and a kidnapping are not helping our cause."

"Now look here, Loman—" Patrick Tucker began.

"You tell that idiot this isn't his turf," Loman said.

"Pete, be reasonable," Stevens jumped in. "None of us can dictate terms. We've all been paid to make this happen and—"

"And the FBI is already sniffing around," Loman finished. "Yeah, I know. What were you thinking, Tucker, trying to prosecute a charge of terrorism? All I asked you to do was to get those Native American radicals out of the spotlight and you made it worse."

"I thought you wanted them to go away. A charge of vandalism isn't going to help us."

"You idiot. Charge them with murder. Get the Don to get us some legit evidence we can plant. Get it fast because this investigation is going to unravel all our plans."

"What if he doesn't agree?"

"Then we can all kiss our careers, our six-figured windfalls, and any promise of more, goodbye. That flushing sound you hear will be us." Loman clicked off.

Loman reached into his deep side drawer and pulled out some Glenlivet XXV. He poured the golden amber liquid into his crystal glass. The light shimmered with gilded flashes as he held it.

He took a sip and held the whisky on his tongue, savoring the spicy tang and the heady aroma of the oak casks it had rested in for so long.

Yes, he thought to himself. He liked the finer things in life and was determined to have them. He's was wasted in this rural backwater. But others had broken out. He knew his destiny spelled out at least a place in the US Senate. He took another sip and rolled it over his tongue. Or . . . maybe even the Presidency. Stranger things had happened.

DARCY PUNCHED IN THE NUMBER THE secretary at Anderson Construction had given her. She slouched low in the uncomfortable captain's chair.

Hank sat across from her, waiting on his landline and looking about as friendly as a bear coming out of hibernation.

Someone picked up Darcy's call. "Is this Terry Anderson?"

"Yes," came the reply.

"This is Darcy Moreland from Channel 23 News. I was wondering if I could have a few minutes of your time to talk about Thompson's Furniture Store."

"What about it? That was three years ago."

"Well, I was just wondering about the bones found on site—"

"Hey, I did all that by the book. I called Coroner Frye just like I'm supposed to, and he said they were just animal bones, so we piled them in a box like he asked and continued with the project."

"Recently, Coroner Frye admitted he'd made a mistake. Did you hear about that?"

"Yeah . . . but my job was done. I gotta go."

"One more thing, Mr. Anderson. Did they look like animal bones to you?"

Darcy knew he would probably hang up. If not, she thought he might try to avoid answering.

"No. They looked human to me. That bothered me, but I did what he told me to do. I gotta go," he repeated, and then hung up.

"I'll be damned!"

"What?" Hank's face brightened in hope.

"That was Terry Anderson, and I asked him—"

"Yeah. I heard your side of the conversation. What did he say?" He rested the phone on his chest. He was still on hold.

"He said he thought they looked human, and it bothered him, but Coroner Frye insisted they were animal bones."

"This connects Frye to a cover-up," Hank said.

"Looks that way. I'm guessing squashing any chance of having the project shut down for a thirty-day investigation was the motivating factor for Frye's initial 'mistake.' He probably got paid to look the other way."

"So, who paid Frye initially and then who paid him to correct the mistake and ID the bones as human?"

"Beats me," Darcy said.

"Why would it be important to ID the bones as Native American?" Hank asked.

Darcy dropped her feet to the floor. "Stop asking me questions I can't answer. You're the detective. Detect."

Hank raised his phone back to his ear. "Yeah. I'm still here. So, no bugs on Frye? Can you give me your best guess?" Hank said into the phone. "Okay. A week judging from the moldy bread on the table? Any trace? Okay, thanks. Get back to me as soon as you can." He hung up and turned back to Darcy. "That was the Albany County Coroner."

"I figured. Now we can go," Darcy said as she started packing up her bag with the items she had scattered on Hank's desk. She threw in her phone, her gloves, half an energy bar, her lip balm, and a packet of disinfectant wipes.

Hank stared at the oddly hypnotizing process. "You could fit a toddler in there."

Darcy laughed. "Yeah, I know. Great, huh?"

"Where do you think you're going now that you've packed up all your expeditionary supplies?"

"I thought I'd tag Netters and have him meet me at Pete Loman's office."

"Why?"

"Well, it occurs to me that Loman is chairman of the State Senate's Indian Affairs Committee, and he might know why Frye changed his determination."

"You're going to ambush him with Netters in tow and ask him what's going on?"

"Got a better idea?" Darcy swung her bag over her shoulder and headed for the door.

"Not at the moment," Hank said softly as he followed her out. Darcy was already calling Netters.

BILL NETTERS WAS THRILLED WHEN DARCY called. All of his fantasies of having a hot chick to hang out with him 24/7 were shot.

Jody Tessler was a professional. After several tactical defeats, Netter gave up and took the couch, leaving Jody his large comfy bed.

Netters grabbed his equipment off the cluttered dining room table, which once belonged to his Grandma Johnson. He packed his favorite Canon XL-H1 HD camera, checked the lenses and tripod, and closed his bag.

"All set," he said to Officer Tessler's back.

She turned and looked at him. "I'll let you know when I've gotten clearance."

Netters shrugged into his Patagonia jacket and wound his knitted scarf once around his neck. "Yeah, well, I'll meet you at Senator Loman's office." He strode to the door.

Jody Tessler was a scant 5'3" but she was quick. She blocked the door before he got there. Hands on her hips and back ramrod straight, she lifted her chin, so her green eyes bored into his. Netters couldn't help thinking of a banty rooster in full fighting stance.

"You are not going anywhere without me."

"Then get your coat, Testy. I'm on a story." He tossed her the bright blue ski jacket from the coat rack by the door.

She caught it and pulled it on. "What did you call me?"

"Testy as in grumpy, cranky, hard to get along with. It fits, huh?" Netters said.

Jody Tessler struggled for composure. She opened and closed her mouth a couple of times, then swallowed whatever retort she had planned. Her phone rang.

She listened, said, "Yes, sir," and then stuffed the phone in her back jeans pocket. "Let's go."

She was halfway down the front steps of his condo, doing a visual scan of the neighborhood before he caught up. He shifted his heavy bag to the other shoulder and shortened his steps to match hers.

Slipping his arm around her shoulders, he was pleased she didn't shrug it off. He knew she wanted to.

"I guess that was Hank saying it was okay?"

"Detective Nelson authorized me to take you to Senator Loman's office, yes."

"Allow me." Netters bowed with mock civility and held the door to his SUV open for her.

He got in his side and put the key in the ignition. Jody put her hand over his to stop him.

"Bill, I know you think I'm being a real hard-ass—"

"No. Why would I think that?"

"This is my first actual assignment outside of investigating lost bicycles or drunken brawls. I'm new to this."

"This is my first time having a protective custodian so I'd say we're even."

"It isn't that I don't find you attractive . . . in a scraggly, sort of artsy way."

"I think I'm going to pink right up and blush if you don't stop, Miss Jody."

She blinked twice, started to chuckle, and then gave in to a gut rolling laugh.

Netters liked the sound. It warmed him.

They pulled into a spot in front of Loman's downtown office. Netters slid the side door open and retrieved his bag as he looked around to see if Darcy was there yet.

Joining Jody was on the sidewalk, she glanced around in time to see Hank and Darcy crossing the intersection to the south.

"You guys look jolly," Darcy said, when they caught up with them. "Here's the deal. We're going in unannounced, so I can't be sure of our reception—"

"Oh boy! Run and gun. My favorite," Netters said as he draped his arm across Jody's shoulders.

Jody laughed and peered up at him. "What are you? A junior high nerd boy?"

"Just try to keep up, Testy." Netters strode past them and into the lobby out of the wind.

"Testy?" Darcy and Hank asked together.

"His not very kind nickname for me," Jody admitted as they climbed the steps together.

"Take heart, Officer Tessler. He calls Darcy Calamity." Hank held the door and Darcy glared at him as she passed.

Netters unpacked his camera and handed the bag to Jody. "Guard this with your life."

"Don't be absurd. I'm guarding you, not your equipment."

Netters ignored her and trailed Darcy into the outer office.

As she entered, Darcy went instantly into full-blown attack mode.

"I just need a few minutes of the Senator's time." Darcy slipped out of her heavy coat and tossed it and her scarf onto one of the chairs in the waiting room.

Netters passed her the mic like a baton in a relay.

Connie Tibbets, Senator Loman's long-time secretary, watched the flight of clothing and reacted like it was a gauntlet being thrown down.

"See here, Ms. Moreland. I don't care who you represent. You don't have an appointment and Mr. Loman is due at a client's office." Although not a steel gray hair on her perfectly coifed head moved, Connie Tibbets' flush betrayed her lie.

"We have a citizen's legislator in this great state of ours to keep our legislators responsive to the questions of the citizens. And since I represent the citizens and their right to know . . ." Darcy paused and gestured over her shoulder at Netters to get the shot.

"What is going on here?" Senator Loman hurtled through his heavy office door into reception. He surveyed the small group, recognized the camera emblazoned with the Channel 23 logo, noted the blinking red record-on light, and shifted his gaze to Darcy. His unruffled calm fooled no one.

"Why, Ms. Moreland isn't it? Did we have an interview scheduled today?"

"No, Senator. We were wondering if you would care to comment regarding some peculiarities in recent events."

"What events would those be?" His hand rested on the doorknob as if contemplating an escape.

"I have been covering a story lately involving the empty Thompson's Furniture store, a severed bison head, and the subsequent murder of Latham Kellogg, a representative of a mysterious consortium. Then there was the murder of former Laramie County Coroner James Frye and your Native American Affairs Committee's recent recommendation that Thompson's be declared

a sacred Native American site and be returned to their governance."
Darcy looked at Hank, Jody, and Netters. "Did I miss anything?"
All three shook their heads.

When she turned back to Loman, he had turned white except
for two ruddy splotches of color on his cheeks.

"I think, Ms. Moreland, you have a monumental tangle of
events which are not necessarily connected. Why don't we go into
my office so we can clarify any confusion you might have?"

"Fine with me." Darcy signaled Netters to stop recording.

Loman stood by the now open door. Darcy noted the fine
sheen of sweat on his upper lip as Hank, Jody, and Netters followed
behind her.

Hank subtly tucked his suit coat back to display his CPD badge
hanging from his belt as he went through the door.

"Hold all my calls," Loman said to Ms. Tibbets before he closed
the door softly. He glided silently across the room over sumptu-
ous dove gray carpeting and slipped behind an ornately carved
mahogany desk.

"Is this to be an official police investigation?" Loman looked
directly at Hank.

"Not unless you want it to be. I'm here as an observer," Hank
paused, "for now."

"Please sit down all of you." Loman's office boasted a dark burgundy camel backed sofa and several chairs scattered strategically.

Hank and Jody took seats on the sofa, Darcy perched on one
of the client chairs, and Netters positioned himself off to the side.

"Should I set up a tripod, Darcy?" Netters asked.

"Would you mind?" Darcy looked at Loman.

Loman's gray-green eyes flicked around the office and ultimately rested on Darcy. "Of course not, Ms. Darcy. I am afraid you
will not find much of a story here, though."

Darcy dug into her bag and pulled out her small moleskin notebook. When Netters finished setting up, she nodded, and the red
record-on button flashed like a ruby. Darcy shifted her shoulders
to the right and her knees to her left.

"Ready?" she asked.

Loman folded his hands on top of his polished desk and looked into the camera like a good-hearted uncle indulging his favorite niece.

"What would you like me to clarify, Ms. Moreland?"

"Why don't we start at the end and go backwards? You are chairman of the Native American Affairs Committee in the state legislature. Is that correct?"

"Yes."

Darcy saw his shoulders relax minutely. "Is it also true your committee has recently recommended the vacant downtown furniture store be ceded back to the Arapaho tribe?"

"Yes, that is true. Our poor treatment of Native Americans sadly tarnished so much of our state history. We try to right our past wrongs when we can and serve justice wherever possible."

"Precisely what wrongs has the Committee committed concerning Thompson's?"

Loman's steady gaze faltered. "It came to our attention that someone uncovered the remains of an older Native American woman and a small child during a recent renovation."

"That renovation occurred in September three years ago. Is that correct, Senator?"

Loman's eyes searched his ruthlessly organized desk for a random file, then gave it up. "Yes, that is correct."

"And why was there such a delay in identifying the remains?"

"I don't really know." Loman shifted toward Darcy as if sharing a confidence. "I think they made some mistake in the County Coroner's office, and it took that long to rectify it. I can assure you as soon as they apprised our committee of the situation, we made arrangements to have those remains interred here in the cemetery."

"Senator Loman, do you think it is a coincidence James Frye, the coroner at the time of the mistake, corrected his report, promptly retired, and was later found shot dead in a hunting cabin outside of Encampment, Wyoming?"

"I don't have any opinion about those events, but to attach that unfortunate hunting accident to the long-ago deaths of the Native American woman and young boy is specious and unfounded."

"A hunting accident?" Darcy raised a brow.

"Well, what else?"

"You tell me, Senator."

"I have no knowledge of Mr. Frye's death."

"How about Mr. Latham Kellogg? Do you have any knowledge about the consortium he was working for?"

"No, I'm afraid not. I only know they informed my committee that Native American remains had been found. We are endeavoring to create something positive from a grievous mistake. I'm sorry, Ms. Moreland. I can't answer any more of your questions."

"Can't or won't?" Darcy asked.

Loman stood from behind his desk. "I really must ask you to leave now." His gray-green eyes glowered at her.

Darcy shrugged, signaling Netters to stop recording. "Thank you for your time, Senator." Darcy held out her hand to shake his. He hesitated only a heartbeat before he took it.

Loman watched the four of them leave. As soon as the door closed, he sank into his chair, dabbed at the sweat on his lip, and picked up his phone.

CHAPTER 23

Officer Randy Cummings bounced over the ruts and small snow-covered boulders in his father's rusty blue 1957 Ford F-100 pickup. It was the perfect vehicle for what he needed. His dad had been reluctant to lend it because he had some cows to feed, but Randy promised to take care of the feeding in exchange for lending the truck.

Randy spotted some of their cows on the low-lying meadow they rented from the BLM every year for as long as he could remember. He dragged the truck into the herd, and the cows began milling around. They recognized the truck.

He made quick work of cutting the bailing wire and tossing the hay off the back. Cows fed, Randy swung into the truck and doubled back to where he had stopped following the black SUV.

Parking on a small bluff overlooking the cabin, Randy looked through his binoculars. He saw the black SUV parked in front of old Gary Lacey's hunting cabin. Randy knew Gary had been laid up this year from a back injury, so he damn sure wasn't in there.

Randy pulled out his phone and dialed the number Detective Nelson had given him.

"Detective Nelson. What have you got for me, Cummings?"

"Sir, you were right. They came right back here. I haven't caught sight of the hostage yet, but the two guys I followed are packing up the car."

"Stay with them, Cummings. If they leave Adkins unattended, wait until it is clear and get him. If they take him with them, follow them. What are you driving, by the way?"

Cummings chuckled a little. "My dad's old Ford pickup, sir. And I am way out of uniform. I'm wearing my haying hat, an old Acme straw. Think it's been run over a time or two."

"Great. Even if they spot you, they won't make you."

"They already spotted me, sir, on the way in. I turned off on county road 54 and fed some of our cows, then doubled back. I look like I belong here."

"Keep on them, Officer. Call headquarters if you need backup."

"Will do, sir." Cummings shut off his phone and picked up his binoculars.

He saw the two perps drag Adkins out to the SUV and toss him into the back seat. Adkins' hands were bound behind his back. Cummings thought Adkins looked pretty good, all things considered. He watched them pull away from the now darkened cabin and head back down the narrow rutted road.

Born and raised in this area, Randy Cummings deliberately drove off-road to another outcropping where he could watch the SUV lumber down the narrow dirt path. From here, he could easily see which way they turned at the intersection. He was pretty sure they were heading back toward Cheyenne, but he'd watch them carefully before he notified Detective Nelson.

VINCE SASSANO TRIED TO STEER AS THEY BUMPED ALONG, heading for the interstate and listening to the man screaming on the phone. Finally, he gave up and pulled off the road, slamming the SUV into neutral.

"Yes, sir," Vince said. "I don't know what we could have done differently. Evidently, his family does not value this little creep."

Adkins whimpered in the back seat. Vince shot Tony an angry grimace. Tony turned from the front seat and jammed the barrel of his gun up under Adkins' jaw to keep him quiet.

"Yes, sir," Vince continued. "Do you want us to kill him? I understand. We'll call you after we've assessed the situation in Cheyenne.

Soon, yes, sir. Soon." He stabbed his phone off and dropped it into the cup holder.

"What's up?" Tony turned halfway forward again.

"That was the old man. That Darcy reporter is still making waves. Boss wants us to dump this punk and go back to town."

Tony jumped out of his door and dragged Adkins from the back. He raised his gun to Adkins' forehead.

"Knock it off. The boss said not to kill him."

"Ah hell! Why not?" Tony whined.

"Because we might need his uncle's good grace later. No point ticking his uncle off permanently if we don't have to."

"Please. Please don't leave me out here. I'll freeze to death. I can pay you. I have money. Please, just take me back to town. I won't tell anyone anything."

"Shut him up, will ya?" Vince said.

He watched impassively as Tony swung and hit Adkins' temple, knocking him to the ground. Adkins screamed, then curled up on the snow in a fetal slump, holding head and sobbing softly.

"What a waste of sperm," Tony commented. As they pulled away, Tony took aim and shot Adkins as they passed.

Adkins shrieked. Tony laughed.

Vince smacked his shoulder hard. "The old man said not to kill him."

"Ah Vince. I got him in the ass. It's a long way from his heart."

Cummings, watching from above, saw the whole drama unfold below. He stood helpless, watching as the perps pulled away, leaving Adkins on the ground.

From here, Cummings couldn't tell how badly Adkins was shot. Everything in him wanted to race down and help the poor guy, but his training told him there was more danger in rushing in before they got completely out of the area. Another bullet could reach Adkins faster than he could.

He waited until he saw them turn onto the interstate heading for Cheyenne, then gunned his dad's old pickup and rattled down the bluff, not bothering to find a road. He jumped out of the cab before the truck came to a complete stop and leaned in.

"Mr. Adkins. I'm Randy Cummings from the CPD. Where are you hit?"

"My ass! My ass! He shot me in the ass!" Adkins screamed between sobs.

"Well, thank God for that. Good thing," Randy said as he cut through the plastic tie binding Adkins' wrists.

Adkins rose to his elbow and glared at the pink-faced kid leaning over him. "Good? Good? Have you ever been shot?"

"Yeah," Randy chuckled. "My brother shot me in the leg once when we were out hunting elk. Hurts like a hell, I know."

"You don't know shit! Get me an ambulance, you moron!"

"I can get you to town faster, Mr. Adkins. Just hold on."

Cummings lifted Adkins under the arms into an upright position, slung one of Adkins' arms around his neck for support, and walked him to the truck.

He gently placed Adkins into the passenger seat. "You might want to sit on your uninjured cheek, Mr. Adkins. The roads are a little bumpy through here, but then we'll be on the interstate, and I'll get you to the hospital in a jiffy."

Adkins leaned sideways on the battered seat and moaned at every bump on the road.

Randy made a call to Hank and reported Adkins' injury and that he was taking him to the hospital.

"THAT WENT WELL," DARCY SAID as she all but skipped down the steps. "If this doesn't stir the pot, nothing will."

"Ever hear the saying about the inadvisability of teasing a rabid dog?" Hank asked as he handed her into his truck.

"But sugar, I have you to protect me." She laughed as he slammed the door in her face.

Netters pulled alongside them in the bank parking lot and Hank lowered his window. "Want me to take this to the station to edit?" he asked Darcy.

"Yeah, I'll meet you there. Fill Zach in on the interview. I know he can't air it until Adkins is recovered, but at least he'll know we're getting the reports out."

Netters saluted and zoomed off. Hank's phone rang.

"What's up, Cummings?"

Darcy watched Hank go rigid. A tentative grin spread across his face. He let loose a whoop of a laugh before he could stop himself.

"Call his uncle and notify Zach Horton at the station. We'll come over and meet you there." He clicked off. Still smiling, Hank said, "We found Adkins."

"Where? Oh Hank, that's wonderful! Is he okay?"

"Well . . ." Hank choked, trying to contain his laughter. "They shot him in the ass, but other than that . . ." Hank gave up and roared with laughter.

Darcy slapped his arm. "Hank be serious. Where is he?"

"Cummings took him to the hospital. I said we'd be there in a minute." Hank wiped the laughter tears from his eyes.

Darcy fished her phone from her bag and speed-dialed Netters. "Change of plans. Meet us at the hospital." She looked at Hank. "Emergency room?" He nodded. She spoke into the phone again, "Emergency room. We've found Adkins. See you there."

The two vehicles reached the hospital almost simultaneously, but while Hank could park in the loading zone, Netters had to find a space in the multi-level parking lot next to the hospital.

Hank flashed his badge at the nurse manning the admissions' desk and she waved them through. They had no trouble finding Adkins. When they reached the emergency room's lobby, he was behind a privacy curtain bellowing about the pain.

Hank turned to Cummings, who hovered just outside of the curtained area. He looked like a cowboy straight from the range with his scuffed boots, faded jeans, and the beat-up Acme hat he kept turning it around in his hands.

Adkins screamed louder as the ER nurse rolled him into a treatment room.

"Go on back to the station and file your report, Cummings. Then go home. Good job," Hank said.

"Yes sir, if you think that's best." He left with a nod to Darcy and one last lingering look over his shoulder.

Darcy sat with Netters and Officer Tessler in the waiting room since they had no official standing.

Hank was back in the hallway that connected the exam rooms. He caught Adkin's doctor as he exited the room. "I am Detective Hank Nelson, CPD." He flashed his badge. "I need to question him as soon as possible. Will the local anesthetic help calm him?"

"I hope so. I'll let you know when you can see him."

"Thanks, doctor. I'll be in reception area."

Hank sat beside Darcy, Netters, and Tessler.

"How's he doing?" Netters asked.

"He's doing ok. He's a little spooked, but the doc said his condition isn't life-threatening," Hank said.

"Is he going to give us an interview?" Netters looked at Darcy.

"Not until he gives me a statement," Hank said. "He's a little shook up. It is possible he may fall asleep by the time I'm finished."

Darcy's phone rang. It was Zach. "Hi. Yeah, he looks okay, but Hank wants to get his statement before we can get permission to interview him. Netters and I will check in with you as soon as we can." She hung up.

"Zach?" Netters asked.

"Uhm hum," she grunted in reply, and went back to leafing through her magazine.

Later, all four of them watched in fascination as Uncle Arnie roared in and through the emergency waiting room.

"Where is he? Where did you put my boy?"

There were some mutters and a few utterings of, "Please be quiet, sir" before Uncle Arnie evidently found Adkins and quieted down. After a brief wait, he came to join the others in the waiting room.

"How is he, sir?" Hank asked.

"Pretty damned shaken up, I can tell you. What the hell is this world coming to when a boy from an excellent family is stolen off the street?"

"Would it be better if Adkins was from a bad family?" Darcy couldn't help but ask.

Arnold Christenson turned on her, his watery blue eyes flashing under bushy white eyebrows. "You watch your tone, young lady. My boy seems to think you are to blame for all this. I told Zach Horton I want an investigation and so help me, if it's true, losing your job will be the least of your worries."

"Wait just a New York minute, Mr. Christenson. Your nephew brought this on himself through–" Darcy sputtered.

"We'll wait over there until I can take his statement, Mr. Christenson." Hank steered Darcy to the far end of the room.

"What are you doing?" Darcy asked in a raspy stage whisper.

"Saving your job. You were about to blast several holes in Uncle Arnie's belief that Adkins is the sun in the heavens. No good can come of that."

"He doesn't know him like we do."

"You go head-to-head with him about Adkins, who do you think Uncle Arnie's going to side with? Let Zach diffuse this one. He's good at smoothing rough edges. That's why he gets the corner office."

At that moment, an older, beautifully groomed lady in an expensive-looking royal blue wool coat flew up to the reception desk.

"I am Mrs. Tamora Tabor Adkins. My brother called and told me my son has been shot. I need to see him."

Before the nurse could say anything, Uncle Arnold had rushed to her side and was guiding her to a chair.

"Now, Tam. He's okay." Arnold pulled out a handkerchief to wipe his brow.

"I sent him to you so you could keep him safe while I kept my other companies going. Somehow, you got him kidnapped and shot. What the hell is going on?"

"I did just like you said, Tam. I got him set up at the station and he fit right in."

Darcy coughed loudly enough to draw attention. "Bad cold," she explained to the room.

"It was all her fault," Arnie accused, pointing at Darcy. "She hated him from the start. I wanted Zach Horton to fire her, but he always took her side."

"As his mother, not to mention the controlling stockholder, you should have apprised me of these issues. You never mentioned them in the weekly reports."

Arnie glared at Darcy. "It was just petty jealousy. She knew Bryce was being groomed to take over some day."

"I don't quite believe you, Arnie. As soon as I make sure my son is okay, I will look into the problems personally. Be advised, if I find anything that doesn't fit your narrative, I will can you, brother or no brother."

"But, but" Arie stuttered, "you can't fire me. I'm a stockholder."

"You are a minority stockholder, and that was a gift to placate our mother who wanted to see you employed before she died," Mrs. Adkins replied sharply. "She's dead now."

A SMALL GROUP GATHERED AROUND A LARGE table at the "Sorry Closed Café so named because Richard Myers who owned the place could never remember to turn the sign over to Open." Condensation fogged up the large picture windows. It diffused the view of the snow wafting slowly outside, much like cheesecloth over a lens to shoot an aging actor during the pre-Botox days.

"A storm is kind of pretty to watch as long as you're warm and dry, isn't it?" Mary Blue Feather commented, trying to cut through the palpable hostility at the table.

She stared at her surly brother, then shifted her gaze to Stuart Johnson, who sat in a rigid mirror image of her brother across the table.

"Look Mary, I came because of the boy, but don't ask me to make nice with Mr. FBI over there," Mike Brown said.

"Mr. Brown," Darren Kincade, John Blue Feather's lawyer, jumped in, "I asked for this meeting. Agent Johnson is here because he thinks he knows why US Attorney Tucker may press for a more serious charge. I think we should listen."

"I'm listening." Mike Brown folded his beefy arms across his chest.

"I did some digging about Latham Kellogg. Seems he is in the system as a Harvard lawyer who specialized in acquisitions," Stuart said.

"What has that got to do with this mess?" Mary asked.

"Well, it seems Sun Corporation–headquartered in Las Vegas, Nevada–put Kellogg on retainer."

"So what? Stop dragging this out, Johnson," Mike Brown said.

"Let Stuart talk Michael," Mary said. She reached over and took her brother's hand.

"Sun Corporation is a conglomerate with multi-layered holdings, but the one that rang my chimes was Lariat Entertainment, Inc."

"What is that Agent Johnson?" Kincade asked.

"Just call me Stuart. This isn't official, it's personal." He winked at Mary. "Anyway, Lariat Entertainment has," Stuart consulted his notes, "entered into development agreements for various Native American-owned casino properties. They intend to manage such casinos when applicable regulatory approvals have been received and other contingencies have been satisfied."

"You mean Kellogg was trying to buy Thompson's old store to make it into a casino?" John Blue Feather clarified.

"Not just any casino. He wanted to make it Native American owned. Isn't that right, *Agent* Johnson?" Mike Brown's face colored darkly.

"Yes, I think that's right."

"But Stuart," Mary wrinkled her brow, "I don't get what this has to do with either Michael or Johnny."

"I'm not sure. There is no paper trail from Kellogg to Lariat, except he has helped them in that capacity in the past. But if it is about somehow acquiring the land for a Native American casino, it would stand to reason that they would be super sensitive about AIM or any other Native American group calling attention to the transactions until everything is all signed and sealed up."

"Is that why you were protesting, Michael? Did you know they were planning on building a casino?" Mary asked.

"I had heard rumblings. Whenever someone from the outside starts investigating the Tribal Council, we face problems. Kellogg was asking about the Arapaho operating and self-regulating class III gaming on the Rez. What else could it have meant?"

"Did you decide to stop Kellogg in the ancient Native American way?" Stuart asked.

"He wasn't scalped, was he?"

"Stop it, both of you!" Mary stood up. "Right now, I am just a mother trying to protect her son and if that means I have to take you both on, I will." She glared at both men.

They both had the grace to look embarrassed.

She sat again. "Now then, why would Tucker try to charge Michael and Johnny with a preposterous charge of terrorism?"

"Probably, because your brother has known ties to AIM, Tucker thought he could get them both on a limited political terrorism charge."

"What does that mean, exactly?" John asked. His face had drained of color.

Stuart looked at his notes again. "Basically, limited political terrorism refers to 'acts of terrorism which are committed for ideological or political motives, but which are not part of a concerted campaign to capture control of the state.'"

"We just left a bison head in front of an old furniture store," John said. "Can they put you in jail for a non-violent protest?"

"The short answer is, yes," Stuart said. "But take heart. It would be worse if they charged you with Kellogg's murder."

CHAPTER 24

BARTON SIPPED HIS TEA AND TRIED HIS BEST to appear composed, though his rigid posture gave him away. Abby was a cleaning dervish, dusting and polishing every surface.

"Sit down, won't you?" Barton said more sharply than he intended. He grimaced. "Sorry, love. I am just as tightly wound as you are over this, but rubbing the finish off the table will do no one any good. Why don't you come over here and cuddle? That would help us both."

Abby put the can of furniture polish on the table with the rag, wiped her hands on her pink velour sweatpants, and sank next to Barton, resting her head on his shoulder.

"That's better," Barton said, and ran his hand up and down her arm.

"I just keep thinking about those men running around shooting people," Abby said. "I worry."

"I know, but right now it's not helpful."

Abby's phone rang, and she dived across Barton to get it.

"Darcy? Oh, thank God you called. I've been worried sick. Is that young fool okay?"

"Yes, Abby, Adkins is doing okay. I just wanted to let you know we are going down to the station. Now that Adkins is safe, we can start broadcasting some follow-up stories. Hank and I think we can rattle their cage a little and maybe force them to do something stupid."

"Isn't that dangerous?" Abby asked, then switched the phone to her other ear to share with Barton, who was hovering at her side.

"Yes, but I have Hank with me. You guys need to stick close, and I'll contact you when I can. Gotta go."

Abby winced at the hollow sound of Darcy clicking off. "Well, I guess we're supposed to stay put and out of the way."

"The hell with that! Grab your coat."

Abby jumped up and raced to the hall tree. Barton was already in his black wool overcoat and draping his bright red cashmere scarf. He took her coat and helped her button up.

"Where are we going?" Abby pulled on her gloves.

"Do you have your cell phone?"

Abby grabbed it off the table and shoved it into her pocket. "I do now, but where are we going?"

"I'm taking you to the Prairie for lunch."

"But I'm not hungry, and . . ." She followed Barton out her apartment door. He was already holding the front door for her. "For an old man, you can move pretty fast when you want to," she said as she passed in front of him.

"I bet you say that to all the boys."

Five minutes later, they strode into the lobby of the historic hotel. A player piano tinkled an old Sinatra tune in the corner.

"That thing gives me the creeps. I keep expecting to see a ghost playing it or something," Abby said.

"This would be the place for it," Barton steered her toward the dining room, then veered suddenly to the front desk.

"Why hello, Lilly." Barton beamed at the titian-haired desk clerk. "How are you doing today?"

"Hello Dr. B. Can't complain."

"Good for you." Barton winked, and Abby bristled, surreptitiously pinching Barton's arm. "Oh yes. This is my good, dear friend, Abigail McNeil."

"Hello," Lilly nodded. Her smooth cheeks blushed and lit up her sea-green eyes. "Mr. B's one of my favorites," she said to Abby.

"Just because I bring you candy." Barton fumbled in his pocket and produced three limply wrapped peppermints and slid them toward the girl. She snatched them up as if they were Godiva chocolates.

Barton leaned toward her and beckoned her to lean closer. "We need a little information, Lilly. Can you help us?"

"I'll try. What do you need to know?"

"Well, if it wouldn't be breaking some ethical code, we'd like to know if two fellas checked in earlier today. They would've been younger, looked a little swarthy and, talked like easterners. Anyone like that?"

Lilly glanced back at the far corner where her boss was intently focused on the computer.

"About 11 o'clock. They looked kind of shifty to me. You're not going to buy anything from them, are you?"

Barton laughed and patted her arm. "No dear. Nothing like that. Are they still here?"

Lilly peered into the dining room and squinted just a little. "I think they're sitting at the bar. They've been there for a while."

"Excellent. Thank you, Lilly." Barton steered Abby toward the dining room again.

"Nice to meet you, ma'am," Lilly said to Abby.

"What are we doing? Darcy and Hank won't thank us for interfering, you know," Abby muttered.

"Two, please," Barton said to the hostess. "Nonsense, we'll just do a little covert snooping, is all. Who would suspect an older couple such as us of being in any way threatening?" Barton slipped Abby out of her coat with practiced grace.

Abby slid into the booth and stared at the backs of the two young men who had been causing so much trouble.

"How did you know they'd be here?" Abby leaned into whisper.

"Just an educated guess. Thompson's Furniture is just across the street so they can keep an eye on it and I'm guessing they wanted a little a little creature comfort after the rough life in the woods. Hence, they're sitting at the bar."

They ordered a light lunch. They were halfway through the Cheyenne Club sandwich they were splitting when one of the men shouted to the bartender, "Hey, can ya turn the TV up?"

The bartender glanced at Abby and Barton, since they were closest to the bar. Abby nodded her assent since she wanted to listen too. A head shot of Darcy filled the screen.

. . . so, the Cheyenne Police Department is asking for your help in trying to apprehend these suspects. Police Detective Hank Nelson has agreed to be interviewed today.

The shot widened to include Hank seated across from Darcy.

Detective Nelson, does the CPD have any theories about the murders of Latham Kellogg and James Frye, our recently retired county coroner? Are the murders related?

Ballistics have confirmed both homicide victims were shot with the same weapon.

Then you are close to an arrest?

Adkins, a reporter for KCWY TV, was kidnapped and found wounded by the side of the road. His wound was a ballistic match for the weapon that killed Mr. Kellogg and Mr. Frye.

What has Detective Nelson said about his attackers?

We cannot interview Mr. Adkins, as he is still hospitalized and under sedation. We wanted to alert the citizens of Cheyenne and the surrounding environs. There is a killer, or killers, at large.

What can the public do to remain safe?

We'd like to urge everyone to be as vigilant as possible. Pay attention to your surroundings and notify the police department if you observe any suspicious behavior or see strangers around your neighborhoods or stores. We will supply a physical description as soon as we are able.

"What the hell are they doing? They know who the murderers are," Barton whispered to Abby.

"I suspect they are trying to trick them into a false sense of security. Darcy said they wanted them to do something stupid. Now shush."

In the meantime, we have contacted a crime scene investigation team from Colorado to do a more thorough sweep of Thompson's store where Mr. Kellogg was found.

What will that accomplish?

We're hoping to gather more forensic evidence to aid the investigation. Colorado has access to more sophisticated technology.

"Shit!" Tony Triolo blurted out, then looked around.

Abby dropped her eyes instantly and studied her sweet potato fries. Just as Barton said something, Abby cut him off. "So, I told Sheila I didn't want to watch her gerbil anymore. Nasty, smelly things."

"What?" Barton asked, very confused.

"People take advantage of me now I'm retired. They think I have no life. Do you have that problem?"

Finally catching on, Barton said, "Yes, I do, though technically, I'm only semi-retired."

Abby nodded in the bar's direction, and Barton turned to watch the two men arguing in a muted conversation, punctuated with waving hands and pointing. A few stray expletives peppered the air.

The taller man stood, pushing his stool back so hard it almost toppled. He threw some cash on the bar and grabbed his coat. The other followed.

Barton grabbed his coat from the hook on the booth. "Move, Abigail. They're getting away." He tossed some rumpled bills on the table.

Barton, with Abby in tow, raced through the side door to the street just as Darcy was wrapping up her interview with Hank.

Outside, they scanned the street north and south, then glimpsed them crossing the street by Thompson's.

"There!" Barton pointed.

Abby pulled out her cell and called Darcy.

"What are you doing?" Barton asked.

"I'm calling Darcy to tell her the ploy worked. She and Hank should come and arrest them."

"Put that away. They haven't done anything yet except cuss and leave the bar. If you call Darcy and Hank too early, they may never catch them with incriminating evidence. There's no way to tie them to the gun. If they terrorized Adkins enough, he may never agree to testify against them."

"Well, what would you suggest, old man?"

Ignoring the jab, Barton steered her back into the lobby of the Prairie Hotel.

"What the devil—"

"Quiet. Just come with me and act like you know where you're going." Barton tucked her hand through the crook of his arm.

They strolled at a leisurely pace past Lilly at the desk. Barton waved to her jauntily but didn't stop to speak. Prodding Abby along, he finally took a jog left down a long corridor containing the restrooms.

Abby stopped and pulled her hand free. "What are we doing? Those men are across the street."

Barton looked quickly up and down the hallway, opened a nearby door marked Staff Only, and pushed Abby through it.

It was dark and smelled of damp. Barton turned on the small flashlight he had on his keychain, and a small golden circle of light pierced the shadows.

"Where—" Abby began.

"Patience. All will be revealed," Barton answered as he splashed the weak light over the wall to their right.

Carefully pushing a mop bucket and mop out of the way, he ran his hand over the wall.

"Ah. There it is." He tapped and pushed, but nothing happened.

"I don't suppose you have one of those old-fashioned metal nail files in your purse?" he asked.

"I think I have, but I can't see a thing in this dark." Abby rustled around in her bag anyway and Barton attempted to aim his light over her shoulder. Abby batted his hand away. "Here it is." She held it up triumphantly, and Barton snatched it from her without thanks.

Barton held the small flashlight in his mouth, shining the weak beam on the wall and holding Abby's nail file like a knife.

Abby wrenched the light from him and re-aimed the beam. "I have no idea what you're doing, old man, but I'm pretty sure holding this with your teeth can't be good for them."

Barton just grunted and continued to pry at a small crack in the wall. Abby watched in silent fascination.

After much loosening and pushing, they both heard a slight pop.

"That did it." Barton said. Pushing harder, a small door swung inward revealing a dust covered wooden staircase.

"I'll go first with the light," Barton explained. "You hold tight to my shoulder and watch your step. I don't think anyone has used these steps in decades."

Abby was too surprised to speak. She placed her left hand on Barton's shoulder and braced her right hand on the uneven plaster wall as they descended. She counted thirteen steps and shivered at the superstition of it. Back on level ground, Abby peered into the dark.

"Now what?"

Barton waved the light around until he saw a turn switch on the wall. It looked like a brown dial from an ancient radio. When he turned it to the right, a free hanging clear bulb sizzled on overhead, flooding the small space with a harsh beam.

Cobwebs festooned the corners, and the dust lay so deep their steps gave mute testimony to the undisturbed passageway.

"What is this place?" Abby turned in a circle.

"This is one of the openings to the tunnel system, which flourished downtown until the early-1900s."

"Oh. Are these some of the old steam tunnels that used to provide heat to downtown buildings?"

"Perhaps some of them are, but the original use of the tunnels was to move the very wealthy to and from the Union Pacific Depot so they wouldn't have to contend with wind, rain, snow, or slush." Barton grasped her hand, and, taking a moment to get his bearings, he guided Abby down the east tunnel directly in front of them. "Latest convenience inspired and imported from the UP station in Omaha."

"Do all the tunnels lead to the Prairie Hotel?" Abby asked, glancing back at the bright hallway.

"Not at all. Some went to the old Intercontinental Hotel down the street, and some wandered over to a cluster of what used to be brothels and saloons on 16th street."

"Where are we going?"

"To Thompson's if I've figured right, it should take us straight there. This way we can get into the store without those guys knowing. We are looking for anything they may try to destroy before Colorado CSI get here."

"Why would there be a tunnel under Thompson's?"

"There are tunnels all over the place down here. Watch your step. There's some rubble just ahead," Barton cautioned. "I suspect, though, that they constructed a tunnel to Thompson's to facilitate the movement of dead bodies from various locations underground to get fitted for a casket. Furniture proprietors often served as undertakers since they did a lively side business in coffins."

"Ewww!" Abby responded inelegantly.

"Ewww, indeed. The initial thought was to spare the gentler sex from being offended by the sight of death. I suspect it was also a convenient way to dispose of bodies not likely to be claimed by kith or kin."

The glimmer of light at their backs was fading, so Barton kept a lookout for more switches. He found one and twisted it on.

The warren of tunnels crisscrossing and disappearing into the gloom fascinated Abby. Occasionally, a tunnel would be identified by its terminus, with a peeling painted sign on the gray plaster announcing the path to the Opera House or Wellnitz's Barber Shop. Soon they arrived at a door painted with a red THOMPSON's sign.

"Okay. Be quiet when we get in. Those guys may already be there," Barton warned. He pulled on the door, wincing as it scraped against the brick floor.

He clicked on his small light again and listened. Above them, they could hear the squeaks and crackles of the ancient wood floor as well as muffled voices. Barton held his finger vertically over his lips. Abby nodded her understanding.

They crept forward, barely daring to breathe. As they got closer to the elevator shaft, they could hear the conversation.

"What the hell are we looking for?" the first man asked.

"I don't know. Just look for anything you might have touched when we were here," the other answered.

"I can't see a thing."

"Wipe off the desk. You may have leaned on it or left a thread or something before you popped him."

Abby's eyes grew round, and she covered her mouth for fear of making any sound.

"I'll check by the loading dock door where we got in. Pick up anything you see."

"Hey. I found a toothpick."

Abby mouthed, "I should call Darcy."

Barton shook his head no, and they turned back toward the door. In the dark, Abby bumped into a stack of wooden pallets, which scraped her shin before they came crashing to the floor. Abby slammed her hand over her mouth, but the damage was done.

"What the hell was that?" one of the men shouted.

"Downstairs. There's someone downstairs. You take the elevator and I'll take the stairs."

Abby and Barton raced for the tunnel door. When they got there, Barton pulled hard on the looped handle and it came off in his hand, but not before the door scrapped again on the brick floor, making a hair-raising screech of protest.

"Who's down here?" the man on the stairs yelled.

The elevator clanked and rattled as it descended to the basement, stopping with a metallic clang, startling Abby, and reminding her of old prison movies. The elevator gate rasped opened.

"You see anything?"

"Naw, but I heard something over in the far corner. Come on."

Leather-soled shoes clicked on the crumbling brick floor, drawing closer to the west side of the storage area. Abby and Barton tried to dissolve into the inky shadows.

Abby decided she'd rather die trying to escape than be cornered like a wild animal. Her foot brushed against a loose brick, which had probably propped the door open in times past. She stooped, picked it up, and threw it as far as she could in the opposite direction, where it clunked and rolled, echoing through the empty space. The men both swiveled in the direction of the sound.

Barton pulled the edge of the door open, and they sneaked through it, pulling the door as closed.

A shot rang out and shattered the old wooden door, raining splinters on Abby and Barton's back as they ran for their lives through the tunnel.

Just as they reached the closest light switch, another shot rang out. Barton turned off the switch, plunging everyone into darkness. He took Abby's hand and pulled her to the tunnel on their left to avoid even the soft glow from the light closer to the Prairie Hotel door.

They listened to the running footsteps pass them, then stopped.

CHAPTER 25

D ARCY PACKED UP HER LAPTOP and grabbed her coat on the run, meeting Hank at the front door of the studio.

"Okay. What now?" she asked as she handed him her laptop case and wiggled into her coat.

"Next, I drop you off at your place, and you bring Barton and Abby up to speed. It shouldn't take too long to get a team down to stake out the store. If they're here and they heard the report, they'll try to go back." Hank opened the door and waited for Darcy to pass through.

"Wait just a second, cowboy. You don't mean I'm supposed to go home, sip hot chocolate, and wait for you to tell me it's over, do you?"

"Darcy, come on. It's cold out here. If you're determined to argue with me, let's do it in my truck."

Hank walked around the back of his truck, bracing for a quarrel.

"You are brain-dead if you think I'm not going to be in on the kill," Darcy said without preamble.

"I may be brain-dead . . . but not because of that," Hank agreed. He started the truck to get the heater churning. "And I really wish you'd tuck your blood lust back in its dark little corner. It isn't attractive. There will be no killing if I can help it."

"You know what I mean and don't pretend you don't."

"Is this where we rehash job descriptions? My job is to catch the bad guys. Yours is not."

"I think our history might prove otherwise, but I'm not arguing with you. Either you take me with you, or I grab a ride with Netters and Officer Tessler." Darcy nodded at Netters who had just pulled up alongside them.

Poor Jody Tessler shrugged. Hank sympathized. He knew short of wasting time by wrestling their charges to the ground, cuffing them, and squandering personnel to pick them up to hold them in protective custody, there was little they could do. Hank shot Tessler a commiserating look then shrugged.

"Here's the deal—" Hank paused. "Wipe that self-satisfied smirk off your face or I'll dump you in the nearest snowdrift."

Darcy chewed the inside of her cheeks to keep from smiling. Hank noted the effort, so he continued.

"You and Netters stay out of the way. If I give you an order—"

"Hadn't we better get going?" Darcy interrupted as she turned and clicked her seat belt.

Jamming his truck into gear, Hank signaled Tessler and Netters to follow. He called headquarters and got patched into Officer Cummings' line.

"Officer, have you found them?"

"Yes, sir. I followed them to the Prairie. They checked in and headed straight for the bar. I watched them from the far end."

"Are they still there?"

"No sir. They watched your interview and slammed out. I followed them out to the street and though I think they may have gone inside Thompsons'; I couldn't get close enough to be certain without risking being made."

"Okay. We're on the way."

"Uh, sir. There is another minor complication."

"Which is?" Hank clenched his jaw in frustration at having to stop for a light by the park.

"You know Ms. Moreland's friends, the older lady and gentleman . . ."

"What about them? Spit it out, Cummings."

"They were at the Prairie too. At first, I thought it was a coincidence, but they followed our guys out, then came back into the hotel when the guys disappeared."

"Where are they now?" Hank shot Darcy a fulminating glance.

"I don't know, sir. I trailed them to warn them off, but I couldn't find them."

"Okay, stay put. I'm bringing Tessler with me, and we'll cover the exits. Call headquarters and request backup. These guys are armed and dangerous. We're pulling up now." Hank tapped his Bluetooth off and pulled his gun from its harness.

"What's happened?"

"Abby and Barton are unaccounted for. Cummings thinks they may try to follow the armed suspects. He couldn't find them to warn them off."

"Oh my God, Hank. They'll be killed."

Glaring at Darcy, Hank got out of his side of the cab. Darcy was out and slinging her backpack over her shoulder by the time he rounded the front of the truck.

"Where do you think you're going?"

"With you or despite you, but I'm not going to sit around while Abby and Barton get shot." Darcy strode past Hank and headed for Thompsons' furniture store.

Hank lengthened his stride to catch up with her. He swung her around, grasping her by her upper arms.

"Don't push this, Darcy."

"Do you want to argue about this, or do you want to catch the bad guys?"

Hank grunted and pushed her behind him. "Stay back and do what I tell you."

They crossed the icy street, stepping over the dirty gray drift of snow that hid the curb. Darcy tripped, but Hank caught her before she fell. They reached Thompsons' front door, walked past casually, then stooped low and peered into the darkened, empty showroom through the partially papered over window.

"I don't see anything. Do you?"

"No, but that doesn't mean anything."

Crouching low, they worked their way back around to the door. Hank reached up to the cold steel handle and pulled. The door opened with a small whoosh. Hank held the door slightly ajar and signaled for Darcy to go through. Clicking on his flashlight, he followed her in.

They sat on the cool, dusty floor and listened in the darkness, trying not to breathe. The crack of an explosion reverberated through the empty building, shattering the silence. Darcy grabbed Hank's upper arm in a vise grip.

"What the hell happened?"

"I think it was a gunshot," Hank whispered, gesturing for silence.

Another crack slammed through the darkness.

Darcy forced herself to whisper when she wanted to scream. "Hank. What if they are shooting at Barton and Abby?"

Hank whispered back, "Be quiet. I'm trying to figure out where it's coming from."

They inched their way in the direction of the sound, listening for every creak, shuffle, or bump. They came to a dead end at what seemed to be a solid wall. Hank gently tapped the butt end of his flashlight against some wood paneling, listening for the hollow sound of the opening. He found a small seam and pried it open with his Swiss Army knife. The thin panel came loose and revealed an old brick archway, with stairs that led into the bowels of the building.

The wood stairs were slick with dust and the staircase sloped steeply which explained why it had been boarded up. It would have been difficult, if not impossible, to carry furniture from the loading area in the basement to the display floor, Darcy thought.

Hank went first, aiming the soft beam of light on the stair treads, while Darcy braced a hand on his shoulder. One stair creaked loudly. Darcy had to force the gasp that rose in her throat.

She squinted beyond the pale light and tried to make out shapes or movement in the room beyond. She could see nothing. It was as if the darkness had sucked all life into a deep black hole.

They reached the bottom of the stairs and she felt Hank tug at her to move to the right. What he saw wasn't clear to her until he flashed his light on the footprints on the dusty floor leading to another doorway.

The door ajar with a sweep of dust in its arc gave silent testimony it had been opened recently. Hank signaled for Darcy to follow as they crept closer. A third crack echoed in the hollow tunnel, and Darcy clutched her chest to keep her racing heart from leaving her terrified body.

Hank reached behind and took her hand. The show of solidarity seemed to steady her as they made their slow way into the deep shadows. Darcy ran her hand along the uneven brick wall on her left, focusing on the rasp of the uneven mortar on her fingers so she didn't have to think about Abby and Barton.

ABBY WAS CERTAIN THE TWO ARMED HOOLIGANS could hear her heart battering against her chest. She and Barton had ducked into a shadowed doorway and stood close to one another.

Any other time, Abby would have enjoyed having Barton's arms around her. His hand clasped the back of her head and pulled her face into his shoulder to conceal her wheezing breath.

As she desperately tried to slow her breathing, she heard the crack of gunfire. Without volition, she squeaked in terror and surprise. Barton's hand pushed her face even harder into the soft wool of his overcoat.

Silence. Abby felt a waft of air past them which, had her senses not been heightened by fear and darkness, she would most likely have missed.

Another crack of gunfire to her right, though farther into the tunnels. Abby pulled her head back and caught a shadowed glimpse of Barton's face. He seemed composed but alert. He even hugged her. She felt herself relax against him and felt his arms slacken around her.

A third crack of gunfire sounded like it came from right beside them. Barton pulled Abby closer reflexively, and she closed her eyes with the instinctual surety from her childhood; if you can't see danger, it can't hurt you.

"Damn it, Tony! Stop firing that gun. Anyone who was here is gone now."

Abby twitched. The men were an arm's length away.

"You're probably right," Tony answered. "What a sweet layout down here though, huh? The boss is going to love this. We found like an entire underground city."

"Maybe."

Abby could smell the heavy cologne one of them wore. Kind of a cross between Pine Sol and whiskey, she thought.

"No really, Vince. Think of how the casino could expand under here. The possibilities make me dizzy."

"Shut up. You were born dizzy."

Abby heard their voices fading away and she stole a glance up at Barton again. He shook his head slightly.

At the far end of the tunnel, they heard diminishing foot-steps and the creak of a door on rusty hinges. Suddenly, the door slammed open. Abby thought she heard wood splintering, and then another shot rang out.

"Drop your gun. You're under arrest."

"Hank," Abby breathed. "Hank is here."

Abby pushed away from Barton and ran toward Hank's voice. The man with the gun grabbed her around the throat and dragged her back against him.

Through the tears in her eyes, Abby saw everyone petrified in that moment. She felt the cold metal against her temple and her knees wobbled beneath her.

"Oh, Abby!" Darcy rushed forward, but Hank jerked her back.

"That's right, Detective, keep your little girlfriend controlled. Vince, get his gun."

Vince wrenched the gun from Hank, then went to join Tony.

Tony tugged Abby backward as they inched their way deeper into the tunnels.

"Stay where you are, and we might not shoot her. We're going to hold on to her until we're out of here, but if you follow us, I'll put a bullet in her brain. Capice?"

Hank nodded. Darcy screamed, "No!" but Hank held her tightly in front of him. Barton stood stoically apart as if good posture and impeccable manners would dissolve this nightmare into a mere bad dream. His jaw was rigid. It was the only way Abby knew he was angry. It was her last view of him as they dragged and pushed her deeper into the tunnels.

"Where all do these things go?" Tony asked Abby as he pulled her along.

"I don't know. I vaguely remember some of these tunnels went to the Union Pacific Depot and the old International Hotel," Abby said.

"Where are we now, ma'am?" Vince asked.

Abby looked at him sharply. "Well, someone tried to raise you right. If your mother knew what you've become, she'd weep."

Vince winced slightly at the direct hit, but asked again, "Where are we?"

"I don't know exactly. My sense of direction isn't good at the best of times . . ."

"Well, figure it out, old lady," Tony said as he pushed the gun barrel against the back of her skull.

"Knock it off, Tony. Scaring her isn't going to help." Vince stopped and looked around. "We came in here from Thompson's, so where in relation to the store would an exit be?"

Abby turned around in a complete circle and squinted into the darkness as she tried to think. If they continued walking this way, she thought they would find the entrance to the Prairie Hotel. At least that way there would be people and she might get away.

"Barton and I came in through the Prairie Hotel. I think if we can follow our tracks back, we can exit through there," she said finally.

"Where is the old coot, anyway?"

"Do you mean Barton? I don't know. He's probably down by the Depot by now," Abby said, hoping it was true.

"Great," Vince said, walking a little ahead, then stooping to peer at the uneven floor. "Here are some tracks. They must be yours. I don't think anyone else has been down here in years."

Tony yanked Abby's arm and led her behind Vince. It took only a short while before they came to the door and staircase leading up to the hotel, as identified by the peeling red paint on the wall.

Tony pulled Abby around to face him. "Now listen old lady, if you want to survive, you'll do exactly what I tell you. Got it?"

Abby nodded stiffly. Idiotically, being called an old lady was more insulting than the gun he held to her head.

"Good. Now Vince there is going up the stairs first. You follow him up and I'll be behind you. If Vince thinks it's all clear, he'll keep going and you can follow him, but if he stops, you stop." He waited for her to nod again. She did.

Abby watched Vince climb the stairs and held her breath when he pushed open the door to a janitorial closet. Vince peered out into the hallway and motioned Abby forward, with Tony close behind. Abby was concentrating on following Vince down the hallway. She didn't see a hand reach out from the women's bathroom and yank her inside. She fell on top of Darcy, sprawling on the cold tile floor moments before Tony fired four rounds into the thick closing door.

Scooting away from the line of fire, Abby and Darcy held each other in a corner of the bathroom and listened to the commotion outside.

They heard Hank repeat the order to drop their weapons. Shots rang out again and were answered. Then silence.

"Do you think it's safe to go out there?" Abby asked.

"Sounds like it," Darcy agreed and helped Abby up from the floor.

Darcy peered around the corner of the door in time to see Officer Cummings handcuffing Vince and Hank standing over a wounded Tony. Hank was calling for an ambulance.

Abby followed Darcy out. Darcy rushed out to the lobby proper and pulled Netters back to get the shot. Officer Tessler trailed behind and answered the sympathetic look of Detective Nelson from across the hall.

IT TOOK HOURS TO GET VINCE SASSANO AND TONY TRIOLO patched up and processed, but by the time they were separated for questioning, Tony couldn't tell the story fast enough.

Vince took a little more time to corroborate Tony's version, but when his public defender lawyer, Donald Westin, suggested he cooperate for the reduced charge of accessory to murder, he rolled.

By the time Detective Nelson and Officer Tessler joined the celebrants at Abby's, it was growing late.

"What took so long?" Darcy demanded as she opened the door. "I thought it was a slam dunk."

"Even slam dunks need a little sweeping up," Hank said as he shrugged out of his coat and accepted a beer from Netters.

"So, tell us, what was going on?" Abby insisted. She was sipping hot chocolate and Bailey's and Barton was hovering.

"Well, it seems the entire plot was pretty convoluted," Hank began and settled into the corner of the settee with Darcy at his side.

"Last year when Thompsons' was being rehabbed, the contractor Terry Anderson found a set of bones. Anderson called the County Coroner, Jim Frye, to identify the remains as required by law. City Councilman Carl Stevens bribed Frye to ID the bones as animal remains, so the project wouldn't be forced to stop for thirty days for a full investigation. The bones went into a box and no one much thought anything about it until a Las Vegas mob boss started nosing around for a potential site for a casino. This is where Tony and Vince come in."

"A casino? In the old Thompsons' store? But why?" Darcy asked.

"Turns out the mob boss didn't care how or where, but he wanted to use the Arapaho Tribe as a front to establish a casino which couldn't be touched by state law. He contacted Wyoming State Senator Pete Loman, who was chairman of the Native American Affairs Committee, to see if he had any ideas."

"He bought a State Senator?" Barton asked.

"There is some question about that. Senator Loman's lawyers are hashing the accusation out, but we think it's probable if you follow the money. Loman contacted his old buddy District Attorney Patrick Tucker."

"I knew that guy was slimy," Darcy said.

"Again, the lawyers are still wrangling about that, but somehow Tucker was paid to smooth any legal problems, including convincing Frye to ID those old bones correctly as Native American. Loman took the bit in his mouth and declared Thompsons' a Native American burial site and the property of the Northern Arapaho tribe. He was in negotiations with the Tribal Council to open a casino on the newly authorized site."

"So that explains why Mike Brown and John Blue Feather were protesting," Abby said.

"Yup. And because they were so effective at throwing wrenches into the carefully laid plans of a mob boss, a state senator, a District Attorney, and a County Coroner, Sassano and Triolo were sent out to clean up the mess."

"Well, why'd they shoot Kellogg instead of John Blue Feather and Mike Brown?" Darcy asked.

"Because Loman was in delicate negotiations with the Tribal Council. It wouldn't look good to have one of their own executed, even a radical like Brown."

"I don't understand why they killed Frye. He'd done what they'd asked him to do . . . twice," Netters said.

"According to Sassano and Triolo, the boss said that Frye got greedy, and he knew too much."

"What a mess. How long before I can broadcast all this?" Darcy asked.

"Since the players are all well connected literally and figuratively, some of this may never be useable. The courts grind slowly and if there are deep pockets to pay the lawyers, this could drag out for quite a long time."

"Great!" Darcy said as she bounced up to get her laptop and make some notes. "This will be a fantastic series of exposés."

TWO MONTHS LATER, DARCY WAS MEETING with Mary Blue Feather to get some background information on the opening of the new Native American Cultural Museum and Heritage Center at the site of the old Thompsons' Furniture store.

"So, is your brother finally satisfied with the disposition of the land?" Darcy asked.

Mary laughed. "Michael will always be a hothead, but I think because I will head the foundation and Johnny will work as a conservator, he will be as content as he ever can be."

"It has a nice symmetry, though," Darcy mused. "The final resting place for a Native American woman and her grandson now becomes a center to educate and inform not only the young people of her tribe but other visitors who are interested in the real Native American contribution to the settling of the West."

"Now, if I could just get my ornery brother to do something constructive with the rest of his life so he'll stay out of mine," Mary said with some heat.

Darcy toasted her with her latte. "Yeah. Good luck, lady."

Stacie M. Keiter photographer

P**AULLA** H**UNTER** **IS** **A** **LONG-TIME** **RESIDENT** of Cheyenne, Wyoming. She lives in a historic downtown area of the city with her husband Roger.

Paulla is a member of Rocky Mountain Fiction Writers, Sisters in Crime, Colorado Author's League, and Wyoming Writers.

She earned her BA from the University of Wyoming in English speech and drama. Paulla taught high school English, as well as writing as an adjunct at Laramie County Community College.

She writes under her given name, Paulla Hunter, and is published by Camel Press, an Imprint of Epicenter Press.

She has a passion for history, reading, theater, travel, and obviously writing.